Hc

Catch and Release

Happy trails

Horse Doctor Adventures

Catch and Release

Elizabeth Woolsey

Catch and Release

ISBN: 978-0-9942972-6-6

Cover design by David Blake

Published in the United States

ewoolseydvm@gmail.com

www.horsedoctorpress.com

In dedication to

My family
My Co-workers
And my clients

Who all graciously allowed me
to retire from active
veterinary practice.

Chapter 1

"Mum, they're crazy over there. They all have guns, and they have murders every day." There was an endless list of reasons my children didn't support my return to America. They didn't want me to leave them. My three children all lived in different states, and I was only flavor of the month in December. Not one of the kids came home for Christmas last year. They had their own families and had moved on. I left them in Australia to return to my native country—God bless America, I hoped. I was starting over.

Old age is not for the faint-hearted, but what's old? Starting my new life in a rural community far from friends and family was scary. My sister and brother thought I was crazy, which I think we'd already established when I upped and moved to Australia to follow my future and now ex-husband.

My kids were furious, and they had every reason to be. Admittedly, I was abandoning them. It was alright and preferential that they moved out and started their own families. Still, parents are expected to stay and be the nuclear family's anchor. I failed my kids and bailed on them. Sorry—not.

I was restarting my life back in the States after twenty-seven years of living in Australia. I pulled into the long driveway to make my way up to my new home. I'd purchased a log cabin on forty-eight acres last year. I told my family I lived in a gated community. An old Powder River gate with a lock protected me from the gun-toting heathens who my children had envisioned.

The gate had seen better days and had a large indentation from a vehicle or a bison. I don't think there are any buffalo here, but I could dream. The gate was well off the road, allowing someone with a truck and trailer to pull into the driveway and be safe when the gate with its chain and ancient lock needed to be opened.

The property looked like a desert with rocks and sage as the only prominent features visible from the road. It fooled me when I came last year looking for retirement properties. I could not imagine wanting to buy this place as I looked up the hill from the road. My realtor, Carol Carter, and I drove over the hill and descended into a small, lush valley with a log home, barn, and fenced paddocks next to a year-round creek abutting a dense forest.

Carol turned to me. "Proceed?"

"Maybe. So, what are the issues? There must be a catch. This place has been on the market for six years. How come?"

"Let's just look before I say any more." Carol pointed to a white speck in a tree. "See her?"

"Is that a bald eagle?"

"Maggie, we can leave, but I think it's worth a look." I observed Carol smiling to herself.

"No, let's at least look around. Any fish in the creek?"

"Some. There's a story, but I think you may just be the one person who can get over a few details." Carol lied. The word detail implied a small obstacle; it was not. Despite knowing the true story, which was far more than a tiny issue, I purchased the property, and now, nine months later, here I was, ready to move in and start the next ten years of my life. I planned to live like this for at least ten years before I went to live in 'the home,' as my children called it.

A bottle of Barossa Valley wine, flowers, and house keys sat on a table on the deck, which faced a cliff and the surrounding forest. My spectacular view was worth every penny. I sat down on the chair next to the table and pulled out my small book of contacts and reminders. Most of my essential details were on my phone. My to-do list was usually written out so I could get the pleasure of ticking the items off. I added a reminder to send a thank you note to Carol. The rocky gravel road would need to be graded and smoothed out. I would add that to a long list of things that would need to be done to make this place livable year-round.

There was an envelope with a list of tradesmen and contact numbers for the utilities and a state fishing license—go Carol! There was a second smaller envelope that contained an invitation to an annual picnic for the locals. Carol mentioned her brother-in-law had an event every year. Attendance was mandatory if I wanted to meet the who's who of the area. I was told not to bring anything but my appetite. The theme was western casual, and it was in two weeks.

Here was my haven from my past life—no more work. No more being on call and no more worries about sick or dying horses. Veterinary medicine had been good to me. I was lucky that I loved what I did, but that life was over.

I left my country of residence, my children, and my profession for a rural life of solitude and recreational fly-fishing. My clients, family, and friends said I would fail at retirement. No one, including me, could imagine I could find joy outside of my professional life. My coworkers were incredibly doubtful. I'd devoted the last fifty years of my existence to veterinary medicine, and to the exclusion of anything else. It was inconceivable that I could find joy in other activities.

They didn't know. I had a secret plan. I was approaching my late sixties when three years ago, I noticed that the joy in my work had finally waned. I no longer looked forward to saving the lives of horses. Most of my contemporaries had retired long before me and found joy in cruises, grandchildren, and hobbies. They encouraged me to do the same. "You can't be a horse vet forever. It's dangerous, and you're vulnerable. Your reaction time is not what it used to be. Remember Larry Childers? You don't want to end up like him."

I never met Larry, but he was a legend in equine veterinary medicine. Larry had been killed when a stallion struck him in the head. He was a good horseman, but Larry took risks. He didn't have my staff. Their number one job was to keep me safe. I'd given up the dangerous stuff years ago. I no longer collected semen from stallions or stuck the first needle into an unbroken colt to be castrated. Still, it was often the most unexpected occurrence that did many vets in.

The reason for my decision to retire was not fear of injury. It was not the midnight calls for help or even the continuous being on call for emergencies. I just had lost interest. I simply found no joy in veterinary medicine. I was at the top of my game, and I didn't want to play anymore. I wanted a new life, and while I was leaving many friends, I wanted new ones.

Living in another country was the best decision I'd ever made. The reason for the original relocation overseas, my ex, did not turn out like I had planned. Still, thankfully it gave me children and a great professional life. I used to say, "Pinch me. They're paying me to do this." Now I have changed the verb to "paid." Sadly, my Australian friends had either died, moved away, or had families and responsibilities that superseded me. We had different interests and, more importantly, different values. I wanted to get back to my people. I had no problems making friends. I thought I might find like-minded people here in rural America. So, I sold up and moved back home to my people and heritage.

Before entering the house, I decided to walk down to the creek. There was an old fence on the other side of the stream. The barricade was damaged in many places. A bear could walk onto the property, and a horse could escape—more for the to-do list. I was aware that bears and mountain lions were known in the area. I saw scat down on the bank and considered adding gun procurement on my to-do list. I left my dogs with my children until I was ready to have them sent over. This might have been a mistake. I was told the dogs were being held for ransom until I came to my senses.

I checked my phone. Only one bar, would that be enough? "Help, I've fallen, and I can't get up." I wasn't that old, and one month ago, I was still wrangling horses. My last call before retirement was a horse with a grass awn in its eye. She was not impressed with me and vice versa. She thought the prick of a needle was a cue to rear. Better living through chemistry, a good vet nurse, and she was on her way home drunk and medicated—good luck on the follow-up. That was my past, and this is my future.

I returned to the cabin and picked up the keys. The door was solid with a heavy-duty lock. I unlocked and opened the door. Phew. The smell of death permeated the great room. I immediately remembered the 'detail' that Carol had explained, which stopped sales for several years. Oh my God, what had I done?

Chapter 2

The smell was overpowering. I stepped back and closed the door. Six years ago, there was a murder-suicide in this house. It was an older couple. The Calhoun's bodies had not been discovered for several weeks. Despite many attempts at removing the smell, bodily fluids had soaked into the floorboards, and the scent of death continued to fill the house. The son of the couple had finally replaced the flooring. Still, knowing the history, buyers shunned the property, and it sat empty.

There was a fire that may have been arson to collect the insurance, so the couple's son might get some of his inheritance. He was interstate at the time and was never charged. If he hired someone, no trace of an arsonist was established. The fire failed anyway, and the damage was minor and easily repaired.

Carol explained the reason for the murder-suicide was never confirmed. Still, the husband had Alzheimer's, and it appeared the wife killed him and then herself. They had only been in the home for two years and were not social. He was an artist, and they moved there so he could paint the scenery.

I negotiated a significant price drop and bought the place well under the estimated value. When I first visited the house, there was no lingering smell. The windows were opened, airing the house for my inspection. But that was a year ago.

Carol promised to have the electricity on, a satellite for cable television, and an internet connection ready. When I picked up the key to the property, the secretary explained the cable guy was unable to come until I was onsite. I needed to explain where the modem and television cables were to be installed.

So, what was the smell? It had to be from something big. Really big. I retrieved a kerchief from the car and covered my mouth and nose. I re-entered the house and immediately began to open the windows. I searched around and discovered a dead snake in the kitchen. I thought of my two cats, which I left at my veterinary clinic. Add cat procurement to my list. I removed the snake. How did it get in? I turned on the fan and opened the doors, but the smell lingered.

There were a few cleaning products under the sink and a spray can of Oust. It was empty. I cleaned the floor, and the smell began to retreat. I didn't have any furniture, and I planned to buy everything new. I had a sleeping bag, and I would sleep on the floor until I had a bed delivered. My sister was arriving tomorrow, and we were going to do major retail therapy as soon as she got here.

The thought of sleeping on the floor where a snake could crawl was scary. I had many friends and colleagues who had died in their first few months of retirement. I was determined to live for at least ten more years. My plan did not include passing anytime soon, and it didn't really include retirement. I was starting my new profession as an author. I'd started it two years ago, but I kept this redirection in my life to myself. I was excited like I had been when I began my veterinary career. Even if I failed, I was getting so much joy out of my new career that I didn't care if I was successful or not.

I checked my phone, which said, 'no service.' I already knew this from my initial visit. The house had a landline, but my plan was for a satellite booster for everything. I considered getting a motel for the night. I wasn't poor. I could afford it, but I decided to tough it out. My sister, Christy, was coming tomorrow and bringing two camping mattresses. We were heading to the big smoke to look at furniture and fixtures for the cabin. I walked up to the top of the hill between my house and the road. My phone immediately dinged, signaling a missed call and message.

"Maggot, I'm ahead of schedule. Be at your place in two hours and I'll be expecting dinner and alcohol. My decorating services aren't free. See you about five-ish."

Crap, I had left the milk and tonic in the car. I walked back down to the cabin, unloaded three bags of groceries, and put it all in the cabinets and fridge. The refrigerator was new and enormous. It was on and cold. There was an inbuilt ice machine, and I decided to try out the ice and water. The initial water was horrible. I had the water tested before I bought the place, and it was clean and filtered. I let it run for a minute and was rewarded with sweet, clean well water. I checked the ice, and it smelled fine. I was ready for gin-o'clock.

I brought my clothes and fishing rod out of the car. The new SUVs had tons of space. My overseas belongings were on their way, but it would be weeks before they arrived. I surveyed the house and walked through each room. I purposely bought a house with three guestrooms and a large sleeping room upstairs for my extended family and friends. I didn't live close to anyone, but this place was ideal, and I would attract visitors who would use my house as a vacation spot.

My immediate plans were to purchase enough utensils and kitchenware and get two bedrooms ready. Christy was on her way to visit her in-laws and was only staying a couple of nights. She and her husband Miles would be back later in the summer for some hiking and exploring. My brother and his wife would come later in the summer. At least one of my children would be over the pond—as we referred to the Pacific Ocean—next year for a few weeks of berating me for leaving the family home.

Most of the house had a timber interior, but the bathrooms, basement, and one room used as an office had walls that needed new paint. The other task was to fix the fences and barn and find a safe horse to ride. I walked around and added to the list. I had so much to do and all the time in the world to do it. When had I ever felt like that?

I went into my bedroom, which faced the mountains and creek. There was a balcony off my room. It was high enough I was safe to leave the doors open. If there were ghosts, then I was happy to share the space. I might even sleep out on the balcony and get a feel for the outdoors. I could hardly wait for my sister to arrive., and I didn't have to wait long. She arrived in less time than she guessed.

Christy looked around and smiled. "Maggot, I could almost be jealous."

"Thanks. I was hoping you would see what I see too."

"Miles and I get saves on the first two weeks in August next year and then the following year."

"Maybe Bill and Lonnie will come too, and you could bring the grandkids."

Lonnie was our sister-in-law. She was tons of fun, which compensated for our brother, who inherited our long-dead father's inability to see the humor in anything. Hey, want to walk down to the creek?"

"Nope. I'm starving, and I need some dinner."

"No prob. I bought steaks, and we can have a salad. Ready for a G &T?"

My sister was smaller than me and had brown hair in contrast to Bill and me. Of course, Bill had let himself go gray while Christy and I kept our "natural" color. We dared each other to let nature take its course, but neither of us was ready to allow the outside world to see us as anything but middle-aged women.

"Where are the pots and pans?" Christy was looking through the cupboards. "Hey, is there a dead mouse in here?"

There was no way in hell that I was telling her about the snake. "Yep. Mickey bit the dust and then the dustpan. I swear there was a frying pan here. I don't even see a tray to catch the drips off the oven grill. Shall we go check out the natives?"

"Is there a place to eat in town?"

"Mabel's. It isn't bad either. I ate there last year."

"Should I dress?"

"Yeah, they don't do naked."

"Do we need to call ahead?" Christy was probably joking. The town was so small.

"Hopefully, not." I wasn't kidding, but we didn't. The café was half full, and the food and smells were delightful. I explained to my sister that, for a short time, I didn't want people to know I had been a vet. I was happy to fly under the radar. Christy thought it was a good idea too. She'd been plagued by people calling for advice and wanting her to come back to work when she retired. We ate and left without notice from the locals.

We returned to the property. As dusk approached, we climbed over the hill, and there was my new home. There was a light on over the garage. I hadn't been in there or the room above the garage since I'd arrived. I still had two boxes of clothes to bring in from the car.

Christy said she wanted to see what was in the room upstairs. She took the key, entered the garage, and headed up to the small room upstairs. She returned and asked if I had been there on my previous visit last year.

"Yes, it could be used for another bedroom if I was desperate, but it was empty when I last saw it."

"You better come up. Someone's been in there."

I went up, and there in the room was a table, chair, and a sleeping bag. There was a notebook with drawings and legends explaining the illustrations. They appeared to be the work of a child.

"What the?" I was at a loss to explain this.

"Goldilocks?" Christy thumbed through the pages.

"Bears?" I joked.

"No, these drawings are more sophisticated than your average bear."

"Some kid has been up here playing house. Maggie, you better call your realtor in the morning."

"Yeah, good idea. Are you sure the door was locked before you tried to get in?"

"No, not one hundred percent. I just automatically used the key to open the door."

"These drawings are pretty advanced, and with cars, houses, and a dog, it's definitely a boy's work."

"Well, Maggot, let's go over and have a drink and maybe watch the stars. Do you know who your neighbors are?"

"Just one, but he hasn't been up here in years. Do you remember the actor, Colin Chandler?"

"Get out! That old geezer? Is he still alive? Maggot, you're holding back."

"He supposedly keeps staff, and his children occasionally visit. He used to have a massive horse facility, but Carol said it was now down to just a few horses and a few stable hands."

"He was a fox in his day. Wasn't he America's sexiest man in the 1800s?" She laughed at her pathetic joke. "He's got to be at least eighty now. You never hear anything about him. Maybe the kid belongs to one of the staff members who live next door on his property."

Chapter 3

Christy set down her wine glass. I had my usual gin and tonic. "Barossa wine, can I take some back with me?"

"It was a gift from my realtor."

"So, what are you going to do to keep yourself busy?" Christy poured a second glass.

"Oh yeah. Well, tomorrow it will be in the news, so you might as well be the first." I went to my suitcase and retrieved the first product of my plan. I came back to the porch, and in the candlelight, I handed my sister a book.

"My new life."

Christy examined the book while I waited with anticipation. She opened the book and saw the dedication. To my children, sister, and brother…. It went on to describe how they helped me in ways they never would have guessed. The book was about the outback men I met during my professional career. I used my maiden name, Margaret Kincaid. The book had been picked up by an Australian publisher, and it was due out next week on Amazon.

What I didn't tell my sister or anyone was that I had a contract for five more books, of which three had been written and edited. They were fiction and were a series about a woman veterinarian who solved crimes. The Australian book was not a big financial deal and was destined for the Australian market. An international publishing company paid me in advance for the fiction series. I was advised to hire a good investment planner. The first book in the series would be out in a month or two. I was contracted to do interviews and book signings if the sales were as expected.

"Maggot, I love the idea. Can I see the other books? Are they in print?"

"I have a reviewer's copy of the first fiction book. It's my only one. You can see it, but I need it back." I went to a box still in the foyer and retrieved the book. "Read this to get to sleep."

The following morning, Christy reported she loved the book and could hardly wait to get her own copy. "Mom and Dad would have been so proud, Maggot."

"Thanks. Want a cinnamon roll for breakfast? I want to get going. It's a long drive to the city."

"Coffee, and let's rock and roll."

"Pun intended on the roll?"

"Yep." Christy had showered and was ready to leave.

My sister was fit and still looked like a woman fifteen years younger than her actual age. She was a year older than me, and she was my role model. She'd taught chemistry at the local college and ran a private tutoring school for disadvantaged kids on the side. She'd won awards for her work with underprivileged kids. Miles had a large construction firm that renovated old buildings in San Francisco. Their children had all married and had kids of their own.

Christy tried to set me up with her single male friends, but I didn't want to meet anyone for fear of being tied to a place that didn't suit my recreational needs. I'd spent the last two years on the internet looking for waterfront properties all over the country. This area suited me for several reasons. While I hadn't met anyone yet, I was advised the population was a mix of people who liked the outdoors and had rural ranching backgrounds.

There was a small group of artists and writers and the occasional ultra-wealthy landowner who jetted in and out but only rarely visited. I hoped to meet both men and women who had similar interests. Still, they would have their own lives, so I could enjoy occasional companionship with a heavy dose of privacy.

As we got into my sister's car, the cable guy, Ralph Childers, arrived. I quickly explained what I needed and where I wanted all the outlets and modem to go. He said he would have it done by the afternoon. I had to arrange to get the system turned on and pay for the service, and he gave me the number to call with my details to start getting the internet. Sweet, I was anxious to Zoom with my kids.

"Ma'am, I'm sure glad you're taking such a chance on the place, given the history. Not many people are willing to live alone and especially in this place with its past."

"You mean the murder-suicide?"

"Well, that's one theory. Most of us locals think it was a double murder, and the sheriff's department didn't investigate it properly."

"Really? This is the first I heard about it." I turned to my sister while she pretended to gaze out the window toward the mountains.

"There are reports there is money still hidden, and the son was still visiting the property just a few months ago."

"I've owned the property for the last six months. Maybe I should change the lock on the gate."

"That's for sure. I'll lock it when I leave, but a new lock would be a good idea." Ralph returned to his truck to retrieve his tools.

We thanked him for the information and drove out. We looked at one another, and my sister said, "Where do you want your ashes placed?"

"Here. Yeah, I better get a new will."

Chapter 4

"Seventy-nine." Christy rolled through the gate and waited for me to get into her car.

"Seventy-nine what?" My sister could be so annoying.

"Colin Chandler. He's seventy-nine."

I was surprised. "He's still alive?"

"According to Google, he is."

"You're driving. Hand me the phone."

Christy handed me her phone, and I continued to read the bio of Colin Chandler. "He's married to a blues singer, Heidi Hayes, and has three children by his first marriage and two step-children by his current marriage. One child had been murdered by her husband, who is currently in jail. Colin Chandler is retired from acting and has several projects he is still involved in. He commutes back and forth between Britain, where his wife resides, and Los Angeles. His acting credits include the movies and the long-running western television series, *Comstock*, which he co-produced, directed, and acted in for over ten years. There's more, but that is the gist of his bio."

"He doesn't look too bad for his age if you can believe this is a recent picture. This must be his wife." I directed the phone, so Christy could see his image.

"Man, we're getting old if that looks good to us."

"Speak for yourself. Thankfully, I inherited the immaturity gene. Sorry for you, but I can't imagine being seventy, let alone seventy-nine." I smugly looked at my sister. I had two years to go.

"It's hard to believe, isn't it? Mom couldn't do half the stuff we do. Can you imagine Mom backpacking or riding a horse at seventy?"

"Yes, I am so proud of how you and Miles carry on. I hope I'm as active as you when I get to be your age." I laughed and punched my sister, who steered the car onto the road while deflecting my punch.

"Seriously, Maggot. I'm so glad you're back, even if you feel the need to live in the boonies. Now get the GPS out and find me some furniture stores. I have a need to spend some of your money and help you back into the twenty-first century."

"I feel like I've gone ahead fifty years already. I now have a self-cleaning oven and garbage disposal. Pinch me." And she did. Hard.

So, we spent the day selecting furniture and kitchenware that would complement my log cabin. I drained my discretionary account and began to use my book advance funds. It was the shopping trip of a lifetime. Christy was a genius at not only selecting high-quality furnishings, but she also bargained with them on prices. The sofas and recliners were going to be made and sent. The themes were western, and I was excited about the material and bed linen we picked out.

Most of the furnishings would be delivered next week. We packed what we could into Cristy's car. We shopped and ate and shopped some more. It was good to have my sister there to guide me on the quality and colors. My art would not arrive for a while, so I would wait until the paintings were here and hung before I finished decorating the house.

As we drove back up over the hill and descended into my beautiful valley, we noticed the light in the room above the garage. We unloaded my purchases, and we both walked over to the garage. As we entered the room, we found it bare except for a glass of flowers.

"Goldilocks has left the building." Christy picked up the glass and flowers. "Your first decoration. Take a picture."

"Great idea. Who knows, maybe he's older and a potential suitor."

"You need someone ten years younger, but my guess is, he's probably sixty years younger."

"I'll call a locksmith on Monday."

Dinner was delicious, with steak, salad, and artichokes. We opened a new Barossa wine we picked up at the liquor store. I'd never been to the Barossa Valley, a well-known wine region of Australia, but it produced many highly rated wines. I had a glass and finished my evening with a port. What a luxury to drink at night and not have to worry about driving to an emergency. I could get used to it. Christy sauntered off to bed and hoped to finish my book before she left.

I opened my laptop and entered my new modem password. Bazinga! I had the internet. It was late, but early for my kids. I knew they would all be at work. I checked for messages and emails. There was one from my publisher with a query about the front cover of the first book. They pretended to care about my wishes, but deep down, I knew they would do what they thought was commercially savvy.

Chapter 5

Christy left early the following morning, and I had the place to myself. Her parting words were to get a security system, keep writing, and send her a copy of the book as soon as I had one. The first order was to check out the creek. I retrieved my rod and tied a fly onto the line. I walked down to the creek and observed three pools that looked "fishy." I did some practice casts and then landed a fly in the riffle of the first pool. I saw a fish rise, but it was not inclined to take the fly. I continued to cast, using the same fly, but had no luck. I tried a second fly and still had no takers. There was an outdoor shop in the neighboring town that appeared to be promising for information and fishing supplies. I used to kid my friends that fly tying was for people with nothing to do. I might have to reconsider this. I looked under a few rocks for nymphs and insect life that might give me a clue to what fly might entice some trout onto my line.

After an hour with no luck, which might better be described as no skill, I returned to the house. I cleaned and explored the rooms. Three rooms needed a new coat of paint. There were no hardware stores open in this small town, but the town east of me might have one. I drove over to the neighboring municipality and searched the main street. Many of the boutique shops reminded me of some of the upmarket townships in Northern California I'd visited over the years. The hardware store did have paint, and I bought enough for the three rooms. Christy had given me color suggestions for each room.

I returned to the cabin. When I went to open the gate, there was a message tacked to the gate. "I know who you are, and I wanted to welcome you to our community." It was signed by Patty Tilmouth. A business card was attached for Mountain Veterinary Clinic with a personal number written on the business card. Well, so much for anonymity. I recognized her name from a veterinary Facebook group, where I was an administrator.

I called her and introduced myself. Her practice was mixed, and she employed two other veterinarians. She knew me from my posts on our mutual vet page and my last post mentioning I was returning to the States and the town where I was planning to live. I explained I would not practice anymore, so I was no threat to anyone's livelihood.

"Oh, darn. I was hoping you would join us for a day or so a week. None of us are hardcore equine vets, but we see a fair number of horses. Any chance I can call on you for an opinion occasionally?"

"Every chance. As long as you keep my previous profession a secret to the public."

"Well, it may be too late. My staff knows, so I'll ask them not to say anything."

"No state license, so I can only advise."

"We would kill to have your advice. I know you have a lifetime of experience. We'd love for you to come by and visit."

"There's one thing I would like to ask. Well, really two. I'm looking for a broke-to-death horse to ride and a mature dog to adopt."

"Doctor, you have come to the right place."

"My friends and enemies all call me Maggie."

"There is a lady on highway 153 that has a dog rescue place. I'll text you her details. As far as the horse, I think there are two places you might have luck. Let me get back to you on that."

"Oh, that's great. My saddle won't be here for several weeks, but I'd be willing to buy a horse if the right one came along. Do you prefer to be called Patty or Dr. Tilmouth?"

"Patty, for sure. My dad was the town doctor. He was a first name kind of guy."

"Is he still practicing? I'll need one of those too."

"No, he passed three years ago, but my brother, Eric, is now the town doctor. I'd go to him if he wasn't my brother. No way is he looking under my hood." She laughed.

"Patty, I'd love to catch up with you. I'm excited to be here. Oh, one last thing. I like to fish, and I need some guidance on fishing. Can you recommend someone to talk to?"

"Eric's a fishing tragic. I'll have him call you. He'd love to find someone to fish with."

"I'm not sure an old lady would be his style."

"No, he isn't that picky, really. Say, how are you finding your new house? Any ghosts yet?"

"I do have a visitor, but I'm fairly sure he's real. Some kid has been hiding out in my garage during the day." I explained what Christy and I discovered.

"Really? Strange. No idea. But seriously, have you got a gun?"

"I've lived in Australia for the last two decades. We don't routinely have guns, you know. Do you think I should get one? How about bears and mountain lions?"

"Cougars have increased in population over the last twenty years. They are a real problem for ranchers. You need a can of bear spray for the bears, and you should carry it, but a gun might not be a bad idea. I was thinking about any riff-raff who might be lurking around your cabin."

"What are your thoughts on the local folklore? Was it a murder-suicide or a double homicide?"

"Juries out. One thing is for sure, the son is a creep. He lives in Florida, but one of my nurses saw him in town just a few months back."

"I bought the place six months ago. Was it around then? Maybe he came to retrieve anything left or sign the papers?"

"I don't remember. I'll ask my nurse, Sherry. She'll remember. He was at the bar where she was meeting her friends for a drink. He came onto her. She knew his face. It creeped her out. She watches a lot of crime television."

"I'll head to the outdoor shop tomorrow. Now that I'm stateside, I might as well be locked and loaded like my fellow Americans." We both laughed.

"Hey, I don't want to give you the wrong impression. This is not a high-crime area, but there are some areas you might want to avoid. There aren't any growers here. Don't get me wrong, we have our drug problems, like most towns, but alcohol is the main problem. The Calhoun's deaths aside, there haven't been any murders in this area for years."

"Good to know."

"How did you do the deed over there if you didn't have a gun?" I laughed. Doing the deed was a common term for euthanasia.

"There are lots of people who had guns, but I mostly used a phenobarbital solution, while some of my colleagues had captive bolt guns. It was never a problem. My funeral director had a gun on the very odd occasion I needed a horse shot."

"Your funeral director?"

"Ron. The guy who picked up the dead horses. The most important man in my life."

"Oh, that's a great moniker. Ours is Dave if you have needs."

"Is he discreet? I might need someone to dispose of the Calhoun heir if he comes around?"

"Nope, you need Larry, the backhoe driver. He's your man for human disposal. Hey, got to go. My work phone is ringing. Let's catch up, and I'll send you the numbers for the dog and pony show."

Chapter 6

Carol, my real estate agent, called to ask how things were going. "Caught any fish?"

"Sadly, no. Did you forget to mention the remote chance the Calhouns may have been killed by someone? What's with their son? Did he need to come and sign the papers for the sale?"

"Maggie, there were rumors. But my cousin is the sheriff, and he was sure it was a murder-suicide. As far as the son, it's true he's a low-life, and he probably did come up and snoop around the place several times. He was sure his parents buried money on the property. We don't think there's any buried money, and we don't think he found any. The sale of the property was his sole inheritance. The Calhouns have a daughter who was severely disabled. She's in a private institution, and there is a trust set up to finance her care until her death. The son's inheritance was the property. When it didn't sell for years, he was frustrated and was quite vocal. He signed the papers in Florida. I did hear he was back up in the area. My cousin said he was just passing through on his way out to California."

"Got a number for a locksmith? I think I need to change the locks."

"Yeah, that's probably a good idea. Anything else? Did you see your invitation to the picnic? You really need to come. My brother-in-law has a party every year. It's a chance for you to meet the locals all at once. I'm sure you will be the center of attention since you bought Calhoun's property. You will love the locals, and Charlie wants to meet you. You can bring a guest."

"Yes, I will RSVP today. I'll be alone unless Larry's available."

"Larry?"

"Larry, the backhoe guy. I have a thing for men who drive heavy equipment."

"Uh, obviously, you haven't met him. He's thirty-two, has no front teeth, and weighs at least two-ninety."

"Carol, I'm sixty-eight. I can't afford to be picky."

"Then I'll let the general public know that."

"That's okay. I don't have time right now. I'm happy with the way things are. I do need a fishing guide, but apparently, the town doctor is going to provide that service."

"You'll love Eric. He'll get you catching fish. He's my doctor—a smart, funny guy. He's single with two teenagers. His wife left them years ago for life in the city. The kids used to stay with her, but they opted to live here and only visit their mother in the summer. They're gone now, and he has plenty of time on his hands."

"Excellent. Eric's sister called me, and she knows I was a vet. That's an emphasis on the verb was. She promised to keep it quiet too."

"I haven't told a soul. Honestly."

"Oh, I almost forgot. Do you know any kids who live near me?"

"There's a kid who lives on the Chandler estate, but I don't know much about him. I think someone said he's a deaf-mute. He might live with his grandparents."

"Who are my neighbors on the other side?"

"National forest. Bears, deer, and elk."

"Beyond that, there is the Bar Double X cattle ranch. Sylvia and Trent West. They're close to your age. They've been here for thirty or more years. You'll love them. They'll be at Charlie's picnic."

"Great, I'm hoping to meet some of the locals. You never mention your sister. Will she be there?"

"Linda died about five years ago. She and Charlie were lovers until the end. He's never really recovered. He worshiped her and cared for her to her dying day. Linda was one in a million. She was beautiful, smart, and never sat down. Linda was a powerhouse in their little empire. They were never able to conceive, so she threw herself into helping him. Hey, I need to go. We can talk later or tomorrow. I'll text you the locksmith's number. See ya."

"Thanks." I planned to search Charlie and Linda on the net. I forgot to ask their last name. I checked the invitation and noted the ranch was called The Sanctuary. I'd see if I could figure it out from there, but there was so much to do. I'd start by painting the bathroom. I taped and covered everything. The floor was tiled so that it would be easy to fix if I spilled anything. I found an old T-shirt to throw over my clothes. This would be a quick job.

I stopped to look out of the cathedral windows over the pasture and toward the creek and forest. Would I ever get tired of looking at this view? There was a boy of about eleven or twelve walking up with a paper bag. He stood outside the house, looked up, and saw me. He didn't appear to be bothered when he saw me watching him. I walked to the door, and he stood observing me. He shyly waved, and I returned his wave. "Hi, I'm Maggie. What's your name?"

He stared and didn't reply. He lifted his bag and appeared to want to show me the contents. I pointed to the chair on the porch, and he walked up and sat down. Curiously, he didn't appear to be frightened. I brought a chair out of the house and sat down next to him. He stared at me and then opened his bag and spilled its contents on the table. There were three arrowheads and a card with a drawing of the boy. On the back of the card, 'Luke' and the single word 'job' were written.

He stared at me without smiling, and I returned his gaze. "Do you want to work?" He watched my face. It took him a few seconds, and then he seemed to understand and nodded. I smiled at him. "Can you read?" He missed my face as he looked over at the garage. I got up, and he began to stand. I motioned for him to wait, and I went into the house and retrieved a piece of paper and pencil.

I sat back down and wrote, "Can you read?" He nodded. I thought for a minute. I then wrote, "Come tomorrow morning and wear old clothes." He smiled and began to gather his arrowheads and card. He stood up and extended his hand, which I took and shook. He grinned broadly and then reached into his bag and handed me one of the arrowheads. Luke ran off through the paddock and toward the trees between my property and the Chandler estate. He turned and waved before running into the woods.

The arrowhead was less than an inch and was made from obsidian. It was well preserved if it was real. I was excited and hoped Luke had found it around here. I would begin my own search for artifacts on the property. I collected them as a child and never found one as nice as this one.

I returned to the bathroom and decided to paint the corners and edges and leave the walls to the young boy. It was a perfect place for him to make a mess. As I finished, my phone rang. It was my book agent. The publishers wanted me to do a video interview for the release of my first book. The talk would be the day after tomorrow, and it would be used later when the book was released. The release date was moved up, and the publishers were going to put the hard sell on, with a promotion ahead of the actual book distribution.

Yikes! I needed to get my hair and makeup done. I was told to dress like a horse vet. No problem, there. I still had a shirt with my vet logo on it. I texted Carol and asked for a recommendation for a hairstylist.

"Oh, already have a date with Larry and his backhoe? You work quickly."

"60 Minutes wants to do an exposé on shoddy real estate dealers who sell haunted houses."

"Pfft, not another one. They need to come up with something new." Carol laughed. "I can do it if you want. I was a hairdresser before I was a real estate tycoon selling haunted houses."

I liked Carol's hair. It was short and highlighted. "Yep, that would be great. I just had it done before I left the island, so all it needs is a coif. I may cut it short soon, but not yet. Can you do makeup too?"

"Honey, that will take Larry and me to fill in the wrinkles, but I'll do my best."

"Can we do it the day after tomorrow, so the hair and war paint are good by ten in the morning? Sorry for the late notice, but they just called."

"I'll get Larry and his backhoe. He charges by the hour. I'll be up by nine, so have the gate opened."

"Oh, thanks so much."

"Don't think of it. It's just part of the post-sales service."

Chapter 7

Luke was at the door at seven the following morning. I looked, and he didn't have a watch. He had on older clothes and brought a paper bag that had his lunch. I wrote a note on a whiteboard I had purchased. "Luke, I want you to come at eleven o'clock tomorrow, and does your mother or father know where you are." He nodded. I hoped he understood and was telling the truth.

I took him into the bathroom and showed him how to use a roller brush. Without speaking, I showed him where I wanted the paint and how to prevent spills. He was tidy and efficient. I hadn't considered it, but we hadn't discussed pay. I would see how he did today, and maybe at lunch, we could discuss compensation. Last night I made a list of things that he might help me with, including making a vegetable garden and restoring the fences near the barn. There was a gate that needed replacing as well. If I was to get a horse, that would have to be done soon.

The barn was in good shape, and the shelter it would provide for a horse in the winter would be essential. As a vet, I knew horses often chose to stay out in the elements rather than stand in a warm or dry barn. The roof seemed to be rainproof. This barn appeared to be robust and would offer protection from the wind and snow. But would a horse choose to go in? Time would tell. At least I could feel good that I gave the horse options.

I like to play music, and while I knew he couldn't hear it, he might feel the beat or vibration of the music. My grandchildren were old enough to like contemporary music. The excellent news with Luke is there would be no disagreement about whose music we played—ah, old people's music. The sixties and seventies were my favs.

While Luke painted in the bathroom, I started the office upstairs. I taped and put drop cloths down to protect the hardwood floor. This room also had a small porch, and the doors opened out to allow the air to flow freely. I stood on the small balcony and gazed over the property extending to the woods. I saw a white spot in the tree and realized it was another bald eagle. I thought Luke would like to see it and went into the bathroom to bring him out. As I stepped in, he didn't react as I expected a deaf person to respond. Luke came, and I pointed to the eagle and smiled. He then pointed to another spot, and I realized there was another eagle a few yards away.

I wrote on the whiteboard, "Eagle eyes." He grinned and went back to the bathroom. He was about halfway finished, and there were no spills. We would be ready for a second coat after lunch, and the bathroom would be done today. Luke was terrific value.

At lunch, I offered him some corn chips to eat with his sandwich. I wondered who made his lunch. I wrote, "Is there someone who I should talk to?"

He emphatically wrote, "No," and he looked intently at me to ensure I understood.

We walked through the bathroom and the study, and I showed him how to clean the trays and prepare for a color change. He finished the second coat in the bathroom, including the corners and trim. He painted like a professional, and I wrote out how impressed I was. I could see it pleased him.

I had to do some book business tomorrow. I thought about what the boy could do, but I had no tools to work in the garden. I paid him, and he tried to hand back some of the money. I wrote: "No, you earned it. You did the work of a grown man."

He wrote back: "Thanks." This kid was keen. He left, and he ran to the wood's edge and was gone. Strange boy, but so polite and so careful. I enjoyed his company. It was fun to have his help and to be able to play my music and sing without him hearing me. My kids would have bellyached all day about old people's music. If I had time, I was going to the local hardware store to get a shovel, rake, and hoe. I would let Luke dig up the old garden bed, and we would get some quick-growing vegetables planted. The growing season couldn't be exceedingly long at this altitude.

Before dinner, I decided to give the creek another go. I took my rod and opted to try a nymph in the pools that were close by. Again, I had no luck, so I walked down the creek to see where it went. I didn't have to go far when I saw it flowed into a more significant and promising stream. The stream was substantial and held more potential than my little creek. The river and the tributary, which ran throughout my property, must have names.

Patty Tilmouth sent a text with several numbers, including her brother, the fisherman. I would seek his services tomorrow. I also had numbers for the dog rescue place and three stables where potential horses were for sale. Maybe I would fix the corrals first. I fished the river and had a decent strike. I didn't land it, but the fight was addictive. I would be back tomorrow. My guess was this was national parkland.

As I walked back up toward the cabin, I surveyed the barn, house, and garage. I was home, but I needed a companion. I needed an extra set of eyes, ears, and a nose. I needed a dog.

Chapter 8

The next day I had so many people coming to the house I left the gate unlocked. Carol came and did my makeup and hair. Some of the furniture arrived, and a locksmith came and redid all the locks. Ralph Childers, who installed the internet, arrived in the afternoon, and did some planning and estimates for a security system.

The interview went well. I was asked about my work as a horse vet in Australia and my inspiration to write the books. I was asked if I was writing any more books, and of course, I said I was. The next book would follow similar lines. I requested that the interviewer not disclose where I was living. I wanted to stay anonymous if possible. I was not going to be a J. K. Rowling. Still, if I even received a small percentage of her sales, I wouldn't turn it down, but for now, I would be happy simply to be a member of the community.

I provided the interviewers several pictures of me working as a vet with horses. The interview took half an hour and would be online in a week or so. They would add it to my Twitter and Instagram accounts and to my website as well. My agent was able to hear the interview on her phone and was happy.

Luke showed up, and I let him paint the corners and trim in the office. We had to cover the new desk and two bookshelves. He painted while I organized my bedroom. Oh, happy day, I had a bed.

Luke gave me a letter that stated his family was not in residence now. I was thanked for providing Luke an opportunity to interact with the outside world in a safe environment. The resident cook cared for him, and he could come and work for me, but he must return by five. He was free to go with me when I went shopping or on errands in the local area. There was a phone number with the letter in case there was an emergency. I called the number and spoke to Mrs. Gillard, the woman who cared for the Chandler estate, and she gave me permission to take Luke on short errands around the local area.

I was keen to look for a dog, and when Luke finished painting the trim, we drove over to the dog shelter. Connie Blanchard greeted us. She had about thirty dogs, which were from chihuahuas to German shepherds. Most of them had been vetted for temperament. I wanted an older dog who was not going to chase stock or horses. There was a brown, mixed breed, neutered male that kept putting his nose under Luke's arm and sitting down next to us. *Suck-up,* I thought to myself. I liked a little Maltese cross, but I saw endless trips to the dog groomers.

I asked if they ever got standard poodles in. I knew they were super intelligent. Connie looked at me like I was crazy. We came home with Baxter, a middle-aged, short-haired dog without a single quality I would have sought. Luke and the mongrel rode in the back seat of my car while I observed Luke stroking and hugging the dog in the rearview mirror. It was pure love. We stopped at the grocery store, and I bought dog food and a bowl.

When we arrived home, I observed the gate was shut but not locked. I'd left it open. I wasn't expecting any more deliveries today and wondered who had closed the gate. As we came up over the rise and looked down into the valley surrounding my house, I saw a horse roaming where the grass grew.

Luke immediately pointed to the horse and nodded, and indicated he wanted the whiteboard. He wrote the name "Digger."

"You know the horse?" I wrote. He nodded.

"Grandfather's horse." He wrote.

"Your grandfather lives there?"

He nodded and bounded out of the car with Baxter on his new lead. As we went toward the house's front door, there was a note pinned to the door.

Thank you for having Luke. Digger is sixteen and needs some work. He is a safe horse and travels on his own in the forest and on trails. I will stop by tomorrow and bring a saddle. If he's not suitable, I will come and get him. The grass is enough for now, but I will bring hay next week. Welcome to our neck of the woods. Gabe Turner

I handed the note to Luke. I wrote, "Is this your grandfather?" He shook his head. I wondered how many people lived and worked for the Chandler estate. It was close to five o'clock. Luke had a wristwatch today, and he knew he must return home. I quickly wrote out a message to thank him for the day. I handed him the note with a written reply to Mr. Turner thanking him for the horse, and I looked forward to meeting him tomorrow.

Baxter wanted to follow Luke, so he had to be left in the house. I inspected the gelding that was a medium-sized, sorrel, quarter horse with two hind stockings and a nice blaze. Digger came straight up to me. I had a thing for chestnuts. My best horse was a liver chestnut that I rode and jumped in my youth. As I got older, I switched to western riding and had a quarter horse mare, like Digger. If he was a good ride, he was perfect. My next project was the corral and barn remodel.

It was time to hit the river. I would test Baxter out and take him with me. As I was leaving the house, my phone rang. I recognized the number as Carol's. I answered, "Welcome to heaven. How may I direct your call?" It wasn't Carol. It was my new potential fishing partner.

"Whoa, and my sister said I was going to hell. This is the Cherokee County fishing guide and body works. I understand you have needs."

Chapter 9

I waited twenty minutes for Dr. Eric Travers to arrive. He drove an old car that had seen better days. Eric was tall and athletic. He had a fishing vest on and carried a walking stick. I noticed a can of bear spray was attached to a belt.

"Madam." He bowed.

"Oh, great leader, show me the way to fish heaven."

"It will be that or hell. I haven't fished here ever. The place is too scary for me to come here alone."

"If you keep the bears away, I'll keep the ghosts and human bad guys at arm's length."

"Deal." We shook hands. "Lead the way."

Two casts and Eric had a fish. "Oh my God, I have a lot to learn."

"It'll cost you, Margaret."

"Maggie is fine."

"I heard you don't want the entire town knowing you're a vet. Oh, how I envy you."

"Your day will come. I had to travel seven thousand miles to get away from it. What are your fees?"

"For what?" He knew what I was asking.

"You said it will cost me." I placed my hand on my hip and waited for his response. I could see he was considering his reply.

"Dinner and regular fishing. I have needs." He dropped his chin to his chest and gave me a severe look but then grinned.

"I'm here to serve, sir."

"I am batching it until school starts. I can get away most evenings and the occasional weekend. There are plenty of places I need to show you. Did you know this is called Dead Man's Creek?"

"Oh, how appropriate." I rolled my eyes.

"Nope, it was named over one hundred years ago. Settlers were attacked by Indians, and an entire family was killed just upstream. The grave markers are still there."

"I have so much to learn about this area."

"I'm here to help. My sister says she'll kill me if I don't make you happy."

Eric handed me a small black nymph with a spot of white. It took forever to tie it onto my leader, but eventually, I could cast it into the second pool. Wham. I had my first fish. I was dying for trout, but it was small, and Eric looked pleased and remarked that we could do better.

We walked down the stream to where it joined the river. The sun was setting, and we only had a few minutes left of light for fishing. Insects were soaring above the water. We found a nice spot on the riverbank where grass draped over to the water's edge. There was ample clearing for a decent back-cast. He pointed to me and nodded. I let out my line with a few false casts, laid down the little nymph a few inches from the grassy bank, and let the fly continue down along the bank, mending my line as it traveled down the stream.

"I'd have sworn that would have caught you a fish. Try again." Eric changed his fly as I cast again and watched the strike indicator travel down the bank without disturbance.

"Your turn." I stepped aside to let him have a go, but instead, he handed me his rod. I shook my head, but he insisted. I stepped up to a spot three feet down the gravel riverbed and practiced casting before landing a fly as close as I dare to the bank. Eric stood on a rock and could see the fly from an advantage of height and shouted, "Now." I'd already begun the motion to set the hook, and the fight was on. The fish and I went up and down the river before the fish tired and found relief in Eric's net. He was a monster.

We smiled at each other, and I knew we were going to let him go. He was just too lovely to keep. We performed the photo ritual and returned the monster to the water. Eric had a turn and landed a nice size trout. After we each hooked a second trout, we high-fived each other and walked back to the house. *Welcome to heaven. How may I direct your call?*

My new dog greeted us and failed the stranger danger test. It was clear he loved Eric. Eric didn't want to drink alcohol in case he was called for an emergency. I laughed, remembering how many nights I did the same. "Well, that was my life until last month. Thankfully, I'm no longer responsible for anything other than myself. How do you like your trout?"

"On a plate and cooked. Giardia is not your friend here." He shucked corn while I deftly opened a packet of microwavable rice.

"Hey, you've done that before. I'm impressed." He placed the corn in the boiling water.

"I'm not just a pretty face. I can open a packet and turn on a microwave before you can say 'gourmet meal.'"

"You won't be single long around here with those skills."

"Want to bet? First, I'm old, and second, I'm not looking. How about you?"

"I'm always looking." He then told me about his wife and kids and their marriage's demise while we ate dinner. "I've dated some, but the kids come first, and there's always the lure of the city. Not many middle-aged women want to live in a rural community. I can hook them, but I lack the skills to land them."

"Any of them keepers?"

"No, not really. I'm still waiting for the special woman who wants a rural life, teenage kids, and an aging country doctor."

"Have you tried any dating apps? Are you around forty?" In truth, I wasn't sure. He had to be twenty years younger than me.

"Forty-five. Yes, but there are few women my age around here. I don't advertise my work. A country doctor sounds pretty romantic, but it's more like getting married and becoming a widow on the same day."

"Tell me about it. How do you feel about the phrase work-life balance?" I spooned the rest of the meal onto his plate.

"A myth. It's all I can do to make it to the kid's sporting events. This area isn't big enough to support two doctors. My sister has enough work to have partners in her vet practice, but there isn't enough for two full-time doctors in Cherokee County. Many people go to the city for their medical needs."

"Ah, a kindred spirit."

We talked for an hour about our history and kids. Eric was lonely. His sister was too busy in her veterinary practice and raising her own children to be available for Eric. I knew we would be fishing partners and would have a meal or two each week until his children arrived back from their summer away with their mother.

Score me. We made plans to meet after work the day after tomorrow. I promised to cook the dinner, and he would take me to one of his many favorite fishing spots.

“Thanks so much for the talk and for dinner, Maggie. This was great.”

“Yep, educational too. Are you going to the picnic this coming weekend?”

“I plan to. You’ll like Charlie. He’s such a down-to-earth kind of guy.”

“Okay. Well, see you when I see you. Oh, one more thing. What’s your theory on the Calhouns?”

“You know, I never met them.”

“Who was treating his dementia?”

“I don’t know. There was a rumor the Calhouns didn’t see any doctors, and they never came to me. As far as a murder-suicide, or a double murder, well take your pick.”

Chapter 10

Luke showed up each morning at least twenty minutes before he was scheduled. He had on old clothes, and he went straight to work. I had a new whiteboard with a list of tasks that he could do each day.

The big one was in the basement. It was empty and was going to be easy to paint. I decided the best way was to team-tackle it. I had picked a light neutral color to make the room appear brighter than a windowless room would appear. I considered putting gym equipment here, but I wasn't sure if I could stay motivated enough to use it.

I worked on the edges and corners, while Luke worked in the middle with the roller brush. I brought down my phone and amplifier. I was confident I could belt away without anyone hearing me. There was no reception, so I would not receive any calls, but it didn't matter. For the first time in thirty-plus years, I was not responsible for anything but me.

I had a list of songs that ranged from folk to contemporary music. I had my favorites, which were often sixties and easy listening. I played several songs and even bopped a bit to the beat. I looked over and noticed Luke bopping too. Curiously, I watched him watching me. He didn't seem embarrassed with me observing him, and he even smiled. This went on for hours. He must be feeling the vibration.

I noticed he was particularly animated when certain songs came on. He liked music with drums, and he stopped and watched me dance to the Four Seasons' song "Walk Like a Man." He was enthusiastic, and I began to dance a little to the music. He and I stood side-by-side, and Luke followed my steps. I enjoyed seeing him relax and began to take more breaks to do some actions with certain songs. I left him to fix some lunch. We had our lunch on the porch, and after, we would sit for several minutes.

Luke would write and draw on a writing pad he brought each day. I wrote and asked him if he went to school. The boy shook his head. I wondered where he learned to read and write, and he just shrugged. I questioned what level of education he had. I took one of the whiteboards and put a math problem on the board. I asked him to add some numbers. He could do it, but it wasn't easy. I gave him some multiplication problems, and he couldn't answer them.

When we returned to the basement. Luke took my phone, turned it on, and began painting. We were finishing the primer at midafternoon, and I went upstairs to get a snack. As I descended the stairs to the basement, I distinctly heard a voice singing the lyrics to "Walk Like a Man." Not only was he singing, but he was also carrying a tune and seemed to know the words. I was shocked. I made some noise and then came down. He stopped singing well before I stepped onto the basement floor. He said nothing, and I pretended I didn't hear him.

We finished the first coat and cleaned up. The basement sink was ample for cleaning. We both washed the brushes, the roller, and the tray for tomorrow. We went upstairs, and Luke had thirty minutes before he had to return home. I pointed to the fishing rods, and he smiled and nodded. We each took a rod and headed down to the small creek below my house. I knew we had enough time to get to the river and have a few casts. I thought Luke could walk up from the river and go directly to his house without any fences. It would be nice for him to take a few trout home for his family.

I helped him cast a few times, and he indicated he could cast on his own. He must have been practicing as he did a beautiful cast, which resulted in a strike. He set the hook and fought the fish until he brought it to shore. It was a huge rainbow and was bigger than anything either Eric or I had caught.

I gestured the option to return the fish to the river or not. At his age, I would have kept it, and that was what he opted to do. He would be so proud to take it home to his grandparents on the Chandler estate. I was reminded I still had not met his family. Did they know he could hear and speak? I decided to wait to confront him. He must have a reason that he pretended to be a deaf-mute.

Chapter 11

I had not heard from anyone from the Chandler estate regarding the horse left in my care. There was a halter with a lead rope, and that was all. I was anxious to give the horse a ride. I called the vet clinic and acquired the number of the wrangler who brought the horse over. Gabe apologized for not getting back to me. He came over within the hour and brought a saddle and bridle and gave me some of the horse's history. He'd been Colin Chandler's personal horse but now was just a ranch horse. Mr. Chandler rode Digger to remote areas to hunt and fish. He was tuned up by the head trainer, and the entire staff was instructed to help me in compensation for the attention I was giving Luke. Luke must be the grandson of the head trainer.

I asked about Luke when we were saddling the gelding. I got a strange response. "We aren't supposed to talk about him. That's an offense that will get you fired, quick-smart."

"Well, I sure am enjoying his company, and he's a great worker. Could you pass that on to his parents or family for me?"

"Yes, ma'am. Do you need a leg up?"

I was nervous about getting on a strange horse at my age, but I summoned my courage and walked him over to a stump to get some elevation and hopped on. I could see the remnants of a small arena, and I walked and then trotted Digger around the old arena several times. His mouth was soft, and he yielded to leg cues readily. I then loped him around a time or two and walked him down to the creek. I wanted to test him before the wrangler left. I walked him back and forth through the stream and down a small embankment. This horse was old-lady-broke-to-death.

"I am officially in love. If you try to take him away, you'll have a fight on your hands."

"Ma'am, I'll pass that on. You're no slouch in the saddle."

"Oh, that's the nicest compliment I've had in some time." The wrangler was about thirty and had a wedding ring on. He was Marlboro-Man, good-looking, and so polite.

"Patty Tilmouth asked me to show you around. I can bring another horse over, and we can go on some of the trails around here. Is next week okay?"

"That would be great. Let me know, and I'll make sure Luke has a day off."

"Shall we say next Tuesday? In the meantime, if you follow that trail on the other side of the creek, you can go for miles, and don't worry about Luke. I'll bring him a horse too."

"Gabe, I can't thank you enough. I think I may have landed in heaven."

Gabe looked up and shook his head. "Or hell. Ma'am, we're all wondering why you bought this place. It gives us all the spooks."

"I like to be called Maggie, and to be honest, I knew about its history, but I didn't know anything had happened since the murder-suicide. Have you got any information I need to know?" I braced myself for his reply.

"There are stories, but chasing you away is also a firing offense too. Patty would have my guts for garters if I allowed you to move. Have you got a gun?"

"Not yet." *Yep, a three-bell-alarm—that would be sorted soon.*

"I'd get one, for sure. Bears and cats are one reason, but the human variety of predators is another thing."

"Duly noted, sir."

Gabe left, and I continued to ride Digger until Luke arrived. He waved and handed me a paper saying he could only stay for the morning. I looked at him and thought whether I should stop the pretense of his inability to hear and speak. The sad thing was I was now inhibited from belting out my favorite songs in front of him. I dismounted and pointed to the saddle.

Luke was about my size, and he mounted and rode Digger like he knew the horse well. He was an excellent rider, and Digger responded to Luke as if they had been together forever. I nodded in approval as Luke appeared happy to continue riding Digger in the arena. Could it get any better? It looked like I had a riding partner. I might have to get another horse.

We unsaddled Digger and turned him loose in the meadow, and I turned to walk up to the house. As we were walking, I notice Luke look up toward the house and stare intently. I touched his arm, and he turned. I mouthed, "Do you see anything?"

He returned his gaze up to the house, studied it for a few seconds, and then nodded. I heard Baxter barking madly. I'd left him in the house when Gabe had arrived. I knew that Luke could hear him but couldn't see him. Yep, this kid was not deaf. Did the Marlboro man know Luke could hear?

We painted for two hours, and then we stopped early and went fishing. Luke was going to spend the weekend at home with his family. I wanted to know more, but I thought I might let him set the pace, and he could decide how much he wanted me to know. I was in no hurry.

We walked down to the river and fished, but we were too early for the evening hatch and feeding frenzy. We walked along the stream much further than I'd been before. There was a set of pools that screamed fish. I let Luke fish the first pool. His casting was improving, and he didn't need any instruction. I fished in the second pool. We both caught and released fish. The third pool was further down, and he walked ahead as I stayed back and watched.

It was now nearing late afternoon, and the light on Luke and his rod and line were optimal for a picture. I stayed back and used my phone to capture several shots. As I stood watching, I heard someone or something come out of the woods behind me. I turned and saw a grizzled old man with white hair and an unkempt beard come toward me, but he stopped short of the creek bed.

"It's custom for people to ask permission to fish on private property. You're on my land." The tall shaggy older man stood and watched Luke fish and used a shaft to prop himself as he gazed up and down the river.

"Sorry, I thought there were riparian rights."

"Not on my land."

"So sorry, sir. We'll leave now." I was embarrassed and pissed. I was sure people could fish along the main rivers in this state.

"No need, miss. Just get permission."

I turned to ask for permission, but he was gone. Who was this old geezer, anyway? Did he work for Colin Chandler? It wasn't Luke's grandfather. He would have said something or at least thanked me. I felt a chill. Luke turned to show me a fish, and I signaled that we needed to return. I wrote and asked him if he had seen the man I had been talking to. He shrugged and shook his head.

I was given a pamphlet with fishing laws with my license. I'd read it and see about getting access to rivers. I sent Luke home and reminded him I would see him again on Monday. As he walked away, I hummed, "Walk Like a Man." He showed nothing that would indicate he heard me. Baxter wanted to follow Luke. This was going to be an issue. A more significant problem was the skunk that wandered near the house just as the sunset. Did Baxter have a rabies vaccine?

Chapter 12

I headed to the hunting store to look at guns the following day. Having lived in Australia, I felt guilty about reaching for a firearm when I'd lived around some of the most deadly animals on the planet without ever owning a gun. I arranged to take a firearm safety course next week and looked at several rifles that might protect me. I purchased some bear spray for travel to the river and mountains with my new horse.

I returned home and dressed for the picnic at The Sanctuary Ranch. I was excited to meet my new neighbors and get more information about the local community. I wore a pink checked shirt and solid pink bandana, my new blue jeans, and my Ariat paddock boots with zippers. I knew that Ariat zipper boots were not sold over here, and I purchased several pairs when I moved across the ocean.

I drove to the entrance and found it was staffed by security people checking invitations from a station house near the road. I presented my invitation. I was checked off the list and given a paper bag containing a wristband with the words The Sanctuary Annual Hoedown and the date. The pack also included a map, a table number and a tee-shirt with The Sanctuary brand, and a woman's picture on a horse.

I was directed to drive up and over a hill. As I came over the rise, I saw a large field for parking and several more security people who appeared to be directing guests to various areas. I spotted a massive house on the second rise, and then down to the left was a large barn that appeared to have an indoor arena. I had no idea about the extent of this enterprise. Who was this guy?

I didn't recognize anyone. I searched and found my table and a place card with my name etched into a wooden nameplate. This was amazingly high-end dining. I gazed at the guests and realized I fit into the crowd and had dressed appropriately. Thankfully, I would blend in. I set my bag in the seat and followed several people over to the barn and indoor arena. It was enormous and could easily accommodate large rodeo or a cattle show. Several men were either riding horses or walking show cattle. The guests were watching, but not many of them were au fait with cattle or horses. They were still impressed. I was too.

I sauntered through the barn and was amazed at the facilities. The cattle were housed at one end of the barn, and horses were kept at the other end of the large building. The indoor arena separated them. Several older men were inspecting the cattle and pointing out various attributes of the bulls. I saw three stallions, which were variations of quarter horse breeds. One was a paint stallion, one was a racing bred stallion, and one appeared to be a cutting bred stallion.

A broodmare that was close to foaling had a foaling alarm stitched to her vulva. The device held a magnet that, when separated as a foal passed through the vulva, would trigger a warning signal to a phone or receiver, alerting an attendant that the mare was foaling. My Australian alarm wasn't that sophisticated and was activated when a mare became recumbent. There were many false alarms with my system.

I walked through the barn and received some greetings from the staff, acknowledging they saw me but didn't know who I was. I could see many out-of-towners with either suits or brand-new western clothes, while the locals dressed in worn blue jeans. The security and employees had on uniforms with the logo of The Sanctuary brand on their shirt. These people were friendly and asked me if I had any questions or needed directions. I thanked them and said this was my first time and I was impressed with the facilities.

The Marlboro man from the Chandler estate saw me from a distance and waved me over to a small gathering of men and women. They were young, and I could see they were ranch hands. Gabe introduced me to his wife, Betty Lou, and the others. They all worked at various ranches around the area. Gabe told them I had moved over from Australia, and I had bought the Calhoun place. They all looked alarmed.

"Ma'am, I sure have to hand it to you. I'd never be that brave." I was introduced to a tall skinny bow-legged man with a mustache. Bobby was chewing tobacco and spitting it into a Coke can.

"Yeah, well, I'm getting the idea the place is haunted or something. Anyone want to tell me why I shouldn't have bought it?"

"Oh, I don't think it's haunted, but everyone who lived there died going back to the 1800s."

A plump pregnant woman standing in between Bobby and Gabe kicked Bobby. "Don't go paying them any mind. We're glad to meet you, and we know you're going to love living here. What brought you here, anyway?"

"I really liked the area, and I like to ride and fish, and this place was perfect."

A bell sounded, and everyone smiled and told me that is the bell that indicated that we needed to head back to the picnic area. The lunch would be served soon. I walked around, peering in several stalls on my way out of the barn. There were mares and foals of every description. One stall had a plaque that read Tinker. An old palomino mare with advanced arthritis slept in the corner. One of the wranglers came up to me and introduced himself. "Howdy ma'am, I'm Roy Higgins. I think you're new here?"

"Yes, I'm Maggie Kincaid. Please to meet you. Is this a foundation mare?"

"She's Mrs. McLeod's mare. She's almost twenty-five. We all have jobs because of her. The boss got into horses and cattle when he married Mrs. McLeod."

"She looks a bit arthritic. Is Dr. Tilmouth your vet here?"

"Yes, do you know her?"

"Well, I haven't met her, but we've talked on the phone." I would tell her about a drug I use that helps animals with arthritis. It makes vets look like heroes.

"You better skedaddle. You don't want to be late for lunch today."

"On my way. Thanks."

Carol saw me as I returned to the picnic area. There were several tables, and over one hundred guests were gathering and beginning to sit at their assigned seats. Carol called me over and gave me a hug. She introduced me to her cousin, the sheriff, Tom Sutton, and his wife and to Sylvia and Trent West, who had the ranch down the way from me. They were at my table.

I saw a table where it looked like the high-end city people were already sitting and eating. Several servers were bringing out plates of salad and meats placed in the center of the large round tables. Each table sat eight to ten guests and had sizable umbrellas that shaded most of us from the sun's glare. Checked linen tablecloths, napkins, and cutlery gave me a feeling of extreme wealth. *Who was this guy?*

I was seated next to Sylvia, who appeared to be in her late fifties. I immediately felt a kinship with this woman. She reminded me of my best friend from college who had disappeared many years ago when I was in Australia. We'd lost contact, and I'd heard she'd been killed in a rock slide. Sylvia was like my old friend, and I felt I had known her all my life. As our food was brought to our table, Carol summoned me. She took me over to the main table, where her brother-in-law sat conversing with a young man who was in a suit. He had missed the cue to dress casually.

Carol tapped Charlie McLeod on the shoulder, who immediately rose and hugged her. Carol introduced me, and he instantly stuck out his hand, and we shook. I hoped he didn't notice how rough my hands had become with my new endeavors.

"Welcome to The Sanctuary. Are you finding everything you need? I hear you're from Australia."

Charlie McLeod was tall with almost white hair. He was probably younger than me but had not aged well. His hand was soft, and I was not surprised. It looked like he didn't do any manual labor. He was polite, but I was quickly dismissed with an apology and a reminder that my food would be getting cold. I could see Carol was annoyed, but I wanted to get back and talk to Sylvia.

On the way back to the table, I saw Eric, and he waved me over. We had fished once again this week, and he introduced me as his fishing partner. The woman next to him was his sister, Patty Tilmouth. She stood up and hugged me.

"I can't believe I'm meeting the famous..." she paused. "Maggie Kincaid."

"It's okay, you can say author." Patty peered at me and cocked her head. "I'm an author now."

She laughed. "Really?"

"Yep. One coming out in a few days here and one in Australia. That's what I do now. I write and fish and ride. Oh, by the way, I can't thank you enough for sending me the horse. He's perfect."

"What horse?"

"Digger, from the Chandler Ranch."

"They sent Digger? You scored big-time. What did you do to snare him?"

"Not sure." I now wondered how I did receive such a gift. The loan of a perfectly trained and safe riding horse was a mystery. We promised to catch up next week, and I briefly talked to Eric. We were going fishing all day tomorrow. He was taking me to a friend's private fishing lodge. I was so happy to be getting these contacts. Why he wanted to fish with an old lady was beyond me, but I wasn't going to turn him down. I returned to my table, and my wine glass had been filled. I sat and watched the people. The air was warm, and clouds skittered across the sky, giving us relief from the penetrating sun. The aromas of garlic, barbeque, and salads were intoxicating.

I observed Charlie McLeod make his way to all the tables. He knew most of the guests, and he talked briefly to everyone. A table was set up for the children. The host even went and sat with them for a minute. Our table was the last table he visited. He stood and talked at length to Sylvia. Apparently, she had been a good friend of his late wife.

He then turned to me and apologized for the short introduction. He talked about his trip to Australia with his late wife. Charlie was polite and attentive. I finally had to admit that I knew nothing about him or his enterprise here in this small remote area. He looked at me and laughed. It was a full-on belly laugh.

"You have no idea who I am?"

"Sorry, not a clue. I was going to do some research, but then the river called, and I went fishing instead."

He laughed again. "Well, you're honest. Carol mentioned you'd lived in Australia for several years. What took you there? I'm guessing it was a man."

"Yep, he's gone, but the kids and work kept me there. But that's in the past."

"What did you do over there?" He appeared to be genuinely interested.

I looked at him and thought for a second too long. This got everyone's attention. "I guess that depends on how honest you want me to be?"

Sylvia looked at me and shouted, "International spy?"

"Nope."

Her husband countered, "Winemaker?"

"Horse vet," I admitted. There it was. I was out. I just couldn't lie. "But I'm retired, and now I write books."

"You're kidding." The two women sitting on the other side leaned toward me. "What do you write about?"

"Fiction and non-fiction."

"Where can we read them?"

"One will be out here in a week or two, but the other is only in Australia."

Charlie had been kneeling. He stood up and shook my hand again. I also stood and thanked him for allowing me to come and see his ranch and join the party. He reached into his pocket, retrieved his wallet, and pulled out a business card. "In case you want to do some research." The card was titled CLM Enterprises. He kissed Sylvia and returned to his table.

Sylvia leaned over to me and whispered, "You really have no idea about Charlie?"

"Not a clue. I'm guessing the man's a big wig. Is that his helicopter I saw as I drove in?"

"Not a billionaire, but close."

Carol came and joined Sylvia and me. "I heard your secret's out."

"Your bro-in-law complimented my honesty. Bastard."

Sylvia gave me a quick rundown of her friendship with Carol's sister, who died many years ago. Carol and Sylvia told me hilarious stories about their adventures. I realized I'd found my new besties. Of course, the wine didn't hurt either. After the main meal was served, we were directed to a dessert table and asked to come and sample the many offerings.

I chose baked Alaska while Carol had a dark chocolate cake, and Sylvia had ice cream. Once again, Charlie wandered over with a glass of red wine. He handed it to me and asked me to have a sip. It was a beautiful wine, and I was convinced I had tasted this once before at my daughter's wedding. I was a wine snob. I found overall Australian wines were superior to American varieties.

"I'll give you a case if you can name the wine." Charlie handed me the glass.

"Penfold's Grange Hermitage. I'm sorry. I don't know what year." I smiled, and Charlie bowed.

"Where do I have the case delivered?"

"Thanks, but I don't normally drink wine since I became a gin tragic. Please auction the bottles and give the proceeds to the local charity of your choice."

Both Carol and Sylvia took a sip of the wine, and Carol proclaimed, "Charity begins at home."

"Or you can give the wine to the Inner Mountain Woman's Better Living Through Enology Club." Carol and Sylvia both high-fived me.

Charlie laughed and said he would deliver the case himself. He excused himself and went down and gathered the children for a softball game. We could see the game from where we sat. The children ranged in age from six to about mid-teens. Charlie helped the younger players, and I could see he was a good player.

"Did Charlie play professional ball?"

Carol responded. "He sure did, he got to triple-A, but then he was injured. If you observe him, he has a slight limp."

Some of the wranglers got involved, and then even a few young women joined the game. It was fun to watch the interaction. Just before sunset, the party began to break up. Everyone was sent home with a box of food and any leftover wine or other nonalcoholic drinks. When Patty and Eric were alone, I went over and talked to them. I told Patty about an arthritis drug commonly used in Australia. I brought some with me to use on a friend's horse, but the horse was sold before I arrived. I had a few vials, and I would be happy to give them to her to try on the older mare in the stall.

"Tinker? Oh, yes, please. I would be considered a saint if I could give this mare another year of a pain-free life."

"I'll drop it by on Monday to your clinic. No need to say where it came from."

"Maggie, I'm so glad you're here. Let's have dinner next week."

"Hey. Pattycakes, she's mine at night." Eric put his arm around my shoulder.

"Eric, go to hell. Sometimes vets need to get together and bond."

"There's enough of me to share. Aren't we supposed to have rain next week? I'm a fair-weather angler. I need to go and feed my new dog. What time do you want to go fishing tomorrow?"

"I'll pick you up at six in the morning if that's not too late."

"Eric, I'm an early . See you then. Oh, I have a combination on the gate now." I texted him the numbers. I went down to where the crowd was dispersing to their cars. Charlie came over and thanked me for coming. He said he was pleased to donate the wine to the club. I suggested he donate one bottle and keep the rest for a special occasion. I shook his hand and left. He wasn't my type, but at least he was in my age range.

I was surprised at how friendly and welcoming this community was. I knew I was a short-timer here. I figured I would be here for ten years before my body would wear out, and I would have to find an easier place to live. This was home, and even though I was an outsider and under scrutiny, I was happy.

Chapter 13

Another day in paradise. Fishing was spectacular, but sadly Eric's mobile phone had reception, and he was called back for an emergency. He dropped me at home and headed to the local hospital. I decided to ride Digger after lunch. I allowed Baxter to come, as well. I wanted to see how things went with both a dog and a horse. Digger eagerly came up to me. I brushed and saddled him, and we headed off on the trail behind the house. I rode for thirty minutes, and Digger was steady and bold. I was in love. Who needed human companionship? I wondered if they would sell me this horse. Digger reminded me of the horse I rode before I moved to Australia.

Baxter kept up and stayed a healthy distance behind Digger. He was going to be a good companion on the trail. He occasionally would pick up a scent that made his hackles rise, but I had my bear spray, so I wasn't too worried.

The trail split in three ways and appeared well used. I decided I would take the easy route and not overwork either Digger or Baxter. We plodded along the pine forest. There were manzanita and other trees that I couldn't identify. I added tree identification book procurement to my list. I thought there was an app, but I hadn't brought my phone. I doubted I would get reception out here. I would kick myself if I saw a bear and didn't photograph it for my kids.

We stopped in a meadow, and I let Digger eat. I was going to have to fence my pasture in. Digger could easily roam there without me. That was going to be my goal for next week. I'd create a large area with an electric fence. I was in love with this beautiful horse. I wondered if he was used in any movies or television series that Colin Chandler had starred in.

I returned to the house and opened my computer. I'd received several emails from my children. I invited them all for a Zoom meeting, and they replied quickly. I set up my laptop so I could show them the views of the scenery from the house. My son, Brandon, was on first. He was followed by Trevor and Colleen. Their spouses were in the background, and I saw all the grandchildren.

After I showed them the inside of the house and the views, I was surprised that they seemed to be more accepting of my ten-year plan. I promised them that when I was too old to live alone in a remote area, I would consider returning to Australia. I had no plans to create any attachments here, Digger aside. I walked outside, pointed the laptop toward the house, and then walked toward Digger and the creek. I was losing the signal. I retreated to the house. We all talked for thirty minutes, and then there was a tearful goodbye.

I was dozing from all my fishing and riding. I felt guilty that I hadn't written anything since yesterday. I usually wrote a minimum of two thousand words a day. I wrote and edited in the early morning before work in Australia, and I'd continued the pattern over here. I planned to power nap and then hit the stream in the evening.

I woke to the sound of a car coming over the hill. I didn't recognize the car and went out to greet my visitor. Eric said he would shut the gate but not lock it. I was hoping Sylvia might come by for more of a chat. When the car stopped, I recognized Charlie McLeod. He brought the bottle of wine and raised his hand in a gesture of friendliness. I waved, and he approached the house.

"Hello to the house." He smiled as he walked toward me. Baxter wagged his tail.

"Hi, Mr. McLeod. Please excuse this failure of a guard dog. You may be licked to death. Baxter, you mongrel. You're a complete disappointment and a wastrel."

Charlie McLeod reached down and patted Baxter's head. Sadly, the dog was obliging. "You didn't have to bring the wine. I was happy to recognize it. It was a lucky guess." My guess was he had another motive for coming to the property. Maybe it was because he heard about the property history and wanted to see it for himself. After all, it was the scene of a ghastly event.

"My friends call me Charlie, and I always pay my debts." He handed me the wine and looked around. He paused, and I invited him inside.

"I'm afraid it's a bit bare in here. I'm hoping my furniture comes soon, but who knows when my personal possessions will arrive from Australia."

Charlie entered and gazed around the great room. "You know, I've never been back here. You have a wonderful view. When you get your furniture and personal possessions, I'll bet this will be a nice spot."

"Can I get you something? I have wine," I said, pointing to the bottle, "Or coffee? Name your poison."

"Coffee would be wonderful. Thank you. I don't mean to impose. I leave for the East Coast tomorrow."

"Charlie, I have a confession."

He looked at me and furrowed his eyebrow. "You're married?"

"Ha. No, worse than that."

"You're gay?"

"Way worse. I just guessed on the wine. I knew it was a good wine, and I also know Americans only know a few wines, and it was just a guess."

"Oh, well. That is a problem."

"No. As I said, auction it off and give the proceeds to a good charity. The dog rescue place where I got your new best friend is a good one." Baxter had inserted his nose under Charlie's arm and was insisting that he be acknowledged.

"Maybe I have a confession to make as well. It wasn't the Grange. It's a Margaret River Shiraz."

It took me a second to realize what he'd done. The bottle he held was the Penfold's Grange. I looked at him and realized he was giving me a five-hundred-dollar bottle of wine. "I'm sorry, I couldn't possibly take that. The joke is on me. Lesson learned."

"No, Maggie. Consider it a welcoming gift."

I thought about it and said I would keep it and save it for a special occasion. We both knew I would only open it with Charlie present. "When do you return? I could have you and a few people over for a meal when I have settled in and have a dining room table."

"I don't know. Probably not for several weeks. I have a lot of contractual obligations." He looked over at the cliff and conifers. He then looked at the small table where the whiteboard and arrowhead sat. He read something I had written for Luke and searched me with a puzzled expression.

"There's a boy who comes to help me around here. He's a deaf-mute. This is how we communicate."

Charlie picked up the arrowhead and turned it over in his hand. "Where's this from? I have areas on my ranch where I've found artifacts."

"I think from around here. The young boy gave it to me. The town doctor, Eric, said there was an Indian encampment here." I pointed down to the creek at the end of the paddock.

Charlie didn't ask anything about the boy. Did he know who he was? I waited, but he simply set the arrowhead down.

"Charlie?"

"Yes?" He stared at me, which was slightly unnerving.

"Do you have a lot of baseball gloves that are only used for your picnic? If so, may I borrow two? I'd like to play catch with the boy."

"How old is he?"

"He's eleven or twelve. I don't need anything fancy, and I would return them. If the boy shows any interest, I'll buy him a glove."

"I have plenty. I'll have a few delivered. Do you need a bat?"

"Yes, that would be great. How do you take your coffee?"

"Milk only, thanks."

"Sorry, I only have nonfat."

"Can we walk down to the creek? I love looking for points and implements."

"Sure." Charlie downed his coffee, and we walked down to the creek. Digger joined us and followed along. It didn't take Charlie long to find a broken arrowhead. He then found a scraper. "This is a great spot. Can I come back and look the next time I'm back home?"

"Is this home?"

"Most definitely. Linda and I love it here. My home is where she is."

"I'm so sorry for your loss. I understand your wife was quite a woman."

Charlie paused and turned away. "Maggie, you would have loved her. You're a lot alike. Carol and Sylvia are lucky to have you."

I didn't say anything. I did put my hand on Charlie's forearm, but that was the end of it. He looked up at the sky, and we both saw gathering clouds. "I better get back to business."

"I still haven't googled you. I'm guessing you are well known."

"I try to keep a low profile. I have many people counting on me these days. My employees are like family."

We returned to the house, and he walked toward his car. He reached in and handed me a second bottle. "You and the girls have a taste of this."

"Thanks, Charlie. Safe travels. Thanks for the use of the gloves and bat too."

"Do you have a gun?" Charlie looked back up at the house and frowned.

"No, but I'm getting one. Don't tell me you think this place is dangerous too?"

"No, it's all just rumors. It pays to be prepared. Unless you are going out again or expecting more company, I'll lock the gate on my way out."

He left, and I returned to the house. There was an email. My book would be published tomorrow. I was told to expect to be interviewed again in a few days.

Chapter 14

Luke arrived on Monday, and he brought some cake. It had been his birthday yesterday. He was twelve, and he wrote on his notepad that his grandmother had made him a cake, and he received a new shirt and some books about fishing. He brought one with him to show me. The book didn't look new, and the inscription was to Colin Chandler. I looked at it and decided not to press the issue. Had he stolen it from Mr. Chandler's library? Maybe it was time we had a talk.

I decided to see how the next few days went first. I explained we were going to set up a fence to keep Digger from wandering into the forest. We drove to the farm supply to get the fencing material and a solar fence charger.

Trent West was getting some barbed wire in the hardware section. He showed me the most reliable charger and stakes I would need to string the electric tape to ensure Digger stayed confined. I bought a new gate for the corral and examined some hay for the horse. It was good quality, but it was expensive. I was getting better at pricing items compared to Australian prices.

Trent had a trailer, and he offered to bring the fencing and gate back to my property. He also offered to sell me hay that was of better quality and at a fairer price. He observed Luke, who was looking at chickens, which were for sale.

"If you want to get into the chicken and egg business, you're going to need a substantial fox and coyote-proof cage."

I looked at Luke and rolled my eyes. "I'll put that on my ever-growing list." I pointed to Trent, who shrugged. I knew not to talk about Luke in his presence. Trent observed the boy and smiled. He went over to him and touched his shoulder. Luke turned and stood. Trent offered his hand, and Luke reciprocated. They shook hands, but Luke didn't make eye contact. Luke turned and bent down to study the chickens.

"Grandson?"

"I wish. No. Luke is my neighbor. Not sure who, but I think he may be the cook's grandson."

"Mira? I don't think so. I've known Mira and Bing Gillard for years. They're still holding out for grandchildren. Could be the handyman they recently hired."

"Is he older and has a wild beard?"

"Um, I wouldn't have said that. The new guy's about fifty and has red hair."

"Someone from the estate told me off for fishing on the property last week."

"Oh, really?"

"He was old and looked like a wild mountain man. Grey hair and beard. Dressed in overalls."

"No idea. Say, Sylvie wants to have you over for dinner. How is this coming weekend?"

"Trent, I'll check my schedule. You know it's hard to fit everyone in with my burgeoning popularity." I opened my phone and smiled. "Actually, it appears I may even be ready for guests myself. There's a message that my furniture is coming this afternoon."

"Do you need any help?" Trent carried fencing wire and staples.

I pretended to open my phone and look at my calendar. "No, I'm sure the movers will put it where I want it. Looks like I'm only free on Monday through the next ten days, so have Sylvia call me. I gave her my number yesterday at the picnic."

"Don't you love that place? Charlie is such a nice guy for his status in life."

"Yes, he does seem like a kind man. He clearly loved his wife. Too bad he can't move on."

"Maggie, that man will go to his grave loving that woman, but he doesn't live the life of a widower. He has his dalliances. Don't feel too sorry for him."

I was shocked. I chastised myself for falling for the long-suffering widow schtick. Thankfully, I wasn't interested in him. *I need an older Marlboro man or an Eric with twenty more years. Oh, for goodness' sake, I don't need anything. If I needed a romantic friend, I could make them up and write a book about the poor bugger.*

Trent followed me home, and we unloaded the fencing material. When we arrived back home, Digger was already on the other side of the creek and could easily escape into the woods. Luke and I would start on the fence this afternoon, after lunch.

As we sat eating, I asked Luke if he liked to play baseball. He shrugged and wrote he didn't know. I then wrote down some multiplication problems, and he just stared at them. I decided that this kid needed more than merely a job. He needed more worldly experiences and a little catching up in his education. I didn't want to offend his family, so I devised a plan to teach him simple mathematics. Maybe I could even get him to talk to me.

We headed down to the paddock and began our fencing. The ground was hard, and we struggled to get the stakes into the soil for the electric fence. The superior outcome would be metal stakes that would be strong and not easily knocked down. We worked on it for an hour when the furniture truck arrived.

I directed the delivery men where the tables, couches, and bedroom furnishings would go. At the same time, Luke and Baxter stayed down, pounding in the stakes. This place was looking like a home. There were rugs and other decorative furnishings that my sister had suggested, which I placed around the house after the moving guys left. I even had a television that the men mounted in the great room. The cable was already protruding from next to the electric socket. The men plugged it in, and I instantly had a television. The furniture movers showed me how to run through the channels. There were over one hundred stations. After Australian television, where you might have thirty, this was a genuine threat to my productivity.

The men left, and I returned to the fencing project. It was time for Luke to go. I took my whiteboard down and wrote a note thanking him for today. I handed him money for the last few days. He smiled and wrote thanks. I wrote that tomorrow we were going to start on the multiplication tables. If he wanted to work with me, he was going to have to learn mathematics as well. I could see he wasn't happy. I wrote, "Your choice. If you come here, you need to learn as well as earn money."

Luke shrugged and then gave Baxter a hug and walked toward his home. Baxter knew his home was with me, and he came and sat by my side while poking his nose under my arm. I yelled, "See you tomorrow." Without looking back, Luke raised his hand. He'd heard me.

Chapter 15

I was ready when Luke arrived the following day. I watched YouTube videos about teaching math to twelve-year-old kids. He should have learned this at least three years ago. I could not teach my kids anything. They had no respect for my ability to do fractions. I hoped I had authority with Luke, and he would listen.

When Luke arrived, we had a small snack and then went out and placed more stakes for Digger's fence. I received a message that there was a delivery at the front gate, which was locked. The quickest way to get there was Digger. I put on his bridle and gave Luke a leg up. He rode him bareback up and over the hill and down to the gate. I showed Luke my phone with the combination. A few minutes later, Tim, one of the wranglers I had met at The Sanctuary picnic, drove up in a pickup, and I walked up to greet him. Luke dismounted and unbridled Digger.

"How did you score that horse?" I could see Tim knew and admired Digger.

"Patty Tilmouth found him for me. Do you know him?"

"I used to work at Chandler's Ranch. No one was ever allowed to ride him except Mr. Chandler."

Tim reached into the back of the king-cab and brought out three baseball gloves, two bats, a net for practicing, and several balls. Luke grinned when he saw this. "Oh, this is great. Thank you so much." I shook his hand and expected him to get back into the truck, but he told me he was asked to set up the net so we could practice without chasing balls all day. After he finished setting up the net, he showed Luke how to hold the bat. He had a softball, and he threw the ball in the air and hit it into the net. He helped Luke do the same. He never said anything, but I suspected he knew Luke.

"There's something else." Tim reached into the back seat and pulled out a twenty-two-gauge rifle. "The boss asked me to give you this until you get your own." Tim handed me the gun and a box of cartridges.

"Thanks, I think. Do I have to have a license to have this?"

"Technically, yes. Practically, no. Are you familiar with guns? Taken any safety courses?"

"I had a shotgun many years ago, but I haven't had one in decades."

"With all those deadly critters In Australia, you didn't own a gun?"

"Nope. We used our bare hands." I watched Luke observing this conversation. He knew what we were discussing.

Tim went over the basics and suggested that I purchase a lockbox.

"Welcome to America, ma'am. The boss asked us to keep you safe."

"Who's us?"

"The entire ranch."

"Well, thanks. My team," and I put my hand over Luke's shoulder, "and I thank you. We'll try to do the same for you." This reminded me I needed to see Patty Tilmouth and give her the arthritis drug I had for the old mare. Tim left, and I received a call from my literary agent.

"Tomorrow's the day. The video you did will come out tomorrow with the publication. Standby for launch." I was ready. Good or bad, I was living my dream. I wrote, fished, rode, interacted with genuinely lovely people, and even could add archeological exploration to my list.

Luke and I went down to the creek just before he left. We looked for artifacts. This area was protected from the wind, which made it an inviting place for indigenous camps. I'd observed arrowheads that had been dated at a museum. I knew nothing about the tribes that roamed around this area. The three artifacts that Luke first showed me were crude and suggested recent tribes. Apparently, the Indians lost their skills over time when modern implements of warfare, such as guns, were introduced. Luke looked up at the sky and then toward his watch. He stood up and waited for me to stand, as well.

"See you tomorrow. May I call you Maggie?"

"Maggie's fine with me." I tried to sound casual. I was elated.

He ran to the edge of the meadow and disappeared into the woods toward his home. I smiled and looked at my whiteboard. *Don't need you anymore.*

Baxter signaled Luke's arrival the following morning. I admonished the dog. "Baxter, could you please at least pretend you love me more than Luke?"

"We're going to do a math lesson and then get to work on the fence." I sat Luke down at my new desk and pulled a chair alongside him. I showed him a few basic math concepts and wrote some simple addition problems. He could add and subtract. He understood the idea of multiplication tables. Still, the lesson was continually punctuated with questions of why he had to know this. He told me he was never leaving the ranch, and he would never need this information.

I asked him to explain, but he would not elaborate. We went through the one times table and then the twos. He used his fingers, and I could see he understood the concept, but he didn't want to take the time and effort to memorize them. After an hour, we returned to our fence building project. That afternoon we went fishing. This kid loved to fish. It gave me an idea. I told him to take home the two times tables and practice writing them out. After today, we would only fish if he could recite and pass a test for the twos. His face fell. I could almost see tears. When it was time, he ran to the edge of the woods without saying goodbye. At least I knew he was human. Did he speak at home?

The next day Luke arrived a few minutes late. He recited the two times tables, wrote them out, and then answered the problems I had written down out of order. I complimented him on his effort. We went over the threes briefly and then went back to work on the fence. The hard ground made it slow going, but we would finish by the end of the week.

Trent and Sylvia arrived later with a truckload of hay. Luke and Trent unloaded the hay while Sylvia and I walked down to the creek. We returned to the house, and I made coffee for the three of us. I noticed Luke reverted to his mute persona while strangers were present. Trent and Luke drove up to the house, and Trent observed our mini batting cage and saw the gloves and bats sitting on the porch.

"Do we have a potential major league star on the rise?"

"You know, we haven't had time to start practicing."

"No time like the present." Trent turned to Luke. "Luke, let's play some ball."

The two boys went out while Sylvia and I sat on the deck outside the great room and watched. Painful was the only way to describe it. Luke had no idea how to throw and catch. Trent pretended it was normal and spent some time just throwing and showing Luke how to throw a ball. He showed him how to toss the ball in the air and catch it to practice independently.

Sylvia and I decided Saturday evening was an excellent time to get together. She was sure that Carol and her husband would be able to come as well. Carol's husband, Hal, worked for a corporation and was often away. This reminded me that I hadn't researched Charlie McLeod's business enterprise yet. I asked Sylvia if she had any idea who Luke's parents were. She didn't, and she'd never met Luke until now. I didn't tell her that he was now talking. I didn't know if he spoke at home. I wanted to know what she knew about the estate and who lived there and ran the place.

"Have you ever met Colin Chandler?"

"Oh, sure. He used to come around all the time. He was a total spunk and a very switched-on man. He did a lot for our community. It's a shame what happened to him and his daughter."

"She was murdered, wasn't she?"

"Yes, by her husband. They were into drugs. The other Chandler kids are okay. They used to come up here all the time, but when Colin remarried, no one liked his new wife, and the boys drifted back to their mother's place. She's in Butte County and has a ranch with her second husband. Rumor has it, Colin hasn't been back here in years. The current wife is a city girl and has him on a short leash. I guess that's why you have Digger. There is no way he would lend that horse to anyone if he was around. My guess is the place will be on the auction block the second he dies. It's not as big as Charlie's, but the rumor is it is still well maintained, and the house is a replica of his television series house."

"Do Colin and Charlie know each other?"

"Oh, sure. I think they see each other often. Colin is based in California now, and Charlie and Linda had a house down there too. I think they still get together several times a year."

"Anything else I need to know?"

"Dinner is at six-thirty, and don't be late. We're ranching people and like to get to bed early."

"What can I bring?"

"It's a little too early for a date, but Carol and I will work on that. How about that bottle of wine? I'm guessing he had someone drop it off already."

"He brought it himself. There's a story on that. I'll explain it on Saturday. Is a salad okay?"

"Sounds good. In the meantime, how about we go for a ride? I can pick you and Digger up, and we can go into the National Forest tomorrow. The weather's going to be nice. Do you have a swimsuit? Is ten o'clock okay?"

That afternoon Luke and I did more work on the fence. I never asked him many questions about himself or his past. We did practice the three times table, and I put on my music from my phone, which connected to my speakers, that I set on a fence post. He smiled, and I could see he was enjoying the music. I decided that singing was his cross to bear, and I began singing the songs on my playlist. I like songs from the rock group Fun and, of course, "Walk Like a Man." Even Luke sang along to that one.

I decided to change gears. I wanted to lock Digger up and be able to use the corral. I had never hung a gate, but luckily the new corral entrance was the same as the old one, and the hinges were still on the main post. We had to lift it together and at the same height to get the bolt hooks to slide into holes that were already in the post. We held up the gate against the post and secured the hinges on the gate. We placed the bolt hooks into the hinges, and then we attempted to lift the gate to slide the bolt hooks into the post. This required us to raise and have the gate level. Luke was strong, but it was difficult for us to coordinate this together. We needed some wooden blocks to help us.

"Okay, Luke. One last try, and then we'll do it by the books and get the damn blocks. So, get your sorry ass over here, walk like a man, and lift this gate." We were both singing and laughing, and we could barely stand up, let alone level the gate to fit the bolts into the wood post. The music was playing, and we were both singing. We didn't hear the two men walk over from the neighboring Chandler estate. Suddenly, the gate lifted as light and steady as could be, and we slid the bolts in, and I turned toward Luke to high-five him. As I turned, I realized we had company. Gabe Turner and an older man were standing next to us and shaking their heads. The old man was the same one that told me off for fishing on the Chandler property.

Luke reached down and turned off the music. He stood between us and stared at me and then at the two men. I wasn't sure what to say, but I thought some humor would be excellent.

"What took you so long? Luke and I were almost ready to give up."

Gabe laughed, but the older man just stared at me and then at Luke. "How's my horse? You're getting some use out of him, hopefully?"

The man had trimmed his beard and had recently received a haircut. Was this Colin Chandler? I observed Luke, who was acting like he was in trouble. He put his hands down deep in his pockets and then sheepishly looked at the old man.

"How's my grandson doing? Is he earning his money?"

Luke is a Chandler? I looked at him hard, and Luke's face reddened. "Mate, you've been holding back. I thought we didn't have any secrets." I laughed, and Luke saw I was kidding. Colin Chandler looked at us both, and I think he recognized that Luke heard what I was saying. Did the man observe us singing? Did he know his grandson was not a deaf-mute? I tried to sound casual. "Anyone want some lemonade or something stronger? I know at least one of us has some explaining to do."

Chapter 16

We headed up to the house. Gabe commented on my electric fence and a few other things I had done in the last week. The two men entered the house, which thankfully now had furniture.

"What would you like? Coffee, lemonade, a beer? I know Luke usually has a beer this time of day."

Colin raised his eyebrows as I reached into the refrigerator and pulled out a root beer. "That'll do me, too," he replied. Gabe just wanted ice water. Colin looked at Luke and motioned for him to go out and drink his on the porch. He was gentle, and I could see Luke was not afraid of him.

"Mr. Chandler, Luke is a great kid. He does have issues, but he's been a terrific asset to me these first few weeks. I'm not sure about where his problems come from, but he is welcome here anytimc. I've quite enjoyed him. He likes to fish, as you know." I gave him a stern look, and he lowered his eyes and laughed.

Gabe downed his drink and excused himself. "I think I'll check out the baseball setup."

"Yeah, Luke could use some help in that department." Gabe went out and took Luke down the steps toward the net with a glove and a bat.

I waited for Luke's grandfather to begin. "I'm not sure what you know about me, but I will say much of it is made up by the press. I had three children, and I'm married to Heidi. She and I live separate lives these days. I travel quite a lot from my home in LA to Europe, where Heidi lives. She never liked coming here. It was my home with my first wife and the mother of my children."

I offered him some more root beer, but he declined.

"Two beers, and I might not make it out the door at my age." I laughed. I knew Colin was about to tell me some dark secret of his and Luke's past, but he did have a sense of humor for an old geezer.

"The children all married and have busy lives. They don't come here often, but we try to meet here once a year. I lost my daughter a few years ago, and she's buried here. Well, her ashes are here on my estate. Luke is her son. Do you know about this?"

"No, sir. I think she was murdered?" I waited while he gazed out the windows looking at the view past my pasture and up into the forest.

"My fucking son-in-law killed her. Do you have children?"

"Three. My kids all live in Australia."

"Well, Sarah was hard work from the moment she was born. She was the second born. Are your kids all good kids?"

"They all had their moments, but basically, yes, they're good kids." I poured us each a glass of water.

"Sarah was a troublemaker from the start. She got into drugs and married a drug dealer. They had Luke, and it seemed that once they had a child, they began to turn their lives around. When Luke was six, my daughter had a miscarriage, which sent her back to her old ways. I don't think Cameron ever stopped dealing, but they hid it well.

"One day, I received a call from my ex-wife. She was hysterical, and she said Sarah was dead. Her husband had killed her. Her ex was in South America, living with her partner. I hate that term, by the way. Partner—damn stupid if you ask me. Anyway, she was on a ranch in Argentina. I was in LA at the time, and I had to deal with it all until something could be arranged for my grandson."

Colin looked around to make sure we were alone. "Luke was in the care of the police and under hospital guard. He had been savagely beaten by his father and needed surgery for internal bleeding. I was there when he awoke, but he wasn't the same. He couldn't hear, and he didn't speak. It's been like that ever since."

"Jesus, I had no idea. I'm so sorry."

"My kids and my ex-wife offered to take and raise Luke, but there's more to it than just that. It seems that the murder was a drug deal gone bad, and Luke saw the whole thing. He might know who was involved, and so my kids and ex all decided to hide Luke until he's old enough to take care of himself. That's why he's here."

I was beginning to understand things now. "Gabe mentioned that talking about Luke was a fireable offense. Your workers are good."

"Yes, I pay them well, and they understand the situation. The police think the whole incident was orchestrated by a very well-connected and sophisticated group of men. We made it clear that Luke was unable to give any details due to his impairment. He would be a target if any of this got out. Do You understand?"

"Is Luke's dad dead or in prison?"

"He's in prison, but he wasn't charged with Sarah's murder, and he is due for release this year. He's already started proceedings to ask for custody. My lawyers are adamant that he won't get custody, but that won't stop this bastard. He's a thug, and he won't stop until he gets Luke back."

"Do you think he genuinely wants Luke? Or is Luke and his testimony what he wants as a trade?"

"In truth, probably a bit of both, but he's not getting him. Since Luke can't speak, it's moot, anyway." Colin looked around the room. I hadn't been to his house, but I knew this place was tiny in comparison. None of my personal effects had arrived, and he would get no sense of who I was from his observations. I tried to decide if I should tell him that his grandson can hear and speak. Obviously, Luke is a master at hiding this. As Luke's friend, I would keep his secret, but I am a parent as well, and it didn't take me long to decide where my allegiance lay.

"Mr. Chandler, Luke can hear, and he has spoken to me."

I think Colin Chandler already suspected this. He didn't look surprised. "Yeah, I had a feeling. My friends call me Colin or Collie. Who the hell are you, anyway?"

I briefly gave him my bio, including my original upbringing in the States, my life in Australia, and my retirement and recent move back to America. "I've been told this house has a long history of death, and my friends are wondering why I chose to live here, but I love it. I'm formally asking permission to cross your property to fish."

He laughed. "Permission granted. Does Luke say anything I need to know?"

"Not so far, and I don't ask any details. Mostly we are just singing to music I play as we work. We've been working on small projects and then fishing in the late afternoon. Still, I think Luke needs to have some other skills, and I noticed he can write and draw, but his education is lacking, and I've introduced baseball and timetables."

This brought a laugh to Colin. "I've been remiss in that department. I should have made sure he kept up, but I did think he had actual brain damage, and I felt he would never function in the outside world. I'm happy to pay you to help him."

"Colin, take your money, and I think, as a former horse vet, you know what orifice you can stick it in. You're my neighbor. You lent me probably the best riding horse I've ever ridden, and most importantly, Luke is my friend and my employee. By the way, I am sure we are breaking a ton of child protection laws. No sense in advertising that."

"What do you like to be called?"

"Maggie."

"Maggie, how do I thank you?"

"You don't have to. Luke's help and the use of Digger are all I could ask for. Well, gate hanging aside."

"If there's any heavy work that needs doing, just call us, and I can send Gabe or one of the other boys over at any time. You have our number?"

"I think I have your cook's number."

Colin wrote down two more numbers. One was his personal number, and one was the estate number. I gave him mine.

"I was told you rarely come here. Is this true?"

"I lie low most of the time. Fame is a powerful drug. It had me by the short and curlies for decades." He looked down and laughed. "Now, there are not many short and curlies left, and I like to keep a low profile."

I thought about my small, pending brush with fame and wondered how it would play out. "Well, the invitation to come and visit is always open for you and any of your staff and family. I suggest that we keep Luke's auditory skills to ourselves at this stage."

"Thanks, Maggie. I couldn't agree more. Charlie's right. You're a good addition to our community."

"Charlie McLeod? I hear you're friends?"

"For many years. Charlie's probably my best friend. He asked me to look out for you. That's why Gabe and I came over. Oh, and to make sure you knew you could fish on my land. When he returns, we plan to have you over for dinner. That is if you don't mind hanging out with some old codgers?"

"I can talk old geezer talk with the best of them, Colin. You're on. How about I have you both over." *Water, water everywhere, and not a drop to drink. So many men and not a single, acceptable bachelor among them. A girl can dream.*

Chapter 17

I received a call from my agent the following morning. She was based in New York, and we'd never actually met, Zoom aside. "Maggie, your book debuted well. The publishers are asking for the next book. They have the first three ready to release, and they are asking for the fourth. Is your editor working on it now?"

"I think it should be ready for a final review. I usually have my daughter back in Australia do that, but maybe we could leave it for the publishers. I'll call the editor and see what she's working on."

"How about the others? Are you writing yet?"

"Uh, well. I've been a bit busy. I'll start tomorrow morning. Pinkie promise."

"Is that an Australian term? Just get going as soon as possible. I have needs, and your writing is what's going to fulfill them."

"I hope your needs are small. I'm quite enjoying retirement and have so much to do around here to get my home comfortable. My gear from Australia is in transit."

I heard a truck coming, and I hadn't fed Baxter or even caught Digger. The fence wasn't complete, and he was across the creek again. I threw on a jacket and went down to see him. I whistled for him, and he came running. *Man, I love this horse.*

Sylvia opened the back of the trailer, and we loaded Digger and were off. We drove for forty minutes to a trailhead and unloaded, saddled, and mounted our horses. The morning was chilly, and I was glad I had layered myself in clothing. Sylvia led the way. Her mount was a young gelding that she was breaking in for the ranch. She and Trent raised cattle and grew hay. On the side, they started young horses for the annual bull and gelding sales.

Along with the bulls, several young horses were sold as ranch horses. The profit was not high, but it was almost guaranteed, and this helped when the market was down or the hay crop wasn't good. They had several years of decent production, but they remembered the bad years, and they were saving for retirement. Their kids showed no interest in the ranch, and the only possible outcome was the eventual sale of the ranch. That was ten years from now unless Trent became incapacitated or died.

Sylvia met Trent at university. They'd attended an agricultural college together and fell in love. Trent's father owned the ranch, and the plan was for him and Sylvia to return and take over when they graduated. Trent's dad was killed in a tractor accident in their last year of college. Trent went back home and was unable to finish his final year. Sylvia stayed and received a teaching degree. She taught in the local grammar school for years, and then two years ago, she retired from teaching and devoted herself to helping Trent on the ranch.

Sylvia didn't hide her age like I did, but other than gray hair, she was fit, with a smooth complexion and toned from her hard work on the ranch. It made me think about myself. I was quickly becoming an old lady in many respects. Three months ago, I was an active horse vet. My nurses were half my age, and yet I still ran from the office to the barn while they walked. I was saddle sore from my first long ride on Digger the other day, and I was muscle sore from pounding in the stakes for the electric fence.

Writing was my new passion and career. It did nothing to help me stay active and fit.

We rode into the woods and then out by a river, which meandered through a canyon surrounded by sheer granite cliffs. The trail was open to the public, and we encountered a few hikers but no other riders. I didn't bring my fishing rod but made a note to come back and fish in here. Did Eric know this place? We stopped, tethered the horses, and ate an early lunch in a grassy meadow. Sylvia spread out a blanket she brought. "Do you have on your swimsuit?"

"I do, but there is no way I'm swimming in this water. It's freezing."

"Follow me, you big baby."

She took me through a narrow break in the cliff, which opened to a small gravel area with a pool protected from the wind and view of any hikers. The water had a smell of sulfur, and I suspected it was a thermal pool. I stuck my hand in the water and noted the temperature was like bathwater.

"I'm in." I immediately took off my clothes down to my swimsuit. Sylvia was already in the water when I stepped in. "Oh, heaven on a stick. How did you find this?"

"Trent took me here when we were first married. We come every year for our anniversary."

"This is unbelievable. It's like the fountain of youth."

"Don't we both wish? Maggie, you're doing pretty well for an old lady."

"Hey. I resemble that remark. Clean living and good genes."

"If you say so."

"Okay, maybe good genes. I got lucky."

We sat, soaked, and I scrubbed the dead skin away from my wrinkled legs. Sylvia asked about my books. I still didn't have any in print, but I promised to give her one when I received my author copies. I didn't want this to end, but we both had to get back. We rode back to the trailer and drove to my property.

"You're keeping your gate locked, aren't you?" Sylvia idled the truck while I jumped out and unlocked the gate.

"Yes, ma'am. What is it with you locals? You seemed obsessed with security."

"Just your place. I can't explain it, but it's like the place is cursed."

"I've never been happier or felt more secure. Sorry to be a downer on your fears." We turned onto my long driveway. As we came over the rise, I gazed down at my cabin and meadow below. My fence was almost complete. Luke, Gabe, and even Colin were down stringing the tape. Sylvia punched my arm. "Well, aren't you special?"

"I told Luke not to come until after lunch. I planned to finish the fence when I returned. Apparently, my neighbors had other ideas. I waved to them and shouted they were trespassing, and I was going to call the sheriff.

Sylvia laughed and helped me unload Digger. We walked over to the new fence. "Hey, Gabe, hey, Collie. Don't think we need the fence today. Digger's plum worn out."

Apparently, they all knew one another. Sylvia went over and hugged Colin and touched Luke to get his attention. She didn't think he could hear. "I'm showing Maggie the haunts. We went to the thermal pool near Magic Falls."

"I hope you two were suitably attired." Colin still had a sense of humor.

"Hey, don't even imagine the visuals at our age." I laughed as I sponged Digger and turned him loose.

"Speak for yourself. My husband doesn't mind looking." Sylvia said as she and I lifted the tailgate on the trailer.

"I'll bet he doesn't." Colin was quick to respond. Gabe was politely not getting into this conversation. Such a hunk but so young and so married. He directed Luke to pick up the tools and put them into his toolbox.

"Can I interest anyone in a beer?"

The men declined, saying they had work to do. Luke went home with his grandfather, and everyone left. Baxter had been let out of the house, and he stayed with me. After a quick shower to get the sulfur smell off my body, I drove to the vet clinic. I was given a tour. It was small and purpose-built. I met two of the vets, and Patty asked me to have coffee. I gave her the arthritis medicine for the old mare at The Sanctuary and explained how to administer it. She wanted to pay for it, but I insisted it was a gift to her and Charlie.

We decided to have an early dinner as her kids had baseball practice. We went and had tacos. OMG, authentic tacos, and corn chips, and I had a Margarita. She had a coke. Patty gazed longingly at my drink. "Retirement definitely has its perks. Someday I aspire to have a drink on a weekday."

"Retirement has its perks for sure, but in a million years, I never thought I would be enjoying it as much as this." I took another taco, making a mess of the whole thing. "I don't feel retired, just repurposed. My agent called, and they are pressuring me to finish two more novels in the next month."

"Novels?"

"Yeah, I'm a writer now. Didn't you know?"

Patty looked at her watch and wiped her mouth. "I have two minutes. What do you write about?"

"Five seconds. You. I write about vets. Mostly cozy mysteries. What ages are your kids?"

"Nine, twelve, and oh my effing God sixteen going on 'I don't have to do what you say, I'm practically an adult.'"

"Ouch. See you in a few years when you reemerge bruised and battered. I might come and see your kids play. I'm helping a kid who I'm trying to teach to play ball. He needs to socialize."

"The kids practice from six to seven on weeknights. The games are on Saturday. How old is your friend?"

"He just turned twelve. He can barely throw a ball."

"Bring him to watch. What's his name?"

"Luke."

"Oh, yeah. Doesn't the lad have some serious issues?"

"Yes. Maybe we can just watch."

"Got to go. Can I call you when I need you?"

"My operators are standing by."

I had missed a call. My belongings from Australia would arrive tomorrow. When I came back to the cabin, Baxter was out waiting for me. I'd left him in the house. This was the second time he'd escaped, or had he?

Chapter 18

"Baxter, you little bastard, how'd you get out?" The gate near the road was locked, and there were no unusual smells, open doors, or windows. I checked the handles, and they were still closed. Did I leave him out when I left? I was sure he was locked inside. Baxter showed no sense of agitation or alarm. He was glad to see me. I looked through the house. There was little that anyone would want at this stage, minus my laptop or my new television.

All my information and books were backed up on a remote server. And yet, here was Baxter, sitting up on the deck waiting for me—my happy brown dog. At least he hadn't run away from the house. Maybe my plans to build a fence to keep him secure outside weren't needed.

My phone rang. It was my sister. Christy was home and wanting to know how things were. I gave her the whole rundown of my neighbors, the townsfolk, and the picnic. I told her I had a dog, a horse, and a fishing partner. In short, life was terrific.

She saw an ad for my book, and she'd already ordered it. This reminded me I needed to do some advertising on my own. I hadn't caught up with Facebook and my other social media. The publishers told me to go my hardest to sell and promote the books.

Christy wanted to bring Miles and come back when I was truly settled. "You mean tomorrow?"

"Maybe early next month. Miles wants to see your place."

"Your suite awaits."

Luke arrived early the following morning. We went through the three- and four-times tables and then did some throwing and catching. We worked in the vegetable garden, and in the afternoon, we went fishing. Luke mentioned his grandfather would like trout for dinner. We did our best, and Luke took three medium-size trout home. I asked him if he wanted to go watch a baseball game on Saturday morning. He was uncertain if he was allowed, so he would tell me tomorrow.

The following day, I had to go open the gate for my expected delivery. The transfer of my personal items was delayed again. I had to leave the gate unlocked. My appointment for my firearms safety class was at ten o'clock in the morning. Man, these people take this seriously, and in the end, I was glad I did it. After the course was over, I purchased a rifle, ammunition, and a lockbox that could be secured to the wall. The gun was guaranteed to be loud, but I was told to shoot at a bear and run like heck because I would probably not kill it. I was back to being a gun-toting American. I felt guilty, but a girl must do what a girl must do. I was officially 'packing' now. I would use the bear spray first.

I arrived home to all my boxes, which were left on the porch. Baxter was in the house, and I was relieved to see him safe and sound. Fortunately, none were so heavy I couldn't move them. Many were framed pictures. This was the best part of moving. I already knew where most of the paintings would be hung, but for many, I was undecided. I didn't have any time to consider this. I was having dinner at the Bar Double X ranch with Sylvia, Trent, Carol, and her husband if he had returned from his travels.

I was not one to dress up, but I showered and dressed in nice slacks and a sweater. The rain threatened. I locked Baxter in the house and checked the doors, windows, and left. The security camera and monitors would be here next week. I almost forgot the wine. I was taking the less expensive one along with the salad. I promised to save the Penfolds for dinner with Charlie. This reminded me, I needed to return the rifle he'd lent me.

I arrived at the same time as Carol and her husband, who had flown back this morning. Hal was tall, like Carol, and dressed in a plaid shirt and khaki shorts. He was very cosmopolitan in comparison to the rest of us. I knew Hal was a pilot. He greeted me and mentioned Charlie had talked about the new vet from Australia. He was disappointed that I didn't have much of an accent.

We all had a glass of the celebrated wine and then a perfectly barbecued steak. The food was delicious. We traded short histories of our past, and then I was grilled about my books. Carol and Sylvia downloaded the e-book and were already into the first book. I wasn't sure if they were polite, but I was pleased.

Hal asked a lot of questions. Carol kept looking at him like there was something fishy going on. I sensed her perplexity. I decided to reverse the questions and asked him about what kind of work he did and where was his company's base. I finally figured out he worked in Charlie's business and was his pilot. He flew Charlie around to his various businesses and residences.

"So, what is Charlie's business?"

"You don't know? Have you been living under a rock?" Carol laughed.

"He owns CLM Enterprises. You've heard of CLM, haven't you?" Hal cocked his head and studied me.

I shook my head. "I've been living on an island, and maybe I need to catch up on the American business front."

Hal began to fill me in. "CLM stands for Charles and Linda McLeod. It has holdings in health care, manufacturing, IT, and resource procurement for other companies. Let's say you need timber or steel for a new high-rise building, you need people to build the high-rise, or you need doctors to care for the people who build the structure. Charlie sources it. His company was named one of the top ten most innovative and progressive companies in America a few years ago."

"Holy moly, and so he sourced the wine we are drinking? He and I need to be better friends."

Trent poured everyone the last of the bottle. "He's a pretty nice guy despite that. He saved us a time or two, didn't he, Sylvie?"

"Yes. We have Charlie to thank for saving us several years ago when the market crashed, and the price of beef made ranching impossible. You know we're all forgetting to mention how loyal he is to Linda and her memory."

"Carol, how did your sister meet him?"

"College. Trust me, back then, he was just a kid, and my parents were sure Linda was making a mistake in marrying him. Oh, if they could have lived to see Charlie and Linda build their empire. It wasn't just him. Linda was an equal partner. Their only regret was they didn't have any kids."

"Why didn't they adopt?"

"It was Linda's choice. She wanted children, but it wasn't a deal-breaker for her as much as it was for Charlie. That man loves kids. You saw him play ball with all the youngsters at the picnic. I think he only has the annual event, so he can play with those children."

"They have charities for impoverished children all over the country," Sylvia mentioned as she cleared the table.

"He sounds a little too good to be true."

"He isn't perfect," Carol stated. I wondered what she meant by that. Sylvia mentioned he must see other women. I felt sorry for him. When my husband left me, it wasn't a tragedy. I still had the kids and the house. We had a mildly contentious divorce, but I got over it quickly, and he was married and having another child within a few months. I dated a few men after the divorce. Still, my lifestyle and work were more than I could handle, and eventually, I just stopped looking.

"Maggie, tell us more about you and your practice."

I told them about my practice and the kids and a bit about my books. I explained that the veterinary practice I had was more like the *All Creatures Great and Small* kind, unlike today's more common ones. I mentioned Patty and said I thought her veterinary clinic was probably closer to mine, except I only did horses.

"Tell us one good story about one of your clients or horses." Hal leaned forward and clasped his hands expectantly. Carol looked at Hal like he had asked me to talk about the surface of Mars.

"What? I think it's interesting. I've always been interested in Australia." Hal looked like he had been caught out.

"Hal, that's tough. Let me think."

"Did you have a favorite client or horse?" Now Hal was really getting the look.

Carol studied her husband and then laughed. "He put you up to this, didn't he?"

I was lost. "Who is he?"

All three responded at once. "Charlie."

"No, I was simply wondering."

"Yeah, sure," said Carol trying to stifle a full-on laugh.

Trent started to hum the tune, "Chuck E's in Love."

"As if. Okay, do you want to hear a story?"

"Yes, please."

I went on to describe a Christmas Eve party when I had eight people coming for dinner and had an emergency an hour before the turkey was cooked and the guests arrived. An older horse had run through two fences and had multiple leg lacerations.

"The owner had left the horse with aging parents, and they could barely hold the lead rope. I was able to clean and dress the wounds on two legs without sedation. When I gave it a tetanus vaccine, the horse went off and ran across a ten-acre paddock. I went and caught her and then once again attempted to inject her. Time was running out. The real owner showed up, and the horse bolted again. The owner wanted her euthanized. She was old, and the wounds were significant, and she was a nightmare to handle. The owner couldn't believe I was able to wrap her legs by myself. I had to inject her with sedation to eventually euthanize her, and that was another drama. I charged them far more than normal, and in my mind, it wasn't enough. I handed them the bill, and they said, 'Is that all?'

"I eventually returned to my Christmas Eve dinner preparations, and as I was pulling into the house to attend the turkey, two friends arrived and helped with the dinner. The phone rang again. A child's pony had severe colic and needed euthanizing. Their vet was away and wasn't able to attend. One of my guests overheard the conversation, and she insisted I go.

"When I arrived, the pony was refluxing, which is vomiting. The pony's abdomen was distended, and the gums were purple. The little girl was distraught. It was heart-wrenching. Her mother took me aside and said her daughter worked for six months doing odd jobs around the neighborhood to buy the pony. Instead of Christmas presents, she requested she could attend pony camp. The pony had a brand-new halter and rope she would use when she went with her pony to the camp for the week.

"I had to pull it together and do the deed. It was difficult because the pony was rolling violently. I eventually was able to sneak in and give heavy sedation and then euthanize the pony. The little girl was taken into the house, and I returned to my car. The parents came over and asked how much this would cost. I told them the last client today paid your bill, and there would be no charge. I drove out of the property and bawled my eyes out. It took me several minutes to compose myself, and I returned to my dinner."

"Did your guests wait for you?" Carol and Sylvia had tears in their eyes.

"Nope, but they saved me a plate, and it was still a great evening. All I said was that I had taken care of the pony. I was not going to ruin the Christmas dinner by attempting to recount this story. I would have recommenced the tear fest."

The two couples were silent for a while. "Can we hear more stories another time? Have you written this up in one of your books? What is the name of the book that just came out?" Hal was not trying to pretend anymore.

"Hal, I can send you my CV, and if you or your boss need any other information, I'm happy to fill in the gaps." I laughed as I stood up. I only had one glass of wine and knew I was legal. I offered to take Carol and Hal home, but Carol declined.

"I'll be set to entertain in a week or two once I've unpacked and the place is decorated. I'd love to have you all over then. Thanks for such a lovely evening and for the ride yesterday, Sylvia."

I arrived home, and Baxter was where I left him. There was a note on the gate, however. Charlie had stopped by and said he wanted to taste the wine. He had returned sooner than he had expected. He wrote his number on the message.

Chapter 19

I called Charlie on Monday. He'd already flown out to Texas. He would be back next Friday, and he invited me to dinner at his house for the following Saturday. I was curious why he would entertain me when I knew he would never get over his dead wife. Still, maybe he was like me and simply enjoyed the company of people without any notions of a pending relationship. I accepted his invitation, and he mentioned I could bring a date if I wanted. That made me happy. There was no one I had met who was suitable, but it took the pressure off the dinner.

"Ha. I wish. I'll bring the wine. Do you want me to bring anything else?"

"No. My staff would be offended if you did that." Again, with fewer expectations on his part—I could get used to that man.

I unpacked and decorated my house over the next few days. Luke was helpful, but he mentioned his grandfather was leaving to attend a Los Angeles family function. Luke's uncle was opening an art exhibit, and Colin wanted to support him. Colin knew his attendance would garner more attention, making the show a success.

When Luke mentioned it, he told me that his grandfather asked him to accompany him to Los Angeles. Luke declined and asked to stay with me until his grandfather returned on the following Saturday.

"Nope, not without your grandfather's permission."

I received a phone call from Colin in less than an hour. He was concerned Luke was taking up too much of my time, and I assured him Luke would work for his keep. We accomplished many tasks, played ball, extended the tutoring from math, added science, and some philosophy. I thought some United States history and teaching of the founding fathers' writings might give him something to consider. Luke could make up his own mind.

Luke and I went to the ballpark and watched the young ballplayers in action before Luke would return to his own home on Saturday. Patty was there with her brood and came up and sat with us. Luke went back to his silent mode, but he watched the boys playing and appeared to take it in.

We stopped at the grocery store after the game, and I picked up a few things and returned home. The week had gone quickly, and soon Luke was heading home. I thanked him and paid for his work. This time he said it wasn't fair that he stayed, ate my food, and then received money for the few things he did.

"Hey, your work was far more valuable than what you cost me this week." He reluctantly took the money. I handed him some math problems to work on while he was home tomorrow. I planned to ride on Sunday, and Luke was going to spend the day with his grandfather.

I had a flat tire on the way to Charlie's house. I was on the interstate when I heard the loud noise coming from my tire. This could not be worse. I didn't even know where the jack was and had to get the manual from under the seat. It seemed simple enough, but I would get dirty, and I was dangerously close to the traffic.

As I retrieved the jack and loosened the lug nuts from the wheel, an old truck pulled up behind me. A man jumped out and asked if he could help. Cars were whizzing by and coming close to me and my SUV. "I would love some help, thanks." He was about my age and slightly overweight. He had a wild white beard, a red, long-sleeved shirt, and suspenders.

He hesitated, and I showed him where the release bolt for the spare tire was. In fifteen minutes, he had the new tire on, and the flat tire stored where the spare had been. As he finished, a highway patrolman pulled up and stopped. I went over to the patrol car and thanked the officer for stopping. He waited with his emergency lights on for extra protection. I went back to my car, and the bearded man suggested I get the tire fixed tomorrow. I looked at my hand, which was dirty from my original attempt to start changing the tire, but his hand was dirty too. What the heck? I stuck out my hand to shake his and thanked him. His name was Nick. "I can't thank you enough."

"Happy to help." He grinned and pointed to my car. "You better be on your way. This is no place to hang out." He turned and went back to his old truck. I retreated to my car. The patrolman signaled for me to pull out and enter the traffic.

I could not explain the interaction. I knew I would not see this man again. His license plate was from another state. He was pulling a trailer that had an old refrigerator covered with a blanket and strapped down. The touch of that man and his generosity in helping me in such a precarious place awakened something in me. It was a man's touch. For the first time in years, I felt a desire I had thought was long gone. I hadn't sought the company of a man in years. I was sure my needs for male companionship were as dead as my ovaries. Well, maybe not.

I arrived at the entrance to The Sanctuary ranch. This time the entry to the property had an unmanned gate with an intercom. I pushed the button, and a woman answered and gave me a combination to key into the pad, triggering the gate to open. I was instructed to drive up to the house. There were several cars parked next to the residence. People were standing on the patio where drinks and nibbles were being offered by staff dressed in traditional uniforms. I didn't know this was another party. They were all dressed formally, while I was in jeans and a sweater. I had dirt on my hands and pants from changing my flat tire. Charlie came down to my car, where I stood, wondering if I had time to go home and redress myself.

"Hi, Maggie. So glad you could come." Charlie smiled warmly. He looked at my clothes, and he bent to kiss me. I held up my hands, and he stopped.

"I didn't realize this was a formal occasion. Do you mind if I go home and change?"

"No, you look great. Don't mind us. I'm happy you're here. I want you to meet some of my associates." We walked up toward the patio, and everyone turned and saw me in my country finest. I wanted to crawl in a hole, but Charlie didn't seem to mind. He escorted me into the house and to the bathroom. "Come on out and meet my other guests. Don't worry about your clothes."

"Are you sure I can't fix some plumbing or maybe see a horse? I feel embarrassed. You have lots of people here. Maybe I can come another day."

He took my dirty hand. "You are the guest of honor. I'm sorry I didn't make it clear about the dinner and my guests. It's I who should be feeling bad."

I cocked my head when he left me in the bathroom. I could hear him as he walked away. "But, if you feel the need, my car needs a tune-up, and the garden could use a good weeding."

I laughed. "I'll get right to it after dinner."

I cleaned myself as best as I could. My jeans still had a streak that would not come out. I emerged and was met by two women who were headed toward the bathroom. They leaned together and laughed, ignoring me.

"Hi. I'm Maggie." I extended my clean hand, and they both looked as if I was the maid and ignored my extended hand.

"Hi Maggie, are you the new gardener or kitchen help?"

I laughed. "Yeah, I can see how you might think that. Oh, by the way. Just a warning, the bathroom could use more toilet paper."

They looked at me, and one said, "Well, don't tell us, Maggie, go get some."

"Yes, ma'am, I'll get right on that." I laughed, but I was internally fuming. I wasn't sure if I should be furious at Charlie for not advising me about this dinner or laugh at the situation. I walked toward a woman who appeared to be on the staff.

"Hi, I'm Maggie Kincaid. I'm wondering if you have some toilet paper?" The woman was upset that the bathroom wasn't stocked and ran to a closet down the long corridor. She returned with several rolls. By now, I could see the humor in the situation. I offered to take the toilet paper to the bathroom, which now had three women in various stages of undress and applying makeup.

"Here to serve. I hope this helps wipe away whatever's bothering you. I tossed the rolls toward the women and shut the door. Walking down the hall toward the patio and party guests, I noticed beautiful artwork interspersed with pictures of Charlie's late wife. She wasn't a knockout, but the images seem to capture a woman that had joy and determination. They were of varying ages and the ones of her marriage day also had a young Charlie. He wasn't outstanding in any way. He had hair that was black and curly. He was slim and tall. Carol was in one group photo. Judging from her, I could see Linda was lanky as well. As I gazed at the pictures, Charlie came up behind me and put his arm around my shoulder.

"We're going to eat now. Can I get you a drink?"

"Sure. What are you drinking?" It smelled like whiskey.

"Bourbon."

"Ah, how about a plain tonic?"

"I hear you're into beer."

I gave him a questioning look. "Huh?"

"Root beer."

"Ah, is nothing sacred? I switch to the hard stuff at night."

"Gin too, then?"

"Not tonight, just the tonic. I need my wits about me. You have a rough crowd tonight."

"Yeah, but don't mind them. These people are all climbing up the social scale and think they can use me to get a rung or two up the ladder."

"Oh darn, and to think all I want is to ride, fish, and live out my life."

"Is that all?"

"Sorry, I don't aspire to much else. I'm shallow. What you see is what you get. No desires to save the world, run for senate, or cure cancer." As I said it, I could have kicked myself. The one person in the world that meant the most to him was his wife, who had died of cancer. Earth, please swallow me. "Oh, sorry."

"Maggie, you don't need to apologize. It's been six years since Linda died. I'm not trying to cure cancer either." We stood silently as we looked at the photos. "How is young Luke? Colin says you have him talking."

"Okay, maybe he is my project. Luke's a great kid. He has a wonderful work ethic, and I'm hoping to get him into some sports. His skills are fairly rudimentary, but I'm working on it."

"Colin says he comes home and plays catch with anyone who will play with him."

"Oh, really. I didn't know that. I sent Luke home with math and science homework. He must complete certain things before I let him work or play. He's a smart kid. I'm enjoying his company."

"Please be careful. If Luke's father gets out of prison, Colin thinks he will try to take him. He told you the story, but I doubt he told you that someone was hanging around last summer, and Colin thought it was a friend of Luke's father."

"No, I didn't know. I got a gun. Which reminds me, I'll bring yours back."

Someone shouted for Charlie to come to the table. There was no formal arrangement for seating, and everyone was seated as close to Charlie as possible. I was left with a seat at the other end of the long table with no one opposite me. The woman I sat next to faced away from me and didn't acknowledge me as I sat down. I gazed down the table and noticed the couples were all much younger than either Charlie or me. I wondered why he invited me. This was not my crowd.

As the food was being served, Charlie got up and picked up his plate and came down and sat at the empty setting across from me. There was silence, and everyone now saw that the poorly dressed woman who delivered toilet paper was the object of Charlie's attention. Charlie tapped his glass and brought everyone to order and silence.

"Good evening. I'm delighted you could all make it this weekend. As you know, I am deciding on a new direction in the company, and the purpose of this weekend is to get your thoughts about what new way we may want to head. I also would like to introduce the guest of honor. This is Maggie Kincaid. Maggie is a recent addition to my local community. She's a retired veterinarian who recently returned from Australia and is now an emerging author. I bought her first book, which has recently been published and sent it here for the occasion. I'm hoping she will sign it." He reached back, and one of the staff members handed him a copy of the book. Even I didn't have a copy.

I was embarrassed and pleased. I gazed at Charlie and nodded. I quickly glanced at the book and thumbed through the pages. The cover had a picture of a young woman dressed as a slightly glamorous vet with the obligatory stethoscope dangling around her neck and a child holding a horse in the background. My picture was on the final page with a quick bio.

I took the pen and wrote: To Charlie, Here's to a new friendship. Maggie. I passed him the book. He read the inscription, smiled, and handed it to one of the servers. He then went on to discuss the book and how far he was into the story. I was impressed. This guy is so lovely. Too bad he wasn't for me, and too bad he had never moved on from his wife. *Give me a man who can change a tire any day.*

The woman sitting next to me turned and began asking me about my life in Australia. She'd visited and, like most, had gone to the usual travel hotspots. She and her partner were here for the weekend to hopefully get some business from Charlie's company. They owned a firm that recruited people for mining. She was active in the company and had three young children who were with their grandparents this weekend.

She quietly told me it was an honor to be invited to The Sanctuary and hoped she and her husband could start working with Charlie and his company. She asked if I had a copy of my book, and I explained only a reviewer's copy, but she could download it off the net. She'd ridden horses as a child, and she hoped her daughter would ride in the future. She and her husband lived in Texas. Charlie flew them and two other couples up, and they would all fly back tomorrow.

All through dinner, I kept thinking about the interaction of my tire-changing savior. I thought how, in my youth, I would have not even considered having anyone but me change the tire. My father taught me basic mechanics, and I even tuned my own car during my college days. The touch of that man made me think about my solitary life. Was my current experience with its freedom better than the companionship of someone that made me remember the joy of a man and the rare intimacy that goes with old age?

I looked over to Charlie, who was engaged in conversation with his other guests. I felt sorry for him. If I wanted to seek companionship, I had no emotional constraints or ties. I just chose not to. He, on the other hand, was living in his past and was still married. Yes, he was at the top of his professional game, and yes, he was the consummate host. He genuinely appeared to care about people he was involved with, but at the end of the night, my guess was he was alone and still grieving.

After dinner, I thanked Charlie and said goodbye to the guest who had taken the time to talk to me. Charlie walked me to my car and apologized once again for not specifying the dress code for the evening. I laughed and told him not to worry. From now on, I would ask him about the required attire if there was ever another invitation. I extended my hand, but he took me in his arms and gave me a quick hug. Charlie said he was flying out again on Monday, and he would call me when he was back at his ranch.

Chapter 20

The next day I did some writing, talked to my kids, and rode into the forest behind my house. I let Baxter come and brought my bear spray. There was a well-worn trail I found and followed it up to a lake. The lake was beautiful, and I saw a man fishing at the other end of the lake. He had waded out a distance from the shore. I waved, and he tipped his rod in acknowledgment. I watched him and observed him bring in a large trout.

I didn't recognize him from a distance, and I moved in closer to see if I knew him. He might be in his mid to late forties, had waders, a camouflage shirt, and a neckerchief to protect his exposed skin. His hat and sunglasses obscured his face. I rode on past and dismounted a respectful distance so I wouldn't disturb him. He cast his line like an expert. I watched for several minutes, but he caught no more fish. The sun was up, and the fish were probably deeper now.

He waded up to the lake's edge and then opened a small box and looked through what probably were the flies he brought. He turned to me and shrugged and shouted. "Are you the vet?"

"I used to be, but not anymore. How do you know me?" I had no idea who he was.

"You're riding my father's horse. I'm Jake Chandler—Luke's uncle. You're our neighbor."

"Well, howdy, neighbor." I walked over, leading Digger.

"Howdy back at ya. I hear you like to fish."

"That would be a fair assessment. I see you're no slouch at this either."

"Dad taught us all to fish. He and I are the only ones who still do. Oh, I think Luke has the bug too. Is your name Maggie? My dad can't stop singing your praises. I hear you even got Luke talking again."

"It's all part of the service. Luke's a great kid, and he certainly perfected his deaf and dumb act successfully. I only luckily picked up that he could hear a sound by playing musical tunes he liked. Are you the artist?"

"No, that's my brother. I teach physics. I'm the boring one." He chuckled as he adjusted his backpack and prepared to leave. "Got to get back. We're having a belated birthday party for Luke, but of course, you're the invited guest."

"Uh, if I am, it's news to me." *Did I forget*?

"I'm sure I heard Luke say you were coming."

"I don't think so. I've never even been over to your family's property."

Jake Chandler shook his head. "I'm sorry. I was certain I overheard you were invited and coming. My wife and I were looking forward to meeting the miracle woman."

"Not hardly. Tell Luke—no, on second thought, don't say anything. If he forgot to invite me, I don't want to embarrass him, and if he didn't want me to come, I don't want to make him feel bad either."

"Maggie, you're too kind."

"Probably." I mounted Digger. I could hardly wait to tell Eric we had a new fishing spot. When I returned home, Luke was waiting down at the barn. He wanted me to come to an afternoon lunch and told me he forgot to invite me.

"Luke, did your uncle tell you he saw me?"

"No. Did you see my uncle?"

"Yes, way into the forest. There's a lake, and your uncle was fishing."

"I don't think he's back. I've been here for a couple of hours waiting for you."

"You sat and waited for two hours? I guess if it means that much to you, I better come."

"The lunch is anytime. Can you come over soon? I want you to meet my cousins."

"It's eleven now. How about I come at twelve?"

"Okay. I'll tell Mrs. Gillard. She wants to meet you too."

"Oh, I don't have anything to bring."

"Just bring a can of beer. Thanks, Maggie. This will be the best birthday party ever."

"Vamoose, cowboy. I need to shower."

Chapter 21

I walked on the well-worn path from my property to the Chandlers. There was a short, dense clump of trees, which then opened to a large grassy area on the other side of a chain-linked fence with razor wire at the top. A large hedge hid the fencing from the view of the house. The gate had a chain and an old padlock. The key sat in the lock and appeared to be intentionally left for me. I entered and locked the gate and brought the key. I'd observed Luke with a key previously, and I assumed he closed the gate as he went back and forth between our properties.

The house was a massive single-story structure. Adjacent to the large house were three smaller houses, two tennis courts, and a swimming pool. A long drive went up to a circular barn and what had to be an indoor arena. I couldn't believe this palatial estate. Did Google Maps hide this?

Jake greeted me with the familiar Chandler smile. Now in shorts and a Hawaiian shirt, he had his father's good looks and muscular build. "Did Luke tell you to bring your swimming suit?"

"No, but that's okay. I'll make an appearance and go. I don't want to interfere with your family time."

"Not going to happen, ma'am. If Luke lets you go home by dark, consider yourself lucky. Come on and meet our family." He strode over to a deck that centered inside a beautiful garden of roses and other flowering plants. Jake gave a whistle. "Here she is, you all. Luke's friend and teacher, Maggie Kincaid."

Two women walked over and introduced themselves. “Hi, I’m Jake’s wife, Megan, and this is my mother-in-law, Helen.” Megan was probably in her mid-forties and was slightly plump, but with straight dyed blonde hair, she could pass for an aging star herself. Helen was much older. I wasn’t sure if she was the first or second wife of Colin.

“Hi, Maggie. I know you’re wondering. I’m Colin’s ex. I’m Luke’s real grandmother.”

I extended my hand. Helen appeared to be in her seventies, had straight, gray hair, and looked her age. “I’m so pleased to meet you, Helen.”

“The pleasure is all ours. We’re all so grateful for what you’ve done for our grandson.”

I saw Colin stride over to us. He smiled and gave me a hug. “Did you bring Luke’s beer?”

Helen looked alarmed.

“Sure did.” I handed Colin the cooler that contained a six-pack. “I had a great ride on Digger this morning. I found a lake, and I met Jake fishing at the lake.”

I gazed up and saw a helicopter hovering over near the barn. Colin peered up and smiled. “That old rascal.”

I looked again, and Colin shook his head. “Never was fond of coming to the front door like the rest of us.” He saw my questioning look. “Charlie. He must have dismissed his associates early. He said he wasn’t coming.” Colin excused himself and began walking toward the barn.

I met a few of the grandchildren. There were eight or so. Helen had brought the other grandchildren from her ranch on the other side of the mountain range. Luke mentioned his cousins stayed with his grandmother most of the summer, but he preferred to stay with his grandfather. Now that he was talking, he was being accepted and treated like a regular family member. His grandmother asked how I did it.

"Music, Helen. He couldn't resist 'Walk Like a Man.'"

"That would be right. I love that song and The Four Seasons."

"Old people's music." As I explained how I helped Luke out of his shell, I heard music from my playlist in the background. "Someone has a similar taste to me."

"I think that's your music. Mrs. Gillard said that Luke received a phone, and he was adding music to it for hours over the last week. He asked to play it at the party. I think it's in your honor."

As I turned and listened, I realized he had duplicated many of the songs I had played for him. It was kind of embarrassing. "If it's a problem, sorry."

Helen laughed. "Thankfully, you aren't into heavy metal."

"He can't duplicate some of the music. I took it off old records I played as a child and teenager. I doubt he can copy many of them."

Colin had gone to meet Charlie. They returned, and Charlie smiled and greeted me with a hug. He had on his suit and tie. "Didn't anyone give you the dress code for today?" I had on shorts. Despite my age, I could wear shorts and not look too bad.

"Touché, Maggie. Hi Helen." He gave Helen a kiss and then asked where the birthday boy was.

Helen gazed around and then pointed to the swimming pool. "I'm happy to say he is playing with his cousins."

"Oh, that's interesting. I have a present for Luke."

Colin called Luke out of the pool, and the boy came running. "Can you say hi to Mr. McLeod? He brought you a present."

"Hello, sir."

"Luke, I hear you want to play ball. Did you know I was in the minors?"

Luke shook his head. "No, sir. What are the minors?"

"Well, that was a team for boys who were good, but not that good. I'd like to help you. Would you like to play some catch?" Charlie handed him a new glove and two balls.

Luke took them and looked back at the kids swimming. Charlie saw where Luke's interest was. "You know Luke, how about you go play with your cousins, and we can play catch another time?"

"Thanks. I do want to play with you."

I shook my head. "Yeah, I don't know why other kids are more popular than old people." I took the glove and tried it. It was just my size, and I pounded my fist into the glove. I tossed a ball up and caught it. Colin and Charlie both watched. "What?"

"What don't you do?"

"Lots."

"Yeah, I bet." Colin turned around as a dinner gong was sounded.

Colin, Charlie, and I sat at one end of a long table. Luke sat beside me. Helen sat on Luke's other side. We had ribs, corn fritters, salad, and I had a real beer. Mrs. Gillard placed a beautiful cake on the table. The birthday song was butchered by us all, and a few more presents were given and opened. Luke stood up and said he wanted to say something. We were all stunned by this.

"Thank you all for coming to my party. Especially my new friend, Maggie." With that, he said, "Last one in the pool is dry."

Helen had tears. I was close, and Colin turned away from us all. Charlie took my hand and kissed it. Megan and Jake came over and said, "Welcome to the family."

"Maggie, 'Walk Like a Man?'" Helen smiled wryly, which might be better described as a smirk.

"Okay, there may have been a cattle prod and bamboo under the fingernails as well."

Colin tipped his glass to me. "We tried that earlier, and that didn't work before. Thanks. Helen and I owe you so much."

"Digger is payment enough. Oh, and full rights to the river on your property for Eric and me."

"Eric?" Charlie was curious.

"The town doctor, my fishing partner, and general boy toy."

"So, you can add cradle robber and Cougar to your resume? I'm impressed." Helen gave me a conspiratorial salute.

"Until I figure out how and where to catch fish, yes. Once I know the local haunts, I'll drop him like I do all my men. In short, I'm a user. I'm really trying to climb the social stratosphere of the town." Helen and I high-fived. Colin shook his head, and he and Charlie gave each other a commiserating look. "And on that short note, I think I'll take my leave. I have a fishing date with a lake before Jake fishes it dry. Thank you all so much. It was truly a pleasure meeting you all. Helen, I'd love to have you over for a coffee if you are around next week."

"Love to, darling. I need to hear more about your life and your children. I'm heading back in the morning, but I'll be back in a week or two if Colin hasn't scared you away from me."

"Fat chance. Us old sisters need to stick together."

Colin walked down to the gate, and after I passed through, he locked it. "Thank you again. Not just for Luke, but for Charlie too. I haven't seen him so alive in years."

I smiled. "I aim to serve." *At least we have Charlie talking too.*

I thought about the man who changed the tire for me. Maybe he awakened long-buried desires in me as well. If I could find that man again, I would love to buy him a cup of coffee. Perhaps it was his smell. Maybe he had pheromones that triggered my need for male company. Anyway, he gave me an unexpected wake-up call.

Chapter 22

The summer was peaking. The weather was holding with an occasional thunderstorm. Lightning was always a concern for me, having lived through the Australian summers and devastating bushfires. Fortunately, the lightning was usually accompanied by rain showers here in my new home territory.

My garden grew while Luke learned, worked, and increased his sports skills. I was still wary of any strangers or people who might want to do harm to the boy. I didn't see Colin or Charlie for several days after the birthday party.

It was time to return some invitations. I had fresh produce I'd grown. I sent Luke home with cucumbers, squash, and tomatoes. I decided to invite Carol, Sylvia, and their spouses to dinner. The house was in enough order to have company. I finally had sufficient cutlery and linen to not embarrass myself. Sylvia and Carol were not the ones to judge my culinary or hosting skills. They were still working women and were only happy to have a meal they didn't have to cook.

The evening they were invited was highlighted with a particularly intense storm. As we sat eating hors d'oeuvres and drinks, we watched the lightning. They asked about the Australian fires and my experiences. I'd cared for burned horses several years ago. I explained I was thankful it only happened once in my local area and declared I never wanted to see a burned animal again. The storm passed over us during the main course. Once again, Carol's husband showed more than a passing interest in my history, much to Carol's amusement.

"Hal, why don't you use your phone to record her stories so you can pass them onto Charlie."

"Good idea." Hal pretended to reach for his phone as Carol batted his hand.

"Charlie is off my list, anyway. I met the man of my dreams a few weeks ago."

They all stopped eating and stared at me as I told them about my encounter with a man who changed a tire for me on the interstate. My guests gazed at one another as I described the man and how bizarrely attracted I was to him. "Sadly, we were both old ships that passed in the night."

Trent sat up straight and appeared concerned. "You have read the papers recently, haven't you?"

Carol asked me to describe the man and my encounter. I laughed as I said he reminded me of Santa Claus. Still, I could see they were disturbed when I mentioned his refrigerator strapped to the trailer he was pulling. "What?"

Carol put her hand on mine. "Oh, my God. You haven't got a clue, do you?"

"Apparently not. Is Santa Claus famous? Did I miss an opportunity to fall in love with someone I should have recognized?"

"Carol, you tell her." Hal glanced at Trent, and both men had stopped eating and sat up.

"Tell me what?"

"Well, she's alive, so I guess she needs to know how close she came to being killed."

"Will someone explain what you're all talking about?"

"Maggie, have you heard about the interstate stalker?"

Alarm bells were sounding. "I guess not. I thought that guy was from California."

"Oh, we have our own out here too. Well, we had our own. Thankfully, he was caught last week." The emphasis was on the word 'had.'

"And you think he was the man who stopped and helped me with my flat tire? No way." I knew he was a nice kind man. His handshake was a lightning rod to me. "If that damn patrol officer hadn't pulled up and interrupted us, I might not have even made it to where I was headed."

Hal reached for his phone. "Yeah, Charlie said you had tire tracks all over you when you arrived." He thumbed through his phone and then turned it to an online news article about the stalker and several women he had abducted, killed, and transported in his refrigerator. I scrolled down, and there he was. It was him for sure. My guests saw my reaction, and we all knew how close I came to meeting a similar fate. I was shaken. I couldn't speak.

Trent was the first to respond. "Jesus Christ. You are one lucky woman. That patrolman saved your life. You better find him and thank him."

I stood and offered dessert and coffee for anyone who would like some. Both Hal and Trent came around and hugged me. They took my phone and put their numbers into my address list and said the next time I had a flat, I was to call them.

"No problem there. Should I call the police and tell them about my close call? I thought he was such a nice guy. You know, I found him physically attractive, and I can't even explain it. I thought it was his body odor."

"Yeah, body odor always does it for me, not." Sylvia waved her hand in front of her nose. "I finally meet a skinny-dipping, horseback partner, and she almost kills herself on the interstate. Your boyfriends won't be too impressed with your lack of caution."

"Yeah." I thought for a second. "What boyfriends?"

"Do you live under a rock? Charlie, Colin, and let's not forget Luke."

"I'm not into kids, and both Charlie and Colin are married for all intents and purposes, and neither is my type. I'm looking for an older Eric, fishing with an occasional dinner and no obligations." I looked at them and then laughed. "Wait a second, between them all, I have the bases covered. I am not looking. Let me make this perfectly clear. I'm too old. I am dead from the neck down, one tire-changing man aside. Am I clear?"

"Perfectly, and we certainly believe you, Maggie. As if." Trent shook his head and laughed. Hal got up and started to clear the table, and Carol and Sylvia both high-fived each other.

"What?" I was still shaking at the thought of my near miss with death.

"Maggie, you can tell this to yourself. We read your first book. No one who wrote what you wrote is emotionally dead."

The lightning began again as my guests left. I sat out on the balcony off my study and watched until rain sent me into the house. One near-miss with death aside, this was a perfect life.

The phone rang early the following day. "Maggie, it's me, Charlie. Can I come over?"

"I guess. Is it an emergency?"

Chapter 23

I now had a combination lock on my gate. Charlie was up at the house within the hour. He asked me to go with him to The Sanctuary. Charlie drove an old Chevy truck with a stick shift. He hardly talked. He asked me what I had done since the birthday party at Colin's place and how Luke was progressing.

He drove up to the barn and escorted me to his wife's old mare. He opened the stall door and put a halter on her. He led her out of the stall and down the shed row. She seemed to have improved, and I observed her trotting briskly.

"What's the problem?"

Charlie came back and stood in front of me. "The problem is there is no more of whatever you gave to Patty who gave it to Tinker, and it seems Patty is unable to procure this here. Tinker needs more."

"I don't think so. I left a course, and usually, it is four injections, and after that, we only give it as needed. Tinker will need more in a month, but I doubt it will help to do any more right now. Would you like me to order some for you?"

"Yes, please. Would you like to come up to the house for some coffee?"

"Sounds great."

Charlie took me to the house and asked an older woman to bring us both some coffee.

"How do you take your coffee, ma'am?"

"Cream, but no sugar. My name is Maggie." I extended my hand, and the woman looked at Charlie, who nodded, and she shook my hand. "I'm Roberta."

"So nice to meet you. Can I give you a hand?"

"Nope, unless you want to hire me. I'm probably going to be fired for even talking to you." She winked at Charlie as she left the room.

"You just can't get good servants these days."

"No, I suppose not. How are you? Do you want me to order some of the arthritis drugs for you too?"

"I talked to Hal this morning."

"And?"

"He told me about the flat tire guy. You should have called me."

"We both know that wasn't going to happen. Charlie, I'm a big girl. I've been on my own for twenty years. Yes, there is no question, I got unlucky, and then I got especially lucky. We're all gonna die sometime. I sure don't want it at the hands of a criminal, but I am careful, and I have no plans of falling off my perch anytime soon."

Our coffee came, and I thanked Roberta for mine. We drank and chatted about Charlie's adventures. He had flown out of Colin's helipad and back to the airport after the party. He followed up the leads he received from the party attendees, went to two other states, and met Colin in Los Angeles on Wednesday. Colin has some court dates regarding the release of Luke's father from prison.

"He's fighting it, but he thinks Luke's father is going to get out on a witness protection program."

"That doesn't sound good. Why would Luke's father need protection?"

"He says he's a victim too. He owes money to dealers, and he says they killed Luke's mother and now want to kill him. He testified against them, but the word out is Luke's father killed his wife in a rage over her drug debts, and two guys are in jail for his crimes. He's a lowlife. Maggie, there are some bad people out in the world. You may have been better to stay in Australia."

"I had a client murdered over there, and I knew both the victim and the murderer." I finished my coffee, stood up, and walked over to his bookshelf. There were many classic and modern books. "Are you a reader, Charlie?"

"Many of those were Linda's. Would you like to borrow some?"

"Sure would. Your wife had great taste."

"She did. She would have loved your book. I finished it, by the way, and I enjoyed it. When does the next one come out?"

"In a month or two. My publishers have me writing as fast as I can. I have to have four books completed by Christmas."

"Will you make it?"

"I'm finishing the last, but the editing is taking longer than I like."

"Would you like to take a short ride with me?" Charlie cocked his head slightly.

"On horses?" I didn't think he rode.

"No, the truck."

I picked up our coffee cups, and while he stepped out for a minute, I returned the cups to the kitchen. Roberta was sitting at the kitchen table and reading the paper. She smiled as I entered with the cups.

"You're going to get me fired, for sure." Roberta appeared to be in her fifties. She had olive skin and was thin. She wore a cross, and her clothing was not a uniform. Her hands indicated she was accustomed to hard work. She had a basket of fresh vegetables and lettuce. There must be a garden somewhere.

"Sorry. The coffee was delicious. Thank you."

"No, it's us that need to thank you."

I was perplexed, and she could see my furrowed brow.

"You've made our boss come alive. He really enjoys your company."

"Mm, no, not really. He's a," but I stopped. Charlie entered the kitchen and gave me a sharp look. I didn't finish what I was going to say.

"Are you two plotting against me?"

I replied, "Not yet, but the day is young."

Charlie opened the door for me on the old truck. We drove up a well-worn track in the vehicle, which seemed to lurch every time Charlie changed gears.

"This was Linda's favorite vehicle. You know she could have any car she wanted, but this was the one she chose."

I didn't respond. It was a junker, but it meant something to him. We drove over the hill and down to a grassy spot next to a small pond. There was a bench, and next to the bench was a grave marker. Charlie stopped the car, and we got out. I walked over to a simple headstone that said Linda McLeod and the dates of her birth and death.

"She was cremated. It was her wish. She is all over here." Charlie swept his arm in a circle. "The stone is for me. Her dying wish was that I do not dwell on her or her memory. She gave me strict orders to get on with my life."

Charlie sat down on the bench and patted the place next to him, inviting me to sit beside him. I was reluctant, but I did sit on the bench, making sure there was a distance between us. It was a little weird. I asked him about his favorite memory of his wife. He smiled and looked away and then began to describe how he and Linda were young and visiting Africa and were held hostage by children in a small village. He then explained how she dealt with the children and then their parents. He said that in the end, she arranged for a new water well and a school and sent teachers down to educate the children.

"Maggie, those were the children we never had. We would visit them every year until she was too ill to travel. I still support the town, but I no longer go there. Roberta goes down once a year to visit and to make sure they are using Linda's legacy wisely."

"She sounds like she was a wonderful person."

"Tell me about you, Maggie."

"There's nothing exceptional about me. I've had a dream career. I wouldn't trade anything I did. The kids were a bonus, but they know I was married to my work. There were good times, and there were not so good times in my life, but I am living a life few could imagine. I couldn't ask for more. My needs are simple, and I can meet them."

We sat without talking, and then he took my hand. Without saying anything, he led me over to the pond and said he had trout planted in the pond, and he wanted me to come and fish it sometime. I laughed. "Do you want to learn to fly-fish?"

"No, I don't ride much anymore, and I don't fish, but I used to. I know you enjoy it."

"What do you enjoy? What makes Charlie McLeod happy?"

"I don't know anymore. It used to be making Linda happy. It used to be wealth accumulation so she and I could fund her projects. I'm happy, but I know I need to find another purpose."

"Maybe stocking all the lakes and rivers with trout might fulfill that purpose." He glanced at me and shook his head. "Have you ever thought it might be time to move on?"

"Oh, don't tell me you're joining the rest of my friends?" He smiled but shook his head.

"You're young, and you appear to be healthy. Tell me you don't ever think about it."

"And you?"

"I just left my marriage." He cocked his head and appeared puzzled. "My work. I was totally married to my work. I've been divorced for a long time, and I'll admit I have had a few boyfriends along the way, but I stopped having any desires until my tire-changing episode. I'm sure Hal's told you." I stopped and waited for a response, but he didn't acknowledge anything. "It made me realize two things. One is that maybe I was still interested in men, and two, I am the worst judge of a person's character."

Charlie didn't respond. We sat, and I watched the pond for fish rising, and Charlie picked a few weeds around Linda's headstone. He indicated it was time to return. He took me by my hand and led me to the truck. We didn't talk on the way back to the house.

"Maggie, you'll be more careful, won't you? I really am enjoying your company, and I would hate to lose you. Promise me you'll call the roadside assist guys next time and stay in your car and lock the doors."

"But he was so lovely and kind, Charlie."

"I saw his picture. I don't see what you saw."

"Who knows why people are drawn to one another. It was probably pheromones. I know I've always been attracted to men wearing Old Spice. My dad wore it, and when I met my future husband, he wore it as well. I was putty in his hands. He was the perfect example of my lack of taste in men."

"Care to elaborate?"

"Nope. He's the father of my children. Not going there, for sure."

"Well, I probably should get you home."

"I'm glad you brought me and told me more about Linda. I can see she would be hard to replace. I'll call a friend and order some of the medicine for Tinker. Don't sit by the mailbox. I'll give it to Patty, and she can dispense it to you." I might even order some for Digger.

We stopped at the house while I retrieved the books I had selected from his library. We returned to my property. Charlie let me out and waited by the house. Baxter ran out and greeted me, and I waved to Charlie, indicating the coast was clear. He mentioned he was leaving tomorrow and would be back next week, and he was hoping we could meet for dinner one night.

"You're asking a lot, you know. My social calendar is fairly full."

"I'd lock it in, but I'm not sure when I'll finish what I need to do."

"Where are you off to?"

"Florida and then Los Angeles. I'll call you when I'm back. Can I invite myself, and we could have some of that wine?"

"Sure. Safe travels, my friend."

Chapter 24

Luke and I continued to pal around. I was struggling to find things for him to do. I took him with me to town for shopping. Still, I was wary of any strangers or situations which might be compromising. I took him to visit the veterinary clinic with Baxter. I needed to test Baxter for heartworms and put him on the preventative program. I also thought it would be an excellent chance to expose Luke to my profession. My Australian arthritis medicine had not arrived. Patty Tilmouth was keen to get some more for her old horse, and I had ordered a large bottle.

Patty could see Luke was interested and offered to take him on calls with her. This would require that I accompany them. We decided next Wednesday would be a good day. Patty had several interesting cases for Luke to see that day. "Are these cases that Luke would be interested in or me?"

Patty appeared to be dumbfounded. "Dr. Kincaid, would I be so underhanded as to dupe you back into practice? Surely not."

I smirked and agreed to accompany her and Luke on the calls. The truth was I was getting withdrawals and looked forward to riding with Patty and observing her cases. Baxter didn't have heartworms, and we started him on preventative meds. There were several pamphlets in the waiting room, and Luke took one of each. "Hey, Luke, if you take them, I'm expecting a report on what you read."

"Maggie, would I dupe you and just take them without reading them? Surely not." This kid was developing a sense of humor for sure. We returned to the house and went fishing along the river that bordered Colin's property. I hadn't seen Colin since Luke's birthday party, but as I watched Luke cast his line, he came out of the woods and stood next to me.

"Hey, Maggie. I see you are still into trespassing." He laughed and put his hand on my shoulder. I was surprised, but it was nice to have an iconic celebrity showing interest, even if he was a married old geezer. I smiled, which let him know I didn't mind. He leaned close and quietly said things had not gone well in Los Angeles. Luke's father might be released in a few weeks, and the rumor was he was applying to get custody of Luke once he was free.

"Have you discussed this with Luke?"

"No, and please don't repeat what I told you. It could be dangerous for Luke if they find out he is talking, especially if he is returned to his father's care." Luke turned around to show me a large trout he had caught and saw his grandfather and waved. He put the fish on a line and let it stay in the water.

"Has Luke ever said he would like to see his father? Does anyone know if he remembers what actually happened?"

"No. I dread my grandson's reply. I think he probably does, and I would say that if he knew his father was being released from prison, it would scare him and be harmful. I talked to the psychologist who my lawyer has hired. She says it could be damaging to even discuss the possibility that his father is released."

"I won't say anything. Keep me updated and let me know how I can help."

Colin hugged me. The hug was a little too intimate for me. I know he is still married, and despite his age, he is still a good-looking man. He is kind and generous, but he is married. Neither he nor Charlie floated my boat. I liked them both, and I enjoyed their company, but my heart was still attached to the serial killer. I'm an idiot, no doubt about it.

"Maggie, I'd like to take you and Luke fishing next week. Are you available on Saturday?"

"Sure am. You know how to make a girl go weak at the knees. I'm in. Where are we going?"

"Just be ready on a week from this Saturday. I want to give Luke at least one good memory if things go pear-shaped. Bring waders. Do you have any?"

"Sure do. I've been letting Luke wear mine. Do you want me to get him some before we go?"

"No, he's growing too fast. I'll find something he can wear."

The week continued. I had Charlie coming for dinner, and the pressure was on. I was not a gourmet chef by any stretch. I planned to use produce from my garden. I was out watering it the next afternoon when I saw the ominous storm clouds approach. I heard the thunder well before the storm hit. Eric and I were going fishing, but he didn't have to call to say he wasn't coming. We fished once or twice a week, and I would cook dinner. The lake deep in the forest was becoming our favorite place. It was called Saddleback Lake for its shape. I often took a picnic dinner, and we would fish, eat, and return before dark.

I looked at Baxter, who was always nervous as a thunderstorm hit. I patted his head to reassure him. He stayed close to my side as we returned to the house. This storm was incredibly intense and had an unusual amount of wind and extraordinarily little rain. I prayed that lightning would not start any forest fires. My prayers went unanswered. I knew when I received a call from Patty around eleven that night.

"Hey, Doc. You awake?"

"No."

"Yeah, well, I need some advice. I think you may be able to help me. There's a fire over at The Sanctuary. There are a few burned horses."

"Oh, my God. Did the barn burn? Were any people injured?" I thought of the horses that were so important to Charlie's dead wife.

"The fire is still going, but the rangers think it won't be too bad. The barn and house were saved, but the horses that were out in paddocks were burned. I euthanized two, but the others don't look too bad. Any chance you could come over?"

Bushfires were a way of life in Australia for the last several years. Sadly, I had experience in treating burned horses—more than I ever wanted, Way more. "What have you got in the way of supplies?"

"Not much."

"Is Charlie there?"

"I don't think so." I heard her turn and ask someone. "No, he's interstate. They don't know where."

"Patty, do you have his number?"

"The men do. They've already contacted him. He's on his way."

"Can you call Eric and see if he has any burn cream? And do you have someone who sells local honey? There won't be too much to do tonight. Make sure Charlie wants to save them. I'll be over as quick as I can. I'll call him. Charlie can source what we need. See you in thirty. Prepare yourself. The next few weeks are not for sissies."

I arrived up at the barn. The smoke was present, and the smell of burnt flesh and hair was evident. It brought back memories I would just as soon forget. Several ranch hands were around arranging to move uninjured horses out of the barn to make way for the burned and injured horses. Both Patty and her brother, Eric, were examining horses and treating them when I arrived.

"I forgot to mention ketamine. You will find that intramuscular ketamine is your friend." I began to assess the horses. Two were in shock. Patty already had them on intravenous fluids. She was no slouch. All the horses were up to date with their tetanus vaccines. They had all received essential pain medication, and they were being placed in individual stalls.

"You know you won't know how bad things are for two weeks, don't you?"

"Yes, but how do I tell which ones aren't savable? I've euthanized two horses so far. Two horses died in the pasture, making four in total. Can you look at the others?"

We walked down the aisle, and I started with the horses on intravenous drips. They were depressed and appeared to be cold. They trembled, and weight shifted. Their skin only hinted that it had been seriously burned, and I was dubious if one of the horses would survive. They all had serum oozing from their coronary bands. I knew this meant there would be some separation of the skin to the hoof.

The men were preparing to ice the legs, but I cautioned them that this would do more harm than good. As I was examining the next horse, Charlie called Patty. Patty handed the phone to me.

"How bad is it?"

"I don't think we'll know for a day or two. I guess you know I've been through this before. It's going to get a lot worse before it gets better. I'm wondering if you can source some supplies we'll need before you come back. I can text you a list of the bandages and topicals I've used in the past. Are you available to come back?"

"Yes, of course, send the list. I'll be back by lunchtime and if I can bring what we need with me, I will. Otherwise, I'll have it sent. How will you know if any aren't going to make it?"

"I think Patty has already made that decision on a couple, but the degree of burns and appetite is what guided me before. It is a long path, and they sure do go through hell initially, but it is amazing how well they can recover. Most of my cases went back and were useful horses."

"I can't thank you enough. Everyone thinks I keep these for Linda's sake and memory, but they are more than that to me. I can tell you about each horse and its pedigree. I want them to live, but I don't want them to suffer."

I remembered how my clients reacted when their horses were so horrifically burned. "I'm sure you and Patty will do the right thing. I'm here to advise her. I wouldn't wish this on anyone. Burns are terrible."

I handed the phone back to Patty. I continued down to observe each horse. The heart rates and demeanor suggested that things were under control for tonight. Patty and I made a list of supplies and texted this to Charlie. Most of the horses would be bandaged with a burn cream combination, which contained silver and honey. Silver was an excellent antibacterial element, while raw honey had many properties that would help in the healing process and conservation of the skin.

I didn't return home until mid-morning, and I promptly fell asleep. Baxter remained quietly by the bed. I was awoken by the phone. I was dazed and disoriented and thought I was back in Australia. I had been asleep for maybe two hours.

"Hello?"

"Maggie, it's Charlie. Sorry to bother you. I'm trying to source the honey. I can have manuka honey here tomorrow. Will that be soon enough?"

"You don't need fancy honey. Raw or unprocessed honey is fine."

"Okay, great. I'll be at The Sanctuary in an hour. Can I meet you there?"

"I guess. I'm sure Patty can take it from here."

"Apparently, she was up all night and has gone home to sleep."

"Uh, well, okay. I'll be there." I should be mad. I've only had two hours of sleep myself. I guessed he was frantic, and remembering my clients, I couldn't blame him. My Australian clients had lost everything. The horses' needs were important to them, but they had lost their houses and anything they didn't take with them. Even though they loved their horses, I didn't hear from the owners for days at a time.

When I arrived at The Sanctuary, the staff were caring for the six severely burned horses. The horses were all eating hay and now had creams applied to the burned areas that could not be bandaged, and their legs were covered where they could be. Five of the horses had corneal ulcers. I suggested eye ointments that would aid in healing and pain control for the corneas.

Gabe, my Marlboro man, had been summoned from Colin's ranch and oversaw the horses. Simultaneously, the rest of The

Sanctuary workers fought the fire, which was almost out. Gabe showed me several horses that were now stalled inside the barn. Many had mildly burned muzzles and corneal ulcers but otherwise would be fine. Charlie arrived and came over to us. He was in shock himself. He had a large stand of timber that had burned, and a few cows were lost, but he walked up to each horse and told me the breeding and what the horse meant to his herd and program. When we finished, and all seemed to be under control, Charlie invited me up to the house. I was exhausted and wanted to go home, but I felt like it would be rude not to have a bite of lunch before leaving.

Roberta had been called, and she had sandwiches and iced tea ready. I told him about my previous experience and what to expect in the next few days. He mentioned Colin and the court case. I told him about my discussion with Colin and our plans to take Luke fishing the following weekend. Charlie asked if he was still invited to dinner tomorrow.

"I hadn't thought about it. You can come, but do you want to?"

"Can I let you know in the morning?" Charlie poured more tea.

"Sure, you look tired. I'll have Roberta drive you home."

"No, I can drive myself. Thanks." I was delirious and wanted to get home.

"Are you sure? How about I drive you, and Roberta can follow and bring me back?"

"Charlie, you are too kind. I'll be fine." Roberta came into the sunroom where we were eating and summoned Charlie to the front door. Roberta said men were reporting about the fire containment. I waited and made the critical mistake of closing my eyes. When I opened them, Charlie was sitting opposite me and smiling. Again, I was disoriented.

"Power nap. I better go. Thanks for lunch."

"Do you know how long you were sleeping?" he was grinning as he set some papers down.

"Five minutes? It's amazing how a little sleep can completely revive me."

"You've been asleep over an hour."

"Bullshit."

"It's two o'clock." Charlie pointed to his watch.

I looked at mine. "No way."

"Every way."

I wiped my mouth. "Did I snore? I know I drooled."

"Drooled, snored, and farted. No wonder you're single." He snorted as he said that.

"Charlie, I'm human, but I didn't really fart, did I?"

"You snored. That's all."

"Thank Christ. You had me going. Sheesh, that would be embarrassing. Let me know about dinner. Would fresh trout be good?"

Chapter 25

I slept for the rest of the afternoon. Patty called to say that the horses were all eating, and she felt she had the pain under control. I said I would meet her tomorrow, and we would go over the horses and strategies to painlessly change the bandaging on the burned legs. The two horses on fluids were now drinking, and the intravenous fluids had been discontinued. One horse had a deep wound near the shoulder, and she was on antibiotics. I advised Patty and her associates not to use antibiotics unless it was essential.

The following day the extent of the burns was becoming evident. One horse had noticeable swelling from the chest to the groin area. Ventral edema can be caused by many factors. Still, in this case, it was the extreme heat, literally causing the red blood cells in the mare's veins to hemolyze or explode.

"It gives new meaning to the phrase, 'this makes my blood boil.'" Patty didn't laugh. She was horrified as she observed the damage to these horses. I remembered my reaction when it happened to my client's horses in Australia.

"Maggie, how do you change the bandages?"

"Ugh, that's not easy. Better living through chemistry. Sedation is the only way."

"Every day?"

"For a while. Gradually many will only need to be changed every other day. You won't know for a while." We discussed strategies, and then I did the first one. It took an hour, and while we were doing the procedure, Charlie came down. He watched for a minute without comment and turned heel and left. He left a message saying he had unexpected company and could we postpone our dinner until tomorrow night.

I read the text, and Patty rolled her eyes when I told her. "You don't want to get mixed up with him."

"No problem there. I don't want to get mixed up with anyone. I like things exactly like they are."

"Suit yourself. There are many nice guys around who aren't complicated. Don't get me wrong, Charlie is not looking, and he will break your heart."

"Patty, perhaps you didn't hear me. I really am not, and I repeat, not looking. There's been only one person that I have been attracted to, and he is behind bars now."

"Huh? Do you have a secret life?"

"I had a flat tire on the interstate a few weeks ago. A nice guy stopped to help. We had a thing, and sadly, we were interrupted by a patrol officer. He turned out to be the serial killer everyone is talking about. I'm hopeless at picking men. I have a long track record. At my age, I no longer require male companionship. I like company, but I want them to go home at night. Baxter is all I want to wake up to in the morning." I turned to see Gabe standing behind me, chuckling. My face reddened, and I stood up and walked out to my car.

I had the gun and books I had borrowed. I thought I would drive up to the house and return them before I headed home. I knew Charlie had company, and I decided to take them to Roberta and went to the side entrance. Even from the kitchen door, I could hear Charlie on the phone. I knocked quietly and opened the door. The only person in the kitchen was a woman who appeared to be in her twenties. She was wearing a man's dress shirt and, by my reckoning, nothing else.

"Can I help you?" She was alarmed when she saw I was carrying a gun. She was looking in the refrigerator, and I quickly explained I was returning some things that Mr. McLeod had lent me.

"You can set them on the table. Is that thing loaded?"

"No, sadly, it isn't."

"Oh, and who should I say brought them?"

"He'll know. So sorry to bother you."

I remembered what Carol said about Charlie having his demons. My guess was she was a dalliance and not anyone special. Did he have a bevy of these women? Not my problem. So, why was I so shocked, and why did I feel I had been gut-punched?

Chapter 26

I returned home to ride Digger. Baxter and I went to Saddleback Lake, where I fished and walked around the lake's edge. I found distinct bear prints and scat. There were small prints, and I guessed there was a mamma bear with at least two cubs. I reached for my bear spray and realized I had forgotten it. I decided to return home.

I needed a break. I wanted to get back to regular people and return to my roots. I called Patty and told her I was going away for a couple of days. I was going on a short road trip. I would be back on Friday, and I was taking Baxter. I called Colin, who didn't answer and then I phoned the cook, Mrs. Gillard. I asked her if Luke was available. He was on the line in a flash. I asked Luke to come and feed Digger for me and water the garden. I explained I needed to visit a sick friend. He said he would be glad to do that and to keep an eye on my place.

"Are you still going fishing with us next Saturday? Grandpa is really, really looking forward to that."

"Me too. Can't wait, cowboy, and yes, I'll be back. Thanks, Luke."

I stuffed a few clothes in a bag, scooped dry dog food, turned off my phone, and left. I had a second combination lock that I hadn't told anyone about. I put it on in place of my regular lock, and I drove away.

What was I thinking? Hanging out with super-rich entitled people. I loved Luke like a grandson, and I would go fishing with him and his grandfather, but that was the end. These people were not in my league. Their values and lifestyles were so different from mine. Colin appeared to have stepped away from his movie star lifestyle, and he did care for his grandson. Still, between Charlie and him, my guess was they both probably had or got what they wanted. I wanted no part of that. I could be happy with the company of regular, down-to-earth people like Carol, Sylvia, and Eric.

I drove for three hours, saw a sign for a pet-friendly lodge, and pulled into the driveway of an old motel. It had seen better days. I was about to pull out when I saw a man who had to be in his eighties walk out of a room and into the main office. There were no cars in the parking bays. I can't explain what made me stop, but I decided to go in. If the rooms were full of old cigarette smells, I would move on.

I walked into the motel office. An ancient woman sat at a desk and smiled. "Welcome, my dear. Are you wanting to stay for a while or just passing through?"

"I need a room for tonight, and then I'll be moving on. I have an aversion to smoke, so I need a smoke-free room. I have a dog too."

"All of our rooms are smoke-free. We allow pets. Would you care to look?" She handed me a key to the room next door. Inside was a beautifully decorated room with an older TV and a coffee machine. It smelled fresh. I looked out the window at the back of the room, and there was a lawn and swimming pool. The older man was attending to the swimming pool, which was clean and inviting. It was quaint, and I only required one night. I would stay here.

I returned to the office, and the woman, who also appeared to be in her eighties, smiled. "Are you staying here tonight?"

"Yes, I'll take the room. Are you expecting more guests? If I could have a room away from any noise, I need a good sleep."

"We have one more guest. She's gone into town for dinner. She's a regular visitor and is quiet. She won't disturb you."

I paid my money and let Baxter out of the car for a quick run. I had so little with me that I didn't take anything into the room. The clerk suggested I get a meal in town and said there were several options. It was a small town. The possibilities were Mexican, pizza, and a café that appeared to have traditional diner food. I chose Mexican and ordered takeaway. I returned to the motel, fed Baxter, and turned on the television. There was news of several small fires from the lightning storm. They even had an aerial view of Charlie's property and mentioned the horses. I turned the television off. I considered opening my phone. I suspected there would be messages from Charlie and others.

I chose to ignore the message bank and called my brother. He was a day's drive from here. He answered and said he was in North Carolina at a continuing education conference. We talked for a few minutes, and he asked if he could come up next month. I suggested he and my sister-in-law come and visit me when our sister was coming, and we could have a family get-together.

I don't remember anything more. I woke up when Baxter put his paw on the bed next to my pillow. The sun was out, and light crept into the room. It was nine in the morning. I hadn't slept that long in years. I threw on some clothes and took Baxter out to a grassy area near the motel's woods. Mission accomplished, and we were back in my room and preparing to continue our journey.

The woman from the motel office knocked on my door. She

had a tray of milk, cereal boxes, and a sweet roll. "How did you sleep?"

"I have no idea." I laughed. "I closed my eyes, and then it was morning."

"This place has that effect on our guests. Will you be staying again tonight?"

"I don't think so. I'm on a short holiday. To be honest, I have no plans. Is there something around here that I should see?"

"Oh, my dear. There are the falls, the museum, the petrified forest, and the quilting store. Do you sew?"

"I used to. I think I'll plan on moving on, but you never know, I might be back."

The other guest came out of her room. She was African American, possibly in her late fifties, and had a dog. She waved at me and took her dog to the same area Baxter used. Baxter shot out of our room and ran to the dog. I chased him, but the two dogs did some butt-sniffing and urinated on each other's spots and then appeared to be enjoying the interaction and company.

"Sorry, Baxter slipped out of my room when he saw your dog."

"No problem. The dogs look like they're enjoying some doggy time. I'm Sandy." She was drinking her coffee, and she watched the dogs play.

"Hi, I'm Maggie. Are you on your way somewhere or visiting the area?"

"A bit of both. I come here every year. I like to hike to the falls, and it's one of the few places you can take dogs. There's a quilting convention here, which starts in a few days. Mrs. Sawyer looks after Molly while I attend. How about you?" I felt she was eyeing me suspiciously.

"I needed a break from life and got in my car and drove. I'm exploring the sites. No purpose and no plans. I recently retired. I can't get used to all this freedom, but I'm learning."

"Half your luck. I'm back at work next week."

"My sympathies."

"No sympathies needed. I'm a teacher. I love my work, and the kids don't come back for another month. We have some training next week, then I have several more weeks before I start up for the school year. How about you? Sounds like you weren't that excited about your former work."

"Nothing could be further from the truth. I loved my work. I only retired and switched professions. I was a vet, and now I write."

"A vet, wow."

"Just horses. I take Baxter to the vet. Don't ask me anything about small animals."

"Would you like to take the dogs up to the falls? I was going to the quilting store, but I haven't been to the falls for a few years. They may not be spectacular since it's been dry here. Did you hear about the horses that were burned in the fire?"

"Yes, that's where I'm living. I saw the horses."

"The man who owns them was on television last night. He mentioned his horses were being treated by a..." She stopped. "Oh, my God. It's you, isn't it?"

"No, I'm only advising the veterinarian who is treating the horses."

"Well, he mentioned you." I could feel my face redden.

We took my car, and as we drove to the falls, I gave Sandy a brief rundown of my history without mentioning Luke, Colin, or Charlie. I talked about my move to Australia and my family and work. I explained I was now writing books, and that was where my passion lay.

"I know you're from the South. Tell me about yourself unless you're a serial killer on the run."

Sandy began her story. She was raised in Alabama. Her great-great-grandparents were children during the Civil War, and they had been slaves, but they all were freed after the war. Her grandparents were educated and taught school, which started a family tradition. Her husband was a banker, but he died two years ago. He had a heart attack without warning. They had three children and several grandchildren.

Sandy started a small school in a rural town in Georgia and taught gifted children who wanted to go to college. She raised money for them and was able to send one or two a year. Her husband set up a nonprofit for her school and tuition for graduates. After her husband's death, she continued her work with help from local businessmen and women.

"I'm impressed. I can't believe how cool this is. I may know someone who could help you."

"If I could find a benefactor, I would kiss you to the moon and back."

"Sandy, I'm not a woman-kissing kind of girl. Even if I was, I'm swearing off any relationships of any kind. I'm too old, one serial killer aside. Baxter is my one and only." I briefly explained my brush with death while she continued her story. She went to the University of Alabama, where Sandy met and married the head cheerleader. "Ours was an interracial marriage, and let me tell you, it was not easy. We raised our children while I finished my teaching degree."

Sandy saw a need to promote exceptional students from poor rural communities. Sandy started an after-school program that grew into a conventional private school that accepted students from all ethnic backgrounds. She could educate them on a shoestring by hiring retired teachers who donated their time. "You know there are many of us who have given up work but still have a passion for helping students who want to learn.

"You need to meet my sister. Christy does something similar in California. I'll give you her number."

"Any help would be appreciated."

I still wasn't ready to tell her about Luke. I was wary of any association with Colin or the custody battle. While I was sure she was someone I could trust, I was reminded of my pathetic ability to judge human motives.

We arrived at the parking lot, from where we would walk a mile to the waterfall. The dogs ran and played along the track. As predicted by Sandy, the falls were not spectacular. There was a family with two small children playing in the pool at the base of the falls. Baxter was in heaven. He found a stick and placed it in front of the children to throw.

I wanted to send a video of this to my children and opened my phone. Surprisingly, the new messages loaded, and despite my rural location, as I videoed Baxter, the phone rang. I didn't recognize the number, and I didn't answer. There were many messages. There was a text message from Patty asking about the control of itching. One of the burn horses was showing the beginnings of pruritus.

"Sandy, do you know what pruritus means?"

"Itching. Why?"

"It's a technical term, but I wondered how much it was known to the average person. I was wondering if I should define it in the book I'm currently writing."

"In case you couldn't guess, I'm not average. My daughter has eczema."

"Sorry to hear that. Have you heard of reserpine?"

"I'm a teacher, of course, I have. I don't think you can get it anymore."

I replied to Patty's message and suggested a dose of oral reserpine if she could get it. It was early for a burnt horse to become itchy, and my thought was that the horse in question would have been mildly burned.

"Maggie, can you use aloe vera on them?"

"It helps some, but in the early phase, it wasn't that helpful to my Australian cases."

I scanned through the missed calls and messages. There were several from Charlie and two from Colin. There was a message from Sylvia asking about our planned ride, which was today, and then one message from my sister. I didn't open the others, but I did open the one from my sister.

"Maggot, answer your effing phone."

I replied, "Talk tonight. Piss off." I also replied to Sylvia and sent apologies.

I could see Sandy was religious and probably didn't swear. I rarely did, but it wasn't her text that set me off. It was the messages from Colin and Charlie. I knew I would see Colin this next weekend. I wouldn't disappoint Luke for anything. I turned to Sandy and asked, "What's next?"

"Want to see some petrified wood?"

"Lead the way."

We returned to the car and drove several miles to a state park. I was cautioned not to take any petrified wood for fear of death. It was tempting, but I didn't. No, I would never do that in a state park. They had collections of arrowheads and other artifacts in their kiosk. It was after lunch when we returned to town. We ate at the diner, and each had a sandwich and salad. It wasn't high-class cuisine, but I was satiated and ready to tackle the quilting store.

That place was amazing. You'd never know how big it was from the outside and the presentation of the different fabrics made it easy to choose some. I wanted to make some quilts for my grandchildren, and that would make a great winter project. When I moved from Australia, I had to switch voltages with converters or get new appliances. I looked at sewing machines and chose one that was like what I had used before.

I thought about how simple my life could be if I kept to myself. I vowed to go fishing with Colin this one time and never accept an another invitation from either him or Charlie. Luke could come and go, but I was sticking to my friends who battled for a living. I knew both men had worked hard, but I wanted to be with people on the same rung of the ladder as me.

I didn't bring a swimsuit, and when we finished for the day, Sandy went swimming while I napped in my room. We would meet for dinner later. I had my laptop, and I opened it without checking my email. I thought about Charlie and his young girlfriend as I lay on my bed. He'd never suggested our relationship was anything more than platonic. I was not attracted to his type. Why should I be mad that he had a girlfriend and not mention it to me? Obviously, Carol knew. I remembered she mentioned that he had his demons. I guess what bothered me was that he pretended to love his dead wife but kept a young lover on the side. So much for the grieving widower. Save that for someone who cares.

If I didn't care, and if I wasn't attracted to Charlie, why was I upset to observe what was really going on? I almost fell into the trap of being seduced by the needs of powerful, rich older men. Perhaps he had good intentions, but I was already plotting to get him to look at Sandy's educational project. Still, now I was going to be the same user he was. I would use him to help Sandy's needy kids. I would trade my veterinary expertise for some do-re-mi to get scholarships. Now I would be a user.

A knock at the door woke me up. Sandy said she would be ready in fifteen minutes for our assault on the town. I quickly showered and put on a new shirt. I called my sister, and she answered, "Dead sister location service."

"What?"

"What do you mean, what? Where the hell have you been? I have sister needs, and you don't even return my calls."

"I'm learning to be spontaneous. I decided to explore my surroundings, and I've been in an area that doesn't have good cell coverage. What are your needs?"

"You don't have a spontaneous bone in your body. You are a creature of habit. So, what gives?"

"Nothing. I'm learning to be free."

"Well, if you say so. Miles and I want to come in two weeks. I want to book a room at the inn."

"Party of two. Hmm, let me check my calendar. Yes, that will fit in nicely. Will you need a lift from the airport?"

"Nope, we're driving out."

"Is that all? I met your twin, and she's doing what you're doing only in Georgia."

"Like what? Would you like to explain? You can be so obnoxious, Maggot."

"Educating poor kids. Getting them ready for college."

"Will she be there so I can meet her?"

"No. We met today, and we're having dinner together. Sandy reminds me of you only in a Bible Belt kind of way. She's cool. I need to go, but I'll get some info, and maybe you could help each other."

"Oh, who's Charlie?"

"Why?"

"He got my number from your realtor, and he was looking for you. He asked if you were okay and where you were."

"Charlie's a local guy, and he has horses that were burned in a fire over here. I was helping his vet. It was a little déjà vu from my horses across the pond, so I decided to step away. Hence the road trip." I have never successfully lied to my sister. I waited for her response.

"If you say so. What do you want me to say if this guy calls again?"

"Say you haven't heard from me. I'll be home on Friday, anyway. I'm in contact with his vet. She can handle it."

"See you soon. Miles is dying to go fishing with you."

"I'll get him a license, and I can guarantee Miles will catch fish. Later, gator."

"Be careful. I don't want you hooking up with another idiot that takes you to another country."

"Pinky promise."

"It's okay to hook up, Maggot. Just let me vet the poor bastards first."

At dinner, I learned more about Sandy's program, and I told her about my sister's gig in San Francisco. We exchanged email addresses and phone numbers. Tomorrow we would hike through a forest, which would take several hours. I needed to become fitter, and to me, this was a great way to keep up since I wasn't working and wrestling horses anymore. The trailhead was thirty miles from our hotel, and we arrived when it was still cold. The motel lady had packed us sandwiches and gave us water bottles. She advised us not to drink the creek water.

The entire walk would take several hours. Sandy appeared fit, but she lived at a lower altitude, and we had to stop several times for her to catch her breath. I was lucky that I was now acclimatized. We rounded a corner two hours into our walk, and directly in front of us was a man in distress. He appeared as if he was having a heart attack. He was pale and sweaty. Sandy immediately put her hand on his arm and felt for a pulse. "Sir, are you okay?"

"My chest and back hurt." Sandy helped him to lie on the ground and used her sweater as a pillow. She turned to me and shook her head. We both opened our phones, and my phone had coverage, but hers only had the SOS indicator. I began to dial triple zero and realized that it was Australian and dialed nine-one-one. The call wouldn't go through. We both tried SOS, and again we could not make a call. We'd crossed a peek twenty minutes ago, where Sandy had opened her phone and received a text message while taking pictures of the view.

"I hate to say this, but you're fitter than me, Maggie. Take both our phones and go back to the peak and see if you can order a helicopter. Sir, what's your name? Do you have a medical condition?" He shook his head, and I took off. I ran as much as I could. It took thirty minutes to reach the summit. My phone began to ring. Effing hell, it was Charlie. I had to answer. What if that was my only link to get some help? This was the first time the phone showed a connection.

"Charlie, I can't talk now. I need a helicopter for a medical evacuation."

"Oh my God, are you okay?"

"I'm fine. I'm on a hiking trail, and we found a man who may be having a heart attack. We need to get him to a hospital now." I hit my location and gave it to Charlie. "Please call someone Charlie. It looks bad."

"Okay, stay on the line, and I'll use my other phone, so I don't lose you."

You have so lost me. I waited while I heard him talking to an emergency operator. It sounded like they would send a helicopter to my location, and then the paramedics would come with me to the man in distress. It would be thirty minutes. I wouldn't have time to run back and tell Sandy, so I could only wait for their arrival. Charlie was still on the line. I thanked him and suggested I should clear the line so the paramedics could reach me. "No, they said to keep you on the line. I need to talk to you. I need to explain."

"No. Not at all. I have no issues that need discussion. We are adults, and while I was surprised, you need to know that there is, and never will be, anything but friendship between us, and what you do in your personal life is not my concern. My personal life is not your concern, either. Just don't play the grieving widower anymore with me."

"It's not what you think. Well, it may have been in the past, but it isn't anymore. I care about you, and I care what you think."

"Not if you knew what I really did think. Charlie. I am living a wonderful new life, and I don't want to complicate it. I'm happy to help Patty with your horses, but that's where it ends."

"Can I see you when you get back?"

"Sure, but you need to understand all I want is friendship, nothing else. I am not attracted to you. You are free to see and screw whoever you want."

"Did you think I was romantically attracted to you? What makes you think that?"

It was my turn to be humiliated, and I was. "Sorry. I guess I'm not used to having men hold my hand and inviting me to dinners with no motives other than to be kind. My mistake—it won't happen again. I'm genuinely sorry. Let's change the subject. How are the horses?"

"They're doing exactly what you said they would do. The eyes and faces are much better, two horses have separation of their hooves, and they're getting easier to handle."

There was a long pause. "I guess I'm not used to social cues anymore. I'm sorry. If you don't mind, I've met someone who I think you would enjoy meeting. My new friend's a lot like your wife. She runs a school for smart, underprivileged students in Georgia. I know you and my new friend would have a lot in common."

"Yes, I'd like to meet her." There was a long pause.

I heard the distant hum of a helicopter. "I better hang up. I can hear the helicopter."

"When will you be back?"

"In a few days. I promised Luke and Colin that I would go fishing with them."

"Collie and I have been worried about you. Please take care."

"Thanks. And thanks for relaying this message. It doesn't look good, but we needed to try to get this man some help."

"Is he a friend?"

"Not yet, but the day's young. Later, dude."

"Touché, my friend." Charlie got in the last word as I hung up and saw the helicopter coming over the treetops.

There was a safe area where the helicopter could land. I didn't know of anything closer. The aircraft landed, and two men emerged and ran over to me. I described the man's condition, and one man took off along the trail while the other man and I carried the equipment and a stretcher.

When we arrived, the man was still alive, and color had returned to his face. He wore an oxygen mask. The paramedic who was with me went to the medical assistant to help with the assessment and treatment. The helicopter pilot was called. Eventually, the man was lifted strapped to the stretcher into the helicopter, along with the paramedics. The patient was evacuated to a hospital for further treatment.

Sandy looked relieved. "That's our good deed for the day. I don't know about you, but I need a stiff drink. Shall we head back?"

"Sounds like a plan. I didn't know you drank."

"I was thinking of a soft drink, but yes, I do drink, and since you ran all the way to the clearing, the drinks are on me tonight."

"You're on, sister. Can we stop so I can pick up a swimming suit? I need some pool time. There's someone else I need to tell you about."

"I knew it. I saw all those text messages." Sandy grinned.

"It's not what you think. Let's wait until dinner." How do I explain my relationship to a billionaire?

We began discussing the man on the mountain. "I'm praying for him. Do you know where they took him?" Sandy looked at her phone. "He gave me his number. I'll wait for a few days and see if he calls, then we'll know he survived."

Sandy and I swam in the motel pool that afternoon. The swimsuit I bought was practical. The suit covered the essentials. I looked down at my aging body. My arms and legs had wrinkles, and my abdomen was losing condition. I thought about the young woman in Charlie's kitchen. There was no comparison. Let's face it, Charlie was younger than me but still looked older. He had no musculature that was at all attractive. Charlie had a paunch, and his arms were thin and white. His hair only hinted at the color he had in his youth.

We discussed our rescue and good deed for the day as wc sat in the pool. Sandy talked to the stricken man when I ran to make the call to obtain help. "I think they were taking him to the hospital in the capital. He was a state senator."

"Did he say much more?"

"No, just that he wanted to let his mother and kids know that he loved them."

I swam and looked around. "Where is the cabana boy? I need a drink."

Sandy laughed. "What is the term you use for men's swimsuits in Australia?"

"Budgie smugglers?"

"Yes, that's it." She paused. "So, who is it you want me to meet? I know you have more going on than you're letting on. How can I be your bestie if I don't know the whole story?"

"I moved into a rural area that is north of here. There are all kinds of interesting people who are kind of low-key in the area but are movers and shakers in the outside world. Have you heard of CLM Industries?"

"No, not really."

"Neither had I. CLM stands for Charlie and Linda McLeod." I went on to describe Charlie and his deceased wife's business and philanthropic endeavors. I told Sandy about how Charlie continued to support Linda's charities, especially with the schools and helping children. I explained how I met Charlie, and it was his horses that were burned in a fire. I didn't mention anything about his personal life or my minor involvement in his life. "He's a nice guy, and I think he could help you and your program. He owes me for helping with his horses, and when I get back, I'll tell him about you. Do you have a website or any info I can pass on?"

"Sure. I saw your phone. He's texted you several times. What's going on with that? His wife's dead? Are you together and having a lover's tiff? Is that why you're here?"

"Nope, on all accounts. He's not my type. He is still married, and I am not looking. I am too old for that nonsense anymore. I only want to write, ride, and fish. He doesn't do any of that." I didn't discuss Colin or Luke. That was too much of a no-go zone. I did describe Carol and Sylvia and how much fun they were.

"What about the books you're writing?"

"One is out, and I think another may be out in a month or two. The books are about a vet who solves mysteries. Kind of like *Murder She Wrote*."

"I haven't heard of them."

"Hmm, I'll have to get a stick after my publicity people. Want to head to dinner in an hour?"

I took Baxter out for his doggy duties, and Sandy emerged with her dog too. "I bought your book, and I'm already on chapter nine. I love it. When did you say the next book comes out?"

"I have no doubt Amazon will alert you."

"I can't believe how lucky I am to meet you and Baxter. You're going to have to come down and visit me now, and I want to come up and see your place."

"Done deal. I'll be seeing Charlie's horses when I get back and most likely him, as well. I'll start my campaign for your school. I'll fall down dead if he isn't interested. You never know. Maybe he's ready to move on. You may be his type."

"I had the best. I'm happy with my life as it is. I found CLM Enterprises too. He's not really my type, anyway. He's a bit too white for me." We both laughed about that.

"Mine either. Charlie's an exceptionally nice man, and you need to wait to judge him after you meet him." Why was I promoting him to her? She deserves better.

Chapter 27

A quick stop at the fly shop, and I was on my way home. I arrived late in the day, and there was Luke down watering the garden and had Digger on a rope walking around with him as he went along. I waved while Baxter galloped down to see Luke.

"Are you still going fishing with us? It's a surprise. You won't cancel on us, will you?"

"Not a chance, mate." I laughed as I thought of how rarely I used that Australian term when I lived there. "I need to do some writing, so how about I see you on Saturday. Am I supposed to come over, or will you pick me up?"

"We'll come and get you. You know I've never gone fishing with my grandfather. I hope I do a good job."

"Luke, you're his grandchild. You can do no wrong." This reminded me of my own grandchildren. I was getting nostalgic. So much has happened. For the first time, I had that empty deep-pitted sensation of homesickness. Had I made a colossal mistake?

I was up early on Saturday morning. I'd packed all my fishing gear, warm clothes, and lunch. I waited for Colin and Luke to drive up to the house, but no one arrived. Finally, I heard the whirring of a helicopter. I looked over into the arena next to Digger, where a helicopter was landing. Digger seemed unperturbed by the commotion, but Baxter was going wild.

When the blades had stopped, Luke jumped out and ran up the hill to my house. I was walking down to the copter carrying my rod and other fishing supplies. I was excited. I'd never ridden in a helicopter and never had an opportunity to fish in remote areas. I waved and climbed into a seat. I prayed I didn't get sick. Oh, heck, I prayed I would survive. The pilot was Doug Cameron, who explained the basics of the copter. I was given a headset, and Colin tapped me on the shoulder and asked, "Are you ready for a great fishing adventure?" I gave him a thumbs-up. "Doug is going to take us to one of my favorite places in the world. Hang on, he's just learning to fly this thing."

I shot a worried look to Doug, who shook his head and said he'd been flying this copter for over ten years and did emergency retrievals during the week. I told them all about Sandy and my encounter with a man having a heart attack and how we called a team to pick him up, and hopefully, he survived.

"Was that the senator?" Doug asked.

I nodded. "Did you hear about it? Was it in the news?"

"It was probably in the news, but I heard about it yesterday in a briefing. It wasn't a heart attack. The senator passed a kidney stone, and the poor guy will never live it down. Was that you that hailed the rescue copter? I'm impressed."

I smiled and nodded. Colin patted my shoulder again. He and Luke sat behind me, and I was in the front seat. It was exciting flying out into the wilderness. I looked down at my house, the nearby stream, and even Saddleback Lake I'd discovered when Colin's son was visiting. We flew for over an hour. Finally, we came to a verdant valley surrounded by granite cliffs. Doug set the helicopter down and began to help me undo my seatbelt, and then he turned and helped Luke. Colin needed no help, and for a man as old as he was, I was impressed with his agility.

Even Doug was going to fish. We all let Colin pick a spot on the riverbank. Luke went upstream, and I went the other way. Colin used a walking stick to help with negotiating the edge of the river. He didn't wear waders. Luke wore new waders that fit him and would need to be discarded in another year while he grew. I had my trusty Orvis waders, which I purchased a few years ago. They fit well and allowed me to wade out into the river from the bank.

Doug went without waders as well. I watched both Doug and Colin cast into the wide river. They were both world-class fishermen. I was far below either man in expertise. Even Colin could cast his line far beyond me. I doubted I would be fishing at his age, but who knew. I watched him fish for a few minutes while he observed Luke. He stopped and went over to Luke and talked to him, and then I could see him instruct Luke on casting his line and fly.

I had my phone, and I stopped to take a picture. I never took pictures of Luke or Colin. Colin was a public figure, and I felt it was an invasion of his privacy. I was particularly wary of photographing Luke. I would only share these with Colin and destroy them if he asked. I wanted Luke to have a memory of fishing with his grandfather. I wanted a picture too, but I would never keep it for myself without Colin's permission. There were very few pictures of the aging film star in the media anymore. I did find one when he attended his other son's gallery opening, but that was the only one I found on the net. I had the memory. That was enough.

That was until I had a monumental strike. The fish hit hard and took my line out and swam way up the river past where Colin instructed Luke. Everyone quickly pulled in their lines and allowed me to play the fish. I slipped and landed in the water but still could hold on to the rod and line and keep playing the fish. I was determined to land this beauty come hell or high water. It was high water, and I fell again and was soaked. If the water was cold, I barely noticed it. The fish finally tired, and I carefully brought him to shore. Doug followed me along the water's edge and used his net to scoop him up. Everyone whooped and hollered.

"I need a picture." The fish was a monster and was more like the giant trout I had caught in New Zealand. My heart was racing, and I noticed the cold and my wet upper body. I kept my camera inside a baggie. I handed it to Doug, who snapped the obligatory fish pic, and then Colin asked to be in the picture. He motioned for Luke to come in too. Doug took a picture of me holding the fish with Luke and Colin on either side behind me. Colin handed Doug his phone and asked for a few photos as well. We returned the fish to the water and planned to keep only the fish we caught later in the day.

Colin looked at his phone. "If this picture isn't framed and, on your mantel next week, I'm going to raise holy hell with you. You understand?"

"Yes, sir." I chattered, now really feeling the cold. I had a sweatshirt back at the helicopter, and I went to change out my shirt.

Colin looked at me and shouted that he was willing to help me change my clothes. I raised my hand without looking back. "You're no good to me dead, Collie. At my age, it might be lethal to see me naked."

"I'll be the judge of that."

"Grandpa," admonished a clearly embarrassed Luke.

I took off my sweater and shirt and laid them out on a nearby bush to dry. The sun would be on them soon, and I could put them on again in an hour. We fished for a few more minutes in the same places until Colin took Luke around a bend. Doug and I stayed. He hooked a beautiful rainbow hen, and I did the honors and netted the fish for him. "Not as big as yours, but still one worth a picture. Will you do the honors?" He handed me his phone, and I took several pictures on his phone as well as mine. "I have coffee back at the copter. Would you like some?"

I looked around, found several places for a girl to relieve herself, and figured I could afford a cup of coffee. We went back to the helicopter, and he poured coffee into two mugs. "What the hell did you do to deserve this?"

"I don't know for sure. I guess it's Luke. Do you know about him?" I peered down the river to see if the pair were returning.

"Yes, Colin told me. I wasn't sure what you knew, so I didn't say anything."

"What do you know?" I wasn't giving anything up.

"Good. I can see you're cautious too. I know about Luke's father, if that's what you mean. I know about the court trial next week, but the last time I saw Luke, he was considered to be deaf. Is this your doing?"

"I guess." I quickly told him about playing music and catching him, singing "Walk Like a Man."

"We better catch up. I don't want to miss Colin catching a fish. It might be his last."

"He's pretty fit for a guy his age."

"So are you, Maggie, if you don't mind my saying."

"Thanks, I think."

We walked up to the bend and saw Luke reeling another large trout in. We ran up and were there as Colin set the fish in the net. I was able to get a picture. Colin turned to us. "These fish are all monsters. This is the best day fishing I've ever had." I took a picture of Luke with his fish, and he asked to have his grandfather and me in another photo.

Colin finally hooked the fish of the day. It was far longer than my whale and outweighed mine by two pounds. "Happy birthday, Grandpa." Luke hugged Colin. That was the most affection I had observed between the boy and his grandfather. Doug nudged my shoulder.

"It's your birthday, Collie? Luke, you are under punishment, mate. You should have told me." I had no idea. Colin Chandler was eighty today. It was hard to believe. He was such a robust man. I didn't mention his age.

"I just found out myself. Grandpa only told me a few minutes ago."

Doug shook his head and put his hands up. "Me neither. Am I under punishment?"

"I didn't plan on telling anyone until later. It slipped out when Luke caught his first fish. Having your grandson catch his first big fish is the best present I could ask for."

This gave me an idea. "I'm going to bring my grandchildren out next year and get them fishing too."

"When's your birthday, Maggie? I never asked. How many children do you have?"

"I have three all grown and married. I have five grandchildren." Colin paused and then motioned toward the river.

We fished for two more hours, and we all caught more fish, but we couldn't outdo Colin's monster. We took pictures of Luke's fish, but the photo session was over for the morning. Doug went back to the helicopter and brought out a picnic basket that Mrs.

Gillard prepared for us. We ate sandwiches and drank root beer. There were cheese and crackers, fruit, and Colin had a real beer. Doug was abstaining due to pilot duties, so Colin pointed a bottle at me. I declined at first, but he wore me down.

The sun was shining, and there was warmth in the sand we sat on. Everyone was feeling the need to shut their eyes. Well, almost everyone. Luke stood up and said he was going back to the river. Doug looked at Colin, who nodded, and he followed Luke. I was succumbing to the beer and sun and leaned back and closed my eyes. Ten minutes later, I heard myself snoring, woke up, and hoped I was by myself. No such luck, Colin was looking at me and grinning.

"What?"

"You."

"What me?"

"You're normal. You drool, you snore, and you."

I cut him off. "I didn't fart, did I?"

"No, never mind. I want to talk to you."

I shot up. Please tell me Colin isn't coming on to me, or he has terrible news, or he's dying. He was now cleaned shaved. He was still a hunk, even at eighty.

"Okay, what about?" I asked hesitantly.

"Charlie."

"What about Charlie?" I wondered what Charlie had said.

"You know he thinks the world of you. He was sick with worry when you took off without telling anyone where you were going. Hell, I think the world of you too. If I were ten years younger, Charlie wouldn't have a chance. If I met you ten years ago, my life would be so different. Even Helen likes you. She told me to dump my current for you. So, as painful as it is, I have to step aside for Charlie and sort you two out."

"Colin." I tried to cut him off.

"Maggie, I liked it when you called me Collie. Just so you know." He smiled and sat forward.

"Okay, Collie. I've been divorced and single for over twenty years. I've had a short relationship or two over the years, but I was married to my work. I got all my kicks out of saving horses and getting my kids launched. When I moved here, I simply wanted to write, fish, and ride my horse."

"My horse." He smiled.

"Yes, your horse. Do you want Digger back?"

"No, he's yours for life."

"I wonder who's going to outlive who? Anyway, I don't know if you know about my chance encounter with the serial killer, but I met him. He changed my tire and my perspective on my life. It could be a movie. We shook hands, and it was like lightning. His touch reignited something. I haven't wanted any intimacy for years and years, and even though I missed his real intentions, for the first time in a long while, I had unfulfilled desires."

"I know what you mean. I've resolved myself to a separate and loveless marriage. My only goal these days is to help my children and their children." He looked over at Luke fishing with Doug. "I guess it's normal and a process of aging, but to have a desire to care about someone and for someone to care about them… I don't know. Am I asking for the moon? Hey, how did this happen? I was supposed to patch things up with you and Charlie, not complain about my life."

"Collie, if you weren't married."

"Maggie, if I weren't married, you and I wouldn't be having this conversation. I sure as hell wouldn't be helping Charlie. I'd be pleading for myself."

"I appreciate your efforts, even if they're questionable, and I can't thank you enough for sharing your birthday with me. I'll talk to Charlie, but you must know, I like him, but that is where it ends. He's in love with his dead wife, and despite that, he has other interests."

"I think he eighty-sixed his other interest that day you walked in on her. Shall we go see if we can catch a few more?" We helped each other to stand. "Oh, you do fart in your sleep."

"Bullshit."

"That wasn't from me. Charlie mentioned it."

I turned from him red-faced. "Well, it's got to come out sometime."

We fished for two more hours. We all caught fish, and Colin helped Luke improve his casting. He even gave me some casting lessons. At the end of the afternoon, we each kept one good trout. Colin wanted us to have a birthday dinner back at his place. He asked Doug to have the helicopter land behind his barn, and we would all walk down and have dinner. Once we were up in the air, he called the house and informed Mrs. Gillard that we were on our way back and we would be eating trout for dinner.

"Uh, maybe tomorrow, boss?" Mrs. Gillard ruled the house. Colin appeared perplexed.

As we were approaching the compound, I saw Colin look down at a spot near the helipad. "What the hell?"

"What is it, Grandpa?"

"A damn mess is the best I can see." A crowd of thirty or more people was standing away from the landing site. "Not what I was expecting. Damn it."

We landed, and while the blades were still hovering, we retrieved our belongings as several well-dressed men and women approached us. One must be Colin's wife. She stepped out of the group, walked over, and threw her arms around Colin. She was probably ten years younger than me and had straight blond hair in a chignon, and a colorful scarf was draped over her shoulder. She had lips that had seen recent action in the plastic surgeon's chair. The others were dressed in almost formal attire and were clearly his celebrity friends. There was a photographer snapping pictures.

"Happy birthday, darling. I was surprised when I arrived and was told you were out fishing with my grandson. I guess I can forgive you." She looked over at me. Luke stood in front of Doug and me. Doug put his arm over my shoulder. The woman walked up and gave Luke a forced embrace. It was awkward. She looked up at me and said, "You must be Luke's teacher. Aren't you a bit old to be with our Luke? And Luke, I understand you can hear and talk now. Apparently, you've been lying to us all this time." I was furious. Doug firmly left his arm over my shoulder and squeezed my upper arm.

Colin turned back toward us and mouthed, "I'm sorry. I hope you're joining us for dinner."

"No, it wouldn't be appropriate. I need to get home, but thanks."

Doug understood that Colin's plans for tonight had changed. "Colin, I'll walk Maggie home, and can I borrow a car? It's getting late for flying tonight. I'll be back tomorrow to pick up my chariot."

I smiled politely toward Mrs. Chandler and Colin. "Doug, you can stay with me, and then we can leave the Chandlers to have their birthday dinner. Thanks for a wonderful day and for the advice. Luke, I'll see you on Monday, and don't forget your homework."

Chapter 28

Doug and I walked through the gate that separated the Chandler's and my properties, and we went up to my house. Baxter waited on the porch, and in the fading light, he saw us emerge from the woods. He bounded down to greet us. I turned to Digger, who called out. I checked his water and threw him some more hay. "Okay, old man, you had the day off today, but you and I are going to the lake tomorrow."

Doug and I each had our trout, which I filleted, and then did some salad and potatoes. I went down to the garden and retrieved a large zucchini and started to cook it as well. Doug and I had a glass of wine. He still had to return to the helicopter in the morning, so he limited his alcohol consumption to one glass. As we sat down at the table, there was a knock on the door. Luke asked to come in. "I hate her."

"She's your step-grandmother. You need to cut her some slack. She's important to your grandfather. Do they know you're here?" He shook his head. "Have you eaten?" he nodded, but I saw Luke eye the trout. "You can stay for a few minutes, but you need to return to your place after dinner."

"Do I have to?"

"Yes. No exceptions. You shouldn't be coming out at night, anyway. I saw a bear go through here last month. It's too dangerous."

I got the teenage look of exasperation. *Oh my God, it's already starting.* Doug saw it and laughed. Luke's presence put a hold on our conversation. Doug was recently divorced and had a daughter. She lived with him most of the time. We decided we needed to get together to fish with his daughter, and I suggested they come after work next week. Doug was on call for flying, but he would let me know. He was going to take Luke back, and I was going to clean up. I had ice cream for the boys, but Luke had gone over to the couch and was already asleep.

Doug carried him to the downstairs bedroom, and I sent a message to Colin that Luke was over here and asleep. If he wanted him to come back tonight, I would wake him up, but he was dead to the world, and I was happy to have him stay with Doug and me tonight. I didn't receive a reply and thought that in a few minutes, I would call Mrs. Gillard.

Doug was tired as well, but he would take Luke back if he wasn't allowed to stay with me. I poured myself another glass of wine, and we sat on the deck in the dark, watching distant lightning. Doug told me about his army training and how he had flown in Afghanistan. He was from Wyoming and had joined the rescue team here. As a side business, Doug occasionally took people up for scenic flights or fishing adventures. He lived near the regional airport and was available most of the summer for fires and rescue. Doug used to work interstate in the winter, but now that his daughter was of school age, he stayed here year-round. He was dating a fellow pilot. He called her and told her he was spending the night and flying back in the morning.

As we sat on the porch, Baxter began to growl. "Bear?" I stood up, and the growl turned to a happy whine.

"Don't shoot. It's an old man."

"How do we know you aren't a bear?" Doug returned.

"You don't, and if I stayed home any longer, I might have turned into one."

"Enter at your own risk. There's a drunk, crazy woman here."

"Hey Collie, not drunk, simply happy. Come on up. Are you doing a grandchild retrieval?"

"No. Can I join you?"

Doug stood up. "Not me. I'm going to bed. Maggie, that was an amazing dinner. I need to leave in daylight. Can I use the couch?"

"Upstairs to the right, Doug. The bathroom is off the bedroom. I'd say enjoy, but I doubt you'll be awake for more than two minutes once you hit the pillow. Do you need a phone charger?"

"No, I have a charger in my kit. Thanks to you both for a wonderful day."

"No, thank you, buddy. Having my grandson and my favorite girl for a day of fishing was the perfect way to spend my birthday. Sorry that it didn't end like I'd planned."

I turned to Doug as he headed back into the house. "Towels are under the sink. Sweet dreams, and let me know about Wednesday."

"Are you two already planning a rendezvous without me?"

"Yes. Doug wants to take his daughter fishing. I suggested we go to the lake, but he may have to work if there are fires." I pointed to the woods, where the occasional lightning illuminated the tops of the trees. We sat in companionable silence.

"Heidi is waiting for me to fall off the perch. She only sees me once or twice a year now. She doesn't know it, but she's only getting her apartment and a small stipend. The rest gets split three ways. Luke won't get his money until he's thirty, but the others get theirs right away. Helen gets some too. I'd divorce Heidi, but she'd get more than that despite our prenup."

"Do they know where you are?"

"No, they think the old man went to bed. I said I'd stay up in the barn, so there would be plenty of rooms for her guests. They won't even miss me until after lunch, and by then, Luke and I will be back."

"So, you think you're spending the night?" I shook my head and pointed to the garage.

"You would put Colin Chandler in a room above the garage on his eightieth birthday?"

"Lucky for you, I have another guest bedroom."

"Lead the way, darlin'. I'm going to crash otherwise."

"Collie, this has been one of the best days of my life. Thank you." We hugged and kissed in a brotherly/sisterly way.

"Don't think that kiss would have been different if I wasn't a good friend of Charlie's."

"Or if you weren't married. Don't tempt me. You're still a fox in my eyes."

"Pleasant dreams, Maggie."

"You too, beautiful boy."

"Are you flattering an old man?"

"Just stating the facts, Collie, Just the facts."

I dreaded tomorrow. I was headed to The Sanctuary to meet Patty. She left a message earlier today to say there were four horses where she needed a second opinion. My goal was to slip in and out without running into Charlie. Well, that didn't happen, did it?

Chapter 29

I was up at my usual time of four in the morning. I went down and made coffee. I had sweet rolls and fruit set out for the men when they woke up. I decided to do my writing while on the couch, so I wouldn't miss them. Luke was up first as dawn broke. He poured himself some juice, selected a sweet roll, and proceeded to sit on the opposite end of the couch and put the blanket I was using over himself.

"Sleep alright?" I adjusted my end of the blanket.

"I guess. How did I get to bed?"

"Doug did the honors. Your grandfather's upstairs. He should be down soon."

"Is Doug still here?"

I heard footsteps on the stairs as he quietly responded, "Right here, ready to kick your ass in a fishing competition Lukey Boy."

"You wish. When are you coming back? Can I meet your daughter?"

Both Doug and I caught that. "She's a wee young for you, but maybe Wednesday. If it's okay with your boss, maybe you can join us."

"Which boss?" Luke asked.

Doug pointed to me.

Colin was now coming down the stairs. Both men got cups of coffee with pastries and sat down in recliners next to the couch.

Luke's feet were reaching for mine, and I kicked him and told him to get his feet away, or he was going back to his room. Colin retorted. "Luke, listen to her. She means it. You don't want to tangle with this woman. I hear she used to make a living by gelding horses."

I smiled. "Ah, the good old days."

"Is that true?" Luke quickly retracted his feet as I nodded.

Doug stood up and asked for a traveling mug. I gave him one, and the three guests departed. Colin turned back. "Be gentle with him, Maggie."

"Don't worry, I sold all my instruments when I retired." Colin gave me a backward wave as he disappeared into the woods between our homes.

I arrived at the gate for The Sanctuary and punched the code into the gate. It didn't work. I called Patty, who said she was still a few minutes away. She replied the code had been changed last week. Charlie had a friend who had been banned from the estate, and she returned several times, so he had the combo changed.

"Did Charlie tell you to say that?"

"No, everyone is talking about it. Six, eight, three, and one."

I entered them into the keypad, and the gate opened. As I entered the gateway, Patty drove up and followed me. We parked outside the barn and were greeted by two ranch hands.

The younger horses were all improving and were allowed onto a grassy area in the morning and late afternoon when the sun didn't scorch their burnt hides. The older horses were the ones who were slow to heal. All four now had extensive separation of the coronary bands and large areas of raw oozing patches on their groins and under the armpits. They were still eating, and despite the hoof issues, were not showing imminent signs of sloughing a hoof.

"I think they'll survive and in nine months will be back to normal. Be sure to keep the skin moisturized, and you may be able to reduce the pain meds to once daily now."

"Maggie, there's a horse magazine that wants to come and do a story about our horses. Can I quote you and give them your number?"

"Sure, no prob."

We were bent over, looking at the older mare, when Patty looked up and smiled. "Hey Charlie, Maggie has given us the thumbs-up. We're going to keep on keeping on for now."

Charlie was standing behind me and leaned over my shoulder as I examined the last mare. I stood up and bumped him, not realizing how close he was. Our heads hit, and he grabbed me to steady me. "Sorry, Charlic." I rubbed my head as he rubbed his chin.

"We do seem to be doing a bit of head-butting, don't we?" I laughed, but I didn't reply. "Do you have time for a cup of coffee?"

I certainly didn't want to seem rude. "Sure."

He asked me to follow him up to his house. I drove up behind his old truck. He emerged and had something in his hand. We went up to the house, he opened the door, and we went out to the sunroom with the adjoining swimming pool.

"How was your fishing trip?"

"It was fantastic. Would you like to see some pictures?"

"I'd like to." He didn't sound enthusiastic, but I showed him pictures of the four of us and our fish.

"I'm sorry, but I can't imagine becoming excited about catching a fish."

"I get that. And that means more for those of us who like hooking the little buggers. You reel in companies while Colin and I reel in fish."

Roberta came into the sunroom and asked if we wanted coffee. "That would be great. Thanks, Roberta. Can I help you?"

She gave me a look and said, "No. I'm sure the boss has more important plans for you today."

I looked at Charlie, who stared out toward the pool. "It's awkward, you see. I'm rarely alone. I want to explain."

"I don't mean to interrupt, but you don't owe me an explanation. We are both adults, and neither of us owes the other any explanations."

"I get that, but I do want to. I feel I owe you an explanation." Charlie was nervous.

Roberta entered the room. "Boss, it's time for me to go. Do you want anything else?"

"No, thank you, Roberta. See you tomorrow. Please say hi to George and give him my best. If he needs any special medication or anything, will you let me know?"

"Thanks. I will. The doctors say it won't be long now. I am praying it's quick and painless."

I was alarmed. Was this Roberta's family member who was dying? After she left, Charlie turned to me. "Pancreatic cancer. George is her brother."

"Oh, how terrible."

"Could I take you up to Linda's grave again?"

"Sure." I gulped my coffee, and we went out to the old truck. Once again, he opened the door for me. I need to talk to my sons about the small things that mean so much to a woman. Has that gesture been discarded considering the #MeToo movement?

We arrived at the memorial site, and suddenly clouds began to gather. Charlie looked up.

"I'm not going to get a break."

"God's punishing you."

"Why?"

"I don't know, just because." I smiled to myself. *Oh, I know why.*

We sat down on Linda's bench, and we heard thunder. It sounded close. "Let's go. I think this is going to be a ripper."

"It looks like there's a little rain with it."

"Thankfully."

"Would you like to come back to my house for lunch? I can cook you some trout from yesterday." Luckily, Doug left most of his trout.

"I would love that. I don't want to impose, though."

"No, I'd like you to come. How about if you come over at noon? It won't be fancy. The dress is casual and what you're wearing is fine."

He hugged me. "I don't want to lose you."

I didn't want to lead him on. "Let's talk, and we can see how it goes. We need to set some rules. You can blame me for expecting more than I should have expected. The rules go both ways."

Charlie took me up to the house, and I got into my car and drove home.

Charlie arrived an hour later and brought flowers and root beer. "You sure know how to weaken my will, Charlie McLeod." He had the same package from this morning. He opened it, and it was a simple box with a glass top. Inside was a perfect arrowhead.

"I don't smoke, so I'm not doing a peace pipe, but I know you like hunting for artifacts."

"You do know how to move me. Thank you."

I offered him a variety of drinks. He accepted sparkling water. The trout was almost cooked, and I added a tossed salad from the garden and microwaved asparagus.

We sat down at the small table out on the porch but under the roof. The rain came and went, and there was an occasional clap of thunder. We scooted our chairs together so we could both watch the sky and yet be out of the rain.

"This trout is delicious. I can see why you like to fish."

I thanked him and offered him more. "Yes, please." I served up the last of the trout.

"Have I created a new addict?"

"You've created something, that's for sure."

I waited for him to continue. Just then, a loud roll of thunder began. I could feel it in my chest. It was followed by heavy rain. "Let's go inside. God is not our friend today."

We gathered our plates, and I placed them on the sink.

"I have cookies, graham crackers, and chocolate ice cream."

"No, thanks. I'm full." I doubted it, but I let it ride.

"I want to say I was embarrassed about your encounter in my kitchen the other day. I wish you hadn't met her, and I wish I'd never met her as well. I don't have an explanation other than it was exactly what you saw. She's been my vice for the last year. Before her, there was another one and another before her. I've had a run of women even before Linda died. Only a few people know."

"Did Linda know?"

"Not to my knowledge, but she was the one to encourage me. Linda was sick long before we ever told anyone, and she encouraged me to seek..." He stopped. "I don't know what you might call it."

I wanted to say whores, hookers, or call girls. "You don't have to put a label on it. It's none of my business. You don't have to say anything else."

"The thing is, I do. When you came over, I was on the phone with a teacher from South Africa. One of Linda's schools had been destroyed by government troops. Talia had arrived a few minutes after I was in consultation, and she assumed we would continue our arrangement. I asked her to leave before I made another call about restoring the school. However, when I came out of my office, she was walking around in nothing but my shirt, telling me you'd arrived and threatened her with a gun."

I rolled my eyes. "I didn't threaten the woman. I might have wanted to, but I didn't. I think you know that. I hope you do, anyway."

"The only woman I cared about is my wife. They all knew that."

"Is it that you were worried I would say something to our mutual acquaintances? I don't understand why you care if I know? I would never say anything. You've talked to Colin, but I never said anything until he confronted me when we were fishing."

"No. I know Carol knows. I've never hidden it. It was an arrangement."

I wondered if he had women in all his ports of call. It was none of my business. "Charlie, as long as we aren't sharing bodily fluids, I have no right to judge or complain. I may choose not to see you, but your private business is not mine to judge."

"That's just it. I do care, and I want your approval. I know it might only result in a friendship, but I want your company. I usually come back here every two to three weeks. You may not know, but I've been coming back every week in hopes that I can see you. If it's only to have dinner and conversation, I'm happy with that."

"I can be bought, you know."

"I doubt that."

"No, really. If you want me to be your friend, it will come at a cost. Seriously."

Charlie looked at me and frowned. "I thought you were different." I could see his dismay.

"Nope. I can be bought. Plain and simple."

"Do you mean I can pay and have sex with you? I don't believe you."

"Oh, no. That would be too easy. Charlie, I'm sixty-eight. Would you pay to have sex with someone my age? I'm flattered."

We both laughed, but he realized I was serious. "What's your price?"

"Stay right here." I went upstairs and retrieved my computer. I sat down on the couch and patted the seat next to me. He came over and looked like he was going to be exposed to unusual porn.

"I'm not into kinky stuff. Do you need glasses?"

"Laser surgery a few years ago. What have you got?"

I opened the web page of Sandy's school. "I met this woman on my, shall we say, retreat. She educates underprivileged, gifted kids in the South and gets them ready for college. She attempts to find scholarships to help them get a university education."

He scrolled down and then hit one or two pages. "Send me the link." I did. "Is this my penance?"

"It's not the key to my inner sanctum. You don't even have to get involved. I just wanted you to look. My guess is this has Linda's mark all over it."

"I think I'll go back to my other women. They are far less expensive."

"You could do both. We are friends. Not lovers. Are we clear?"

"Do I have a chance?"

"If Colin gets a divorce, or the serial killer gets out of prison, you have no hope. Otherwise, a year or two of good behavior and a serious look at my friend's program, and you never know your luck."

"That's good enough for me."

Sandy called later that night as I was headed to bed. "Hey, sista. How do I thank you?"

"I'm not sure. Did Charlie call you?"

"I have twelve full-ride scholarships to begin with and more to come if half of my students complete their studies."

"You're kidding. Damn, now I'm going to have to be nice to the bastard?"

"Be genuinely nice. This means the world to my students and me."

Chapter 30

I was sure the ringing phone signaled an emergency. I tried to orient myself. Where is the call? Was it a colicky horse or a foaling mare? As I reached for the phone, I knocked it off the side table. I was back in Australia working at my clinic. I could not get to the phone in time before the ringing stopped. I prayed my phone registered the number so I could call the person back. I turned on a lamp and retrieved the phone, which dangled from the charging cord below my bed.

As I drew the phone to within reach, the ringing began again. I pulled the phone up and saw the caller was my sister. A flood of relief washed over me. No, it wasn't a sick or injured horse. I was not on call. I would never again be the person that a desperate horse owner called, expecting immediate help. I did miss my life in Australia, and I was possibly a little bored, but I was adding sewing to my hobbies. Moments like this reminded me to be thankful that my life was different, and I was free to enjoy every day.

"Hello?"

"Maggot, we'll be there in four."

"Where are you? It must be midnight in the Golden State. Even I'm not up."

"Dust off your welcoming mat. We're on our way, and we're trying to beat the desert heat. Bill called last night and said you didn't answer. What's with you?"

"I had the phone turned off. I was fishing."

"Okay, so who are you, and when did you invade my sister's body. My real sister never turned off her phone in case some sick horse in outer Mongolia needed her."

"Yeah, isn't that the truth? Now hang the damn phone up and call me back in a respectable hour."

"Thirty minutes, okay?"

"Jesus, Christy."

"I'll call in an hour."

She hung up, and I lay in my bed, attempting to orient myself. I was waiting for a call from Colin or Charlie. They were both in Los Angeles. Colin and his former wife, Helen, were attending a parole hearing for Luke's father. Charlie was there on business. Charlie called every few days to give me updates on the parole hearing and the new non-profit he'd set up for Sandy's school. It was way too early for any word from California. I was impressed with how quickly Charlie McLeod's company, CLM, had responded to my request.

I must admit that was first base on a ticket to my inner sanctum. Playing catch with Luke and teaching him how to throw, catch, and bat a ball almost got Charlie to second base. I wasn't falling for this guy without a return on my investment. I hadn't decided on my next 'need.' I didn't want anything for myself. I simply wanted things for others. Playing ball with Luke didn't cost Charlie anything and was satisfyingly pleasant.

Colin was no slouch in the baseball department, either. The two old geezers even let me revisit my softball glory days and play with them. We played flies and grounders using a softer ball when I played. We often played at Colin's until dark, and then Mrs. Gillard would call us for a late supper. I only played when Eric was a no-show for fishing. I knew this would be a time that Luke would remember forever. His skills improved dramatically. Once again, Charlie went up a notch on his quest to conquer my fading attempts to resist him.

Bill phoned me an hour later, announcing that he and Lonnie would be here later this afternoon. We had not been all together since our mother's funeral. This was going to be a remarkable family reunion. Bill asked for last-minute directions and if I had Scotch and beer.

"Sure do. Pabst Lite and some other brand."

"They don't make Pabst Lite anymore, so nice try. We'll stop and get the beer. Lonnie wants to know if you need anything else for dinner?"

I gave my standard answer. "A man. Isle seventeen, halfway down on the left. Get a sturdy one. I need some wood chopped."

"Christy says you have a toy boy."

"Uh, no. I've got a friend, but he's still hung up on his dead wife. Hurry up. I can't wait to show you around."

"Magster, we're on our way."

Christy and Miles arrived at ten o'clock. Luke and I were finishing making the beds and airing the rooms. I ran down and greeted them. Luke stayed behind and only came down when I waved to him. Baxter was in full force when they arrived. He circled them and gave a welcoming, long, "woo-woo," while wagging his tail and smiling.

"Christy, Miles, this is my intruder, Luke. You remember the artist?"

Christy went to shake his hand, but Luke hesitated. He had been cautioned by his grandfather to assume his deaf-mute persona in front of strangers. "Luke, this is my sister and her husband. They're good people, and you have no fear of them. Well, Christy likes to give noogies, and Miles will have you in the construction business faster than you can say 'Bob, the Builder,' but otherwise, they're safe."

Luke shook hands with both. He tentatively and quietly said, "Hello."

"Are you the artist I heard about?" Miles motioned to Luke, who came to the car trunk and helped him carry in the suitcases.

Christy smiled and nodded. She gazed around the property. "I'm impressed, Maggot. Did you do this all yourself, or did you have help?"

"I had help, but Luke is my main man. He and I have been busy. Come on in. Let's get some lunch going. Bill called, and he and Lonnie won't be here for a few hours. We can eat, and then you can have a nap or go for a hike. You can ride my horse if you like. He's old lady broke to death."

"I'll take you up on the nap. I did the driving while Miles studied the inside of his eyelids most of the way this morning."

We went up and made sandwiches and had chips. Luke stayed and took Miles down to the barn and corral and then over to the creek. Christy slept for an hour while I walked down to the creek and joined the boys.

"Maggie, I can see why you bought this place. I love it. Luke and I discussed building a bridge over the creek and making a small dam to hold fish that migrate through. We saw some fingerlings. We can even make a smoother path from the house down here, so when you're using a walking frame, you can still get to fish." Miles gave Luke a conspiratorial nudge.

"Eat dog feces and die, Miles. That will be you before me."

Miles turned to Luke and winked. "What did I say?"

"You said she would kick your donkey from here to Christmas about everything except the dam."

"Oh, I see Miles is already corrupting you. Hey, it's the wrong time of day, but how about you and Luke hit the river and see if we can get a couple trout for dinner? Miles, I bought you a temporary fishing license."

"You are singing my song, Maggie. Are you game, old man? Or should I say, young fella?"

"Sure thing, Mr. Maguire. Maggie, should I get him a cane?"

"Hey, kid. I prefer Miles, and there's no need for any elderly aides. Although a good caning might make you more respectful."

I gave Miles my good rod and a small box of killer flies. Luke had his rod, and they headed out over the creek and toward the river and Colin's property. I would give everyone the lowdown on my friends and neighbors tonight at dinner. If Luke told him who his grandfather was, I would be surprised.

I was out in the garden when Christy woke up. She'd changed into shorts and had a wide-brimmed hat. She came down to the vegetable garden, and we picked squash and corn for dinner. "So, how are things? Are you meeting the neighbors and making friends?"

"Yep, and then some. The people here are nice. Almost everyone still works, but I've become close to some. I invited a few friends over for dinner tomorrow night. Have you talked to my new friend Sandy?"

"The one who has the school for underprivileged gifted kids?" I nodded. "No, but we emailed a few times. Sounds like you set her up with a large corporation. How did that happen? How did you and Sandy meet? What happened to my workaholic-set-your-clock-by-her-movements sister?"

"Yeah. What did happen?" I thought about how my life had changed in the last year. I knew I had a great life, beautiful kids, and a to-die-for job. Outside of my unusual career and life in an exotic location, I never thought I was exceptional. Okay, writing books was different, but all of that took time and dedication. I was a creature of habit. Taking off and hitting the road without an agenda was not the real me. Or was it now?

"Do you want to have a ride on Digger? He'll make you want to return to your youth."

"Okay, let's test that theory."

We saddled Digger. I held the opposite stirrup while she mounted off my tree stump. Even in shorts, she could still ride like when we were kids. I led Christy to the arena. Christy was tentative at first, and then she began to trot and even lope around the arena.

"I'm in. This horse is heaven. Where did you get him?"

"He belongs to Colin Chandler. He was sent over as a welcoming present. He's mine to use as long as I want."

"The real Colin Chandler? Did you sleep with him?"

"Not yet. He's married, in case you forgot."

"And that's stopping you?"

"Actually, yes and no. Don't think I didn't think about it, but it would complicate things. I guess you didn't look at my mantel. There's a picture of Colin and Luke and me fishing. It was Colin's birthday, and he invited me to go helicopter fishing. He's Luke's grandfather. There's more to it, but basically, I've helped Luke come out of his shell. Colin thanked me by loaning me his horse, allowing me to fish on his property, and taking me on an extreme fishing adventure."

"Wow is all I can say. Is it Colin's corporation that's funding your new friend's school?"

"No. That's Charlie McLeod's doing."

"Maggot, you've been holding out on me."

"It's complicated. I did meet the man of my dreams, but alas, as we all know, I'm a pathetic judge of character. I'm happy with my life as it is. Sharing it with someone else is too complicated. Luke is enough company for me right now."

"Does he go to school?"

"Not yet. There are issues I can't discuss. We're going to have to leave it at this for now. I'll give you the whole story when I'm able."

"You know the parole hearing for Colin's son-in-law is all over the news, don't you? Is he Luke's father?"

"Hell. I had no idea. I can't believe it's in the news."

"Living in Oz made you so unaware of American news. It's not all about the government. Tragedies and good things are going on all over this country. Colin's campaign to keep his son-in-law in jail is front-page news." We heard a car come over the hill. "Hey, our broski has arrived."

"Why don't you ride up on Digger and greet him? I'll finish picking some corn for dinner."

Baxter did his usual greeting, and as I joined Bill, Lonnie, and Christy, he began to circle us all, wagging his tail and howling. I hadn't seen Bill and Lonnie in three years, and I was tearful as we hugged. Bill wouldn't let me go. Bill had aged, and Lonnie wasn't far behind him. Bill was the oldest, but only a year older than Christy and three years older than me. He walked with a limp, and his hair had thinned dramatically. Lonnie made up for Bill's lack of humor. Despite her gray hair, she was tan, fit, and athletic looking.

"How's the swimming team?" Lonnie competed in senior swimming events. She gave up tennis a few years ago.

"I am on the injured reserve list. I had my shoulder injected a week ago. I'm getting old."

"Aren't we all?" Christy took one of the suitcases, and they went up to the deck while I returned Digger to his paddock. I observed Bill and Lonnie entering my beautiful home. Bill came out onto the deck and signaled his approval with a thumbs-up. I'm so happy to have my brother and sister here. I was living the dream. I returned to the kitchen to prepare some nibbles and drinks.

"Oh, Maggie. This is beautiful. I had no idea. I love the wood interior and the cathedral windows. I'm officially jealous."

"Thanks, Lonnie. I have to get through my first winter, and then I'll know if I made a huge mistake or not." I showed them to their room and returned downstairs. Christy was pouring a glass of wine and examining my picture from my fishing adventures with Luke and Colin.

"He doesn't look too bad for his age."

"No, he doesn't. He's really a nice guy. He is on top of his game. He bowed out before he acted in some stinkers and ruined his reputation."

"How well do you know him?"

"Not that well. We play baseball once or twice a week, and then Colin comes over occasionally and sees what Luke is doing. He's good friends with Charlie McLeod, and I think his mission is to get Charlie and me together, but that won't happen. Want some cheese and crackers? We can sit out on the deck and maybe catch a bald eagle."

Bill and Lonnie emerged from their room and took the tour. "Maggie, this is a great place. I love what you've done with the decorations."

"Thanks, Bill. Ready for a beer?"

We sat out on the porch and watched as Miles and Luke emerged from the woods. Miles raised his hands, indicating he had success. Dusk was approaching. Luke and Miles came up to the deck and showed us four medium-sized trout. Luke quietly told me he was expected for dinner and left.

Miles and Luke fist bumped. "Later, dude."

"I'll be ready at seven, Mr. Nicholson."

Miles turned to us and grinned. "My new fishing partner. What a find, Maggie. Beer o'clock?"

My cell phone rang. The call was from Charlie. He and Colin were flying in, and they had a proposition for me. They would discuss it tomorrow when they arrived. I explained that my brother and sister were visiting, but they said it was urgent. They hated to interrupt, but could they come over tomorrow afternoon. I asked if Luke was in present danger, and they only stated no, and they would discuss it when they arrived.

Lonnie and Bill overheard my conversation. Bill glanced at me and then at the picture on the mantel. "Magster, you have some 'splaining' to do."

Trout, steaks, and homegrown vegetables were on the menu. Dinner was a success. We talked about old times and discussed our children and grandchildren. Lonnie asked about my kids. "Maggie, how do you feel about the separation from your grandchildren? I don't think I could do it." I shrugged and glanced at Christy and laughed, knowing that Christy only saw her children about twice a year.

"It's only been four months, Christy, and we've Zoomed once a week. The older grandkids will come over next year, and I'll be back to work for a month when the new practice owners want some time off. I said I would give them a month the first year."

We went out and sat on the deck until the mosquitos drove us back in. Lonnie asked if I had seen a bear. "One, and he was a big one. I've seen bear tracks. The one thing that scares me is mountain lions."

"Maggie, you need a wildlife camcorder to record the animals that are invading your valley. Bill and I could get it tomorrow and set it up for you. I need to go to the hunting and fishing store and get some waders. I'll bet they have some camcorders in the store. Wouldn't that be cool?"

"Yeah, boy. I'm in." This might scare the pants off me if I saw a bear or mountain lion near Digger, but it would be interesting. I offered dessert and a liqueur.

I knew what was coming. My brother and sister spent the last ten years attempting to find me a partner. They had loving relationships, and they wanted me to have the same. I couldn't blame them, but I had stopped looking years ago. I don't know when I stopped caring, but I was happy as a single person. I didn't really feel the need to seek companionship. I was satisfied saving horses' lives and writing stories about women who saved lives while solving crimes. If it wasn't for that chance encounter with the serial killer, I would laugh at their attempts to help me.

I was grilled about who I'd met and if any of the men were possible suitors. We finally all retired for the night. I sat on the upper deck outside my bedroom and watched the moon come over the tree-lined mountains and cast a partial moon shadow over my little valley. I wondered what Colin and Charlie had in mind. I googled the news reports about Colin's former son-in-law, Michael Lonergan. His case was in review, and the parole board appeared to be siding with him based on his behavior in prison and his possible work once he was paroled.

The reports were suggesting a reunion of Colin's son-in-law with his son. I wondered how Luke felt about seeing his father. Maybe he wanted to see him. I decided not to broach the subject. It was not my role to get involved. I was Luke's confidant and his friend. If he wanted to discuss it, I would listen. I was on his side and not anyone else's. I tried to protect him.

Chapter 31

Luke arrived early, and Bill and Miles went with him to the lake. It was about forty minutes on foot. I stayed with Lonnie and Christy, and we hiked into the forest next to my property. I hadn't been on this trail and found it challenging with lots of ups and downs. Christy and Lonnie found it particularly difficult due to the altitude. We didn't go far. I was surprised how well-trodden the trail appeared. There was a spot where I could see the top of my house. That was a bit of a shocker. I decided I better not do the au naturel thing anymore.

"Do you go around the property without your clothes on often?" Christy smirked.

"No, and I won't be doing it again for sure. Those days are long gone. I don't know if Luke watches the house from the woods. Ain't goin' there for sure." We had a picnic lunch and found a blackberry patch that had ripe berries. There were bear prints in the wet spring near the bushes. Thankfully, I had a can of bear spray.

We returned in the midafternoon. The boys were already back from their fishing adventure and a trip into town. They were installing the camcorder. As the afternoon faded into early evening, I received a call from Colin. They would be back around six. He asked to come over after dinner to discuss his concerns and options for Luke. I explained I had my family as well as Carol and Sylvia coming for dinner.

"Maggie, we really need your help. I wouldn't ask, but I know you are Luke's confidant, and I think you are the best person to help us protect him."

"How can I help?" My anxiety was rising.

"I can't discuss it on the phone. I only need thirty minutes of your time. Can you come over after dinner? We'll all be here."

"Does Luke know anything about what's going on?"

"No. We've tried to keep him out of it all."

"Well, is ten o'clock, okay?"

"Oh, that's great. We can't thank you enough."

"I'll send Doug over to get you. I'm not keen on you walking through the woods at night by yourself."

"Colin, I'll be fine. Have bear spray, will travel. See you later."

I decided it was best not to discuss what was going on. I hoped my family would be in bed and not miss me. We had a wonderful dinner, and Sylvia offered to take Christy and Lonnie to the hot spring tomorrow. We would take Digger, and she had horses that were safe to ride. Lonnie was apprehensive, but she agreed to go.

When everyone was in bed and I was alone, I slipped out of the house and took Baxter over to the woods that separated my property from Colin's. As I walked along, I heard the distinctive crunch of a large animal. I stopped to listen and readied my spray can. The crunching noise appeared to be coming closer.

"Hello?" I was shaking with fear. My voice reflected my anxiety.

"Maggie? It's me, Doug."

"Oh, Jesus Christ, Doug. You scared the crap out of me."

"Sorry, the boss insisted I come and get you." My helicopter hero pilot stepped out from behind a tree, and his flashlight shone into my face, almost blinding me.

"That is a heck of a torch. Can you dial it down?"

"Oh, sorry. Really glad it's you."

"Were you expecting anyone else?"

"I guess not. Let's get over to the house. They're all waiting to see you." Doug took my hand and guided me to the gate and then up to the house. We entered, and I was surprised to see Colin's ex-wife, Helen, as well as Charlie.

Colin was the first to greet me with a hug. Charlie followed him, and even Helen hugged me. "Okay, what's going on?"

"We need your help, Maggie. Luke's in grave danger, and despite everything, we can't protect him from what may come down. I don't know what you've read in the press, but much of the true happenings aren't in the public domain." Colin looked at Helen and nodded.

She continued. "We love our grandson and want to protect him, but we're concerned that we are too well known, and even our other grandchildren will be targets if we don't do anything. Luke's father is a well-connected man, and his friends are not nice people. If we get Luke into hiding, we think we can take the pressure off both him and his father. They all think he is the key to the murder, but we think Luke knows more than simply who really killed Sarah. Her husband has paid his dues, and if he gets out, he'll be pursuing a wrongful conviction. He knows Luke could help him. The other scenario is that Luke could sink him too, or if Luke really did see the murder and knows who killed his mother, then he is still a target."

"I'm a bit confused, but essentially Luke may or may not know who really killed his mother. And you want me to find out?"

Charlie spoke up. He had been quietly listening to Colin and Helen. "No, we don't want to have him relive this. We want to protect him. How does a trip overseas sound?"

No one spoke. Everyone sat forward and stared at me as I took this in. Colin came over and put his arm around me. "You wouldn't be on your own. Doug will go too."

"So, who is or are Luke's legal guardians?"

"Collie and I are." Helen went on, "We have guardianship until and only if Luke's father doesn't seek to have Luke returned to his care. He's already signaled he plans to do that when he's released."

Charlie went on to explain, "Collie and Helen have all the rights to do what they want unless there is a custody dispute. Then Luke will have to remain here in the States until the custody dispute is settled. If you leave in the next few days, you'll be legal, and with our permission, you could get him out of the country and away from any harm."

"Where do you want me to take Luke?"

"Australia," they all chimed in at once.

I was dumbfounded. I wanted to race out of the house. I could see how this might end, and I was having no part of it. I would leave with Luke, and they would pretend he was abducted, and then I would be hunted for kidnapping, and they would be innocent victims.

"I'm not interested in an international custody jail sentence. I'm sorry, but I'm a law-abiding citizen most of the time, and I don't look good in stripes. Let me ask you. Has any of this been discussed with Luke? Has anyone asked if he even wants to see his father? How sure are you that he even has the knowledge or memory of the events that may or may not have occurred?"

Helen and Colin glanced at each other. "You tell her, Collie." Helen clasped her hands and stretched her arms. She looked exhausted. She was looking much older than the day I met her at Luke's birthday party.

"When Sarah was killed, Luke was beaten so severely that he was placed in an induced coma. He never spoke until you came along. We knew Luke could hear several months after the beating, but we also knew Luke chose not to listen. If we discussed anything that might have to do with his past, he would run into his room and barricade himself in his closet. You can see why we don't discuss it. Therefore, we want you to go with him and protect him. He trusts you. Helen and I will sign any documents you like to say you are doing this with our blessings. Charlie can verify them. The one small issue is that we need to get Luke out of the country without using his real name. The crime family has far-reaching extensions, and we don't want to alert anyone where he is until we can ensure that Luke will be safe."

I shook my head and glanced at each person in the room. Doug spoke for the first time. "Maggie, I am a card-carrying, honest, law-abiding citizen. I understand how you feel. I'm in on this, whether you are or not, but we all know how much Luke respects and is comfortable with you. Your Australian connection is the perfect link to pulling this off. It isn't forever. It's only until the parole and custody hearings are settled. I hope you'll go with me. We could go to New Zealand and fish if that sweetens the deal."

I chuckled. "Oh, now that does change things. One or two weeks of fishing in New Zealand for a lifetime of jail might be a fair trade. Charlie, why are you involved? What's in it for you?"

"Yeah, what is in it for me? Well, I've enjoyed playing ball in the evening with you and Collie and Luke, and I don't want to lose that. Is that enough?"

"You all know this is crazy dangerous, and I'll be the one taking the rap if this fails. How do you get Luke a passport?"

Colin reached into his coat pocket and tossed me a passport that showed Luke with brown hair, and for all the world, it looked legitimate. The name was Luke Kincaid. I looked up, and before I could respond, Helen said. He's your grandson. I looked at the document, and it showed he was an American citizen. My children were dual citizens, but only two of my grandchildren were duel. Colin then tossed me a second passport, which was Australian. It had travel details showing he had arrived three weeks ago from Australia. Both documents were well worn and had embedded holograms that looked authentic.

"How did you," I started, but Charlie cut me off.

"Don't ask."

"I don't suppose we could go, first class?" *What am I saying? I'm giving in.*

"Yeah, I'll second that." Doug glanced at Colin, who stared at Charlie.

"Anything else?" Charlie had an exasperated look.

"Well, yes, but first, I need to think about it. How long do you think we might need to be away? Where will we stay? Will we be in danger? What if the immigration border patrol doesn't allow Luke into the country? Where will we live? Who's going to take care of my dog and my horse?" I hope Colin got the possessive "my" regarding Digger.

"So, you'll consider it?"

"I need details. I'll want to see my own children at some stage. I'm not saying yes." Helen and Colin smiled.

"No, we've got that. Collie and I love this boy so much, and we want to protect him. If either of us could get him out of here, you know we would."

"I need to get back to my place. My family is there, and I need some sleep. I'll let you know in the morning."

"Maggie, you can't tell them anything about Luke. You could say you are making an emergency trip over for one of your grandkids or to see a sick friend, but this needs to stay in this room."

"I understand. I'll let you know tomorrow. I'll let myself out. If I decide not to do this, you have my assurance I won't say anything."

Charlie got up. "I'll walk you to your house."

"Charlie, I'm fine. I have my bear spray."

"You need a gun at night. March, Maggie, I'm not taking no for an answer."

I saluted him. "Yes, sir."

"That's more like it. I like a woman who knows her place."

"You wish."

We walked over the grass where we played ball, through the gate, and then through the woods to the clearing where I could see my house.

"You better stop here. My family will think I snuck out to meet you to go snogging."

"Snogging?" Charlie cocked his head.

"Kissing, making out. I guess I was in Australia too long. I think it may be more of a British term."

"I could oblige your family." Charlie shyly smiled.

"Yeah. But then I would have to kneecap you. I still don't get how you figure in all of this."

"Collie and Helen were both friends of Linda's. When we knew Linda wasn't going to survive, Helen flew home from South America and came to nurse her every day. Both she and Collie were there to the very end. Nursing Linda brought them back together. Of course, Helen and Collie were both remarried, but both knew their marriages were not working out. Helen was happy to get out of her marriage, but Collie's kind of a traditionalist and he feels the need to try to stick it out."

"Why did he leave Helen then?"

"Yeah, that's what the media and public think, but it was Helen who wanted out. Can you imagine being married to one of the world's most sought-after movie stars?"

"Well…."

"Margaret Kincaid!"

"Hey, we all have our get out of a relationship option card. Mine was James Garner and Robert Redford. So far, it hasn't happened."

"Since he's passed, if the James Garner thing works out, let me know. I would say, Audrey Hepburn and Sandra Bullock."

"Have you met her?"

"Audrey Hepburn, no."

"You know who I mean."

"No, I haven't met her, either."

"So, back to the important people. Helen was the one who left?"

"Yes, despite what you heard or read, she left him."

"I didn't know. I was overseas working my butt off, raising kids, and trying not to kill too many horses."

"When Linda died, Collie was the one who dragged me out of bed for a year. I owe him."

"I think I get it now. I need to get to sleep. I'll think about it tonight."

"Can we come over in the morning?"

"I'm supposed to go riding with Sylvia, my sister, and sister-in-law."

"Could we come over later, then?"

"I'll be back in the midafternoon. Is that okay?"

"I know my family would like to meet you all, so that's probably a good time. The boys are going fishing with Luke and Eric."

"Maggie, any chance I could snog you?"

"Have you got a protective cup on?"

"I know karate. I'm willing to take a chance," and he did.

Chapter 32

It took me a while, but I finally fell asleep. I had so much to consider. I might ruin my life if I was caught abducting a child. I knew the consequences, but I was also worried sick about Luke and what might happen if he was returned to his father. I'm a law-abiding kind of girl. As a child of the fifties and sixties, I was taught to do the right thing, no matter its consequences. Then there was a chance for a first-class ticket home to see my kids, and finally, there was a matter of a kiss.

Everyone was awake when I came downstairs the following morning. The boys were all watching the video from the webcam of the creek. There were several deer and even a porcupine. There were no big animals or anything that would scare me, thankfully. We had breakfast, and then as we prepared to leave, Sylvia called and said she had two flat tires on her trailer and asked if we could postpone the ride until tomorrow.

My guests were feeling lazy, and they began to play bridge while I wrote a few chapters of my next book and then saddled Digger for a quick ride. I hadn't fished for days. I had so much on my mind. I needed some solitude to think about what was happening to me. I didn't regret moving back to the States, but the truth was I missed the easy access to my kids and the occasional visits of my grandchildren.

It would be nice to surprise them, but then would I be able to see them? Doug was keen on using New Zealand as our destination. The fishing and the diversity of the country attracted him. I could go either way. I wanted to talk to him and hear how this was going to work for him. What was he going to do about his daughter, and what if we got into trouble?

Phone reception was poor where I was riding, and I turned back to the house. As I was riding along the trail, I noticed Digger became agitated. He snorted, and I could see he was staring into the woods. I suspected it might be a bear. I stroked Digger's neck and tried to calm him, but he would not be appeased. He shied and then bolted. I barely hung on and lost my footing in the stirrups. I grasped the horn and tried to stay in the saddle. He finally slowed down as we emerged from the woods and crossed my little creek. I unsaddled him and hosed him off. He was sweating and only then began to be the horse I knew. I stared back at the woods. He did too and then walked over to some hay and started eating like nothing had happened.

I returned to the house, where everyone was still playing cards. I'd only been gone for half an hour. Miles glanced up and gasped. "Jesus, Maggie. What happened to you?"

"What?" I touched my face where I had been scratched by a branch when Digger bolted. Blood was everywhere. I hadn't noticed at all. It was only a scrape, and I used a napkin to wipe it clean.

I had to change my shirt, and when I returned, the boys were down at the creek with picks and shovels, creating a small dam and pool to retain water. Lonnie and Christy were sitting and turned to me. "So, do you want to talk about last night?" Lonnie wasn't one to hold back.

"Pardon?" I was quite sure my face reddened, but I stared blankly at them both.

"You went next door. Miles saw you head into the woods. Isn't that where Luke comes from every day. By the way, where is he?"

"His grandparents are back. He's with them today."

"Do you go over there late at night often? Is there something you aren't telling us?" Christy was giving me the family evil eye.

"No, not really. Colin called and asked to speak to me about Luke. They feel he's going to be in danger if his father is granted bail, and they wanted to discuss how best to protect him."

Christy set her book down. "Maggie, are you sure you should be involved with these people? It isn't your problem, you know."

"I'm not really," I lied. "By the way, they may come over this afternoon. You can meet the famous Colin Chandler."

Lonnie shot up. "I need to coif." Then she sat down. "He's almost ancient."

"He's only six years older than Bill, and he is still pretty fit, but sadly he's married. I met his current wife." I gave the thumbs down motion and then continued, "But his ex is all right, though. They get on well, and I think she'll come over too."

"Are we going to meet your millionaire friend?"

I hoped my face didn't betray the feelings I was having. "Probably closer to a billionaire. Not sure." I would prefer to keep this all to myself. The boys were heading back, and I began to prepare lunch. My phone rang. It was from Helen.

"Hi, Maggie. Did you get any sleep last night?"

"Hi, Helen. Yeah, some, how about you?"

"Not much. Collie and I wondered if you and your family would like to come over and have a swim. We're planning a barbeque and would love for you all to join us."

"I don't want to put you out. Maybe just a swim."

Christy was standing next to me, cutting cucumbers, and could hear the conversation. She was making signs indicating a barbeque would be perfect. She pointed the knife in my direction, and I could see she was pretending to threaten me. "Helen, on second thought, a barbeque would be lovely. What can I bring?"

"How about some of your vegetables and lettuce?"

"Are you sure that's all? How many people are you having over?"

"Just us and maybe Charlie if he's free. Are you still thinking about our discussion last night?"

"Yes," is all I answered. Christy looked at me and cocked her head.

"The pool is open anytime, and dinner will be at seven."

"Thanks, Helen, and tell Collie thanks too." I hung up and began to slice some salami.

"Collie?" Lonnie had come over. "You call him Collie?"

"And he calls me Maggie, get over it. We're neighbors. His friends all call him that. I'm nobody special."

"If you say so." Christy and Lonnie looked at each other, and both rolled their eyes.

"I'm going to shower and shave my legs." Lonnie inspected her legs.

"Do you have hair left? Mine all went when I turned sixty." Christy laughed.

Then Bill and Miles came in from a quick trip to the creek. "Bill found something that looks suspiciously like an arrowhead."

Bill pulled out a beautiful spear point.

"Wow. Bill, that's exceptional. However, since it's on my land, I think it's only fair…"

Bill came over and put me in a headlock. "You were saying."

"Only fair that I give it to you."

"Magster, that was the right phrase. You can resume your life now."

Christy shook her head. "Hey, you two. We're invited next door to swim after lunch. I hate to channel Mom, but we need to wait an hour before we can swim, and I'm dying to meet the infamous Collie Chandler, so let's eat and start the timer."

Miles responded while reaching for a beer from the fridge. "Bill, want to join me?"

"Yeah, I need to get ready to defend our honor with these women and the sexiest man of the—was it 1950s or 1960s?"

"Yeah, we better watch out, Miles. You never can trust a screen star with women as good-looking as our babes."

"Anyone want to defy Mom and get in the pool a few minutes early?" I suggested.

Christy gazed up to heaven and addressed our long-deceased mother. "Mom, that was Maggot. You know I was always the one who went by the rules. I'm sure she was kidding."

"Isn't it true? How many things do we still do when we know it's BS because Mom said so?"

"Did you ever wear white when visiting San Francisco in the winter? I live there, and I cringe when I see white belts and purses on women, let alone men."

"Lonnie, did you make the kids wait for an hour after lunch?" Christy poured iced tea for Lonnie. She tipped the jug toward me, but I declined.

"Of course. I was honest, though. I told the kids the rest was for me, not them."

I smirked. "I was never around. I farmed the little bastards out any chance I could. Of course, when I put a pool in at the house, that all went down the gurgler. They were older then and as teens, I would not miss them if something unfortunate happened."

"Ah, the joys of single parenthood." Bill gave my shoulder a squeeze.

"Don't you miss them, Maggie?"

"Yes. Sure, I do, but the kids are all in other states, and they were all going to the in-laws for Christmas. Who knows, if my books take off, I might be able to fly over and do a book tour." *Hmmm, maybe this was an excellent way to get a hall pass with my families' blessing.*

Miles and Bill both went and took showers. Lonnie and Christy followed.

"I think you guys forget our past. Remember Mom said If we swam, we didn't have to have a shower." We walked over to Colin Chandler's two hours later. The pool was empty, and we had it to ourselves. Lonnie was the swimmer in the family. She had competed in many Masters Games and had numerous ribbons and trophies. Bill, Christy, and I had all competed as children in our local town swim team, but Bill's main interest was football while I was a horse girl through and through.

We swam and sunbathed for an hour. Finally, Helen emerged with Luke. He had been told to stay inside and allow us some time to ourselves. I introduced Helen to my family while Luke jumped into the pool. Lonnie was watching him and began to help him with his swimming strokes. Helen mentioned Colin was with Charlie, and they were doing some planning. I wondered what she meant by that. Were they purchasing tickets?

I avoided Helen's stares by lying on a towel with my arms folded and resting my head while we discussed the barbeque. A few more people had been invited, and I was asked to bring more vegetables. Helen mentioned she was leaving tomorrow to attend her small ranch. The other grandchildren were coming for one more visit before starting school. She was hoping to take Luke, but so far, he declined to leave Colin's ranch. "You know why he won't leave?" she whispered.

"Better fishing?"

"Better fishing partner. Just saying."

"Noted. I better get some clothes on, or I'm going to fry."

We left after swimming with Luke, and we went home to prepare the vegetables and a salad for dinner. The boys went down to have one more go fly-fishing before we were expected for dinner. Luke met them down at the creek, and they disappeared into the woods.

They returned with several trout, which Luke took back home. This would be added to the dinner. When it was time, we all ambled over to Colin's property. Us girls wore summer dresses while the guys dressed in sports shirts and shorts. I had a feeling we were overdressing, but I didn't care. Despite the acclaim and notoriety, Colin was a down-to-earth kind of man. He didn't seem to care what I did if I helped his grandson. But was he going to like me when I told him I decided not to go?

Chapter 33

Of course, we were early. Other than last night, I had never been inside the house. How could I have missed the beautiful architecture and the paintings? Some were Colin's, and some were done by famous artists. Christy, Lonnie, and I carried in our vegetables and home-grown salad ingredients. Mrs. Gillard and two other women took our food and shooshed us out of the kitchen.

We returned to the porch area that had umbrellas and chairs over several tables. Luke came out and greeted us. He asked if we wanted to take a tour up to the barn. We walked up and viewed a few horses and a beautiful indoor arena. The equestrian facility was not as big as Charlie's Sanctuary facility, but it was well maintained. I hoped to ride there in the winter.

As we walked back down to the house, several people were ambling toward the patio. Eric and his two teenagers, Patty with her brood, and Carol and Hal arrived. I made introductions, and finally, Colin came out of the house. He smiled when he saw me and came directly over and hugged me. As he hugged me, he whispered in my ear. "Come to my library after dessert." I nodded and then introduced him to my family.

Colin was so gracious and insisted on showing the guys his gun collection. He spent several minutes talking to Lonnie and Christy. Colin and Helen knew all about Christy's nonprofit and asked how they could help. I was wary he was doing this all, so I would agree to take Luke overseas for God knew how long. I didn't blame them, but this could put me in jail. Maybe Luke would be happy to go with Doug.

Luke stuck to me like we were joined at the hip. He and I sat together at dinner. Colin insisted on sitting with my family, but Luke and I sat with Helen, Doug, Eric, and the kids. As we were sitting down to eat, Charlie arrived and handed me an envelope. I introduced him, and he sat with Colin and my family. He looked over and smiled. I have to say it gave me pleasure to see him. Carol was at my table, saw the interface, and kicked me under the table.

I glanced toward Carol and gave her a perplexed look. It didn't fool her, and she returned my gaze with an eye roll. Fortunately, no one else observed the interaction. After dinner and dessert, Colin stood and said he would be back in a few minutes. After he left, I told my group I was going to the bathroom. I entered the house and then the library, where Colin sat on the edge of his desk. I shook my head, and his shoulders slumped.

"I can't talk you into it? Is there anything that will make you change your mind?"

"Collie, I love your grandson, and frankly, I am fond of both you and Helen, but this is illegal. If you asked me to take him and not lie about who he was, I would do it in a heartbeat, but I guess that would defeat the purpose, wouldn't it?"

Colin stared out a window. He turned back and said, "When this is over, we'll still go fishing on my birthday next year. I understand."

"I'll talk to Luke if you wish and see if he wouldn't be happy traveling with Doug."

"I guess we can try. Luke does like Doug. Your brother says they are leaving the day after tomorrow. If I bring Luke over, can we talk to him then? Is that too late?"

"Sure. You never know."

"Maggie, you're so lucky to have your family. I lost my sister when she was nine and then my daughter. Well, you know. I would give anything for Luke to be safe and away from any of this."

I went over and hugged him. Even in his eighties, Colin still carried the pain of that long-ago and more recent loss. I hated myself right then.

We returned to the barbeque, and both Helen and Charlie turned to him. Colin didn't need to say anything. They could see the resignation on his face.

I thought it was best to leave and let them make their plans. Colin planned to bring Luke over after my family was gone. Luke was going fishing one more time with Miles and Bill. Eric had to work tomorrow, but the chance for a quick fish was too enticing. He would be over at six in the morning. We thanked everyone and said goodbye. Charlie stood and hugged me. I almost didn't want to let go. Almost.

Chapter 34

Christy didn't hold back. "I don't know what's going on, but you and your friends are up to something."

"I can't talk about it. I know it looks that way, but I'm not involved in anything. You have one more day. What would you guys like to do?"

"Let's either ride or hike to your secret warm springs," Lonnie suggested, and everyone agreed. We sat out on the porch for a while and watched the stars. It was a new moon, and with the house lights turned off and no clouds, the stars were spectacular. Bill reacquainted me with northern hemisphere constellations. All I remembered was the Big Dipper and the North Star. As we gazed toward the heavens, Miles watched the horizon and down in the little valley where Digger grazed.

"Hey, did you see that?" He pointed to the woods near the creek.

"No, what?" Bill walked over to where Miles was standing.

"I swear I saw a light right over there."

"That would be interesting. Maggot, got any friends sneaking around to see you?"

"Uh, no." I tried to think about who would be there. I wonder if Luke snuck out at night. I remembered the son of the couple who died in the house, but more likely, it was nothing. I recalled my ride this morning in which Digger responded to some unknown threat. We watched, and no one saw anything.

After we went to bed, I took the envelope that Charlie handed me and opened it. The envelope contained a locket and a note saying he enjoyed the kiss and hoped there might be more. It was signed with the letter "C." That was random. I think he's socially awkward. He probably hadn't dated in the traditional sense since college. I don't think there were many social interactions with the women who visited him over the last few years. I have to say, the locket was lovely, and I enjoyed the kiss as well, but since he didn't ride or fly-fish, he didn't fit my criteria for a 'soulmate.'

The boys left early for their last fishing expedition and returned with two nice fish. Eric and Luke left after they returned. Sylvia called and said she was sorry, but she would have to drive up to the sale yards. Trent had bought a new bull, and they needed that bigger trailer to bring him home. I decided we would walk to the springs. We packed lunches, and we all wore our swimsuits. I called Mrs. Gillard and asked her to tell Luke that I would be gone today and would be back in the late afternoon and invited Luke to dinner tonight.

The boys went through the webcam recordings, and this time there were several deer and a raccoon. Miles examined the recording during the time where he thought he saw what may have been a flashlight. He observed nothing suspicious.

We hiked to the spring, and all sat in the warm water. Christy splashed water onto her shoulders. "Does this mean we don't have to take baths tonight?"

"Not unless you want to sleep alone." The sulfur smell was pungent. We all moved to a second colder area to remove the scent of 'au de rotten eggs' from our suits and bodies before emerging.

We discussed old times and our family. The subject of children and grandchildren resurfaced. I could see my brother and sister were concerned that I had abandoned my kids. I admitted I had misgivings about whether I could stay away, but for now, I was happy with a yearly visit.

I planned a return to Australia during the worst of winter here and spend at least a month visiting my children and another month working for the couple who had bought my veterinary practice. I only agreed to one year, and maybe when I was too old to travel, I would return permanently. "This place is my ten-year plan. So far, I think I'll stick it out. Then, who knows where I'll go." I fingered the locket which I was wearing.

"Nice locket, Maggie."

"Thanks, Bill. I just got it." I wasn't ready to say anything about where it came from. I had mixed feelings. I felt both Charlie and Colin were using me, and despite the enjoyment that I received from their attention, I had a feeling it came with a price.

We returned to the house in the late afternoon and decided to have dinner at the neighboring town's bar and grill. It was a common meeting place for the locals. I'd rarely been there, but both Carol and Sylvia liked it. Luke had stopped in before we left for dinner but said he was expected home, and he and his grandfather were going fishing together. Then Charlie was coming, and they were going to play catch. I was jealous and wanted to come. Used or not, I enjoyed their company.

The dinner was delicious, and the waitress even said hello. She mentioned she'd read my first book and was interested in the next one. I was asked to sign her book when I came in next. We strolled down the main street and peered into the shop windows. The town was quaint. The stores were primarily tourist boutiques and would never support a township.

We returned home and played cards before retiring. I received two text messages. Colin asked to come over in the late morning after my family had left, and the other one was from Charlie, also asking to come and visit.

It was raining the following morning, which followed a thunderstorm that had rolled through earlier. There was steady rain following the initial weather front. My sister and brother all hugged and said their goodbyes. We promised to make this an annual event. We weren't going to commit to holidays as they were set aside for our individual families. This was precisely how I envisioned my retirement and one of the many reasons I chose this place.

Luke had come over to see them off. He was soaked, and he went into the house. I gave him a sweatshirt to wear and threw his shirt and jacket into the dryer. "Would you like some hot chocolate?"

"Yes, please." His voice was wavering, and I could sense he was upset. He didn't say what was bothering him, but as much as I wanted to ask, I knew he didn't want to discuss it.

"You know, I'm happy to hear your thoughts. I am the no judgment friend. I won't even respond unless you ask me for an opinion."

"No, thanks. You won't help, anyway."

"Okay." Did he already know I turned down the trip to Australia?

Luke sat for a long time without further comment. I waited, and finally, he looked up from his hot chocolate. "Did you like your father?"

"Sure did. My dad was gone quite a bit, but we loved him. It was always fun when he was at home. He was the fun parent. My mother was the disciplinarian. She was tough, but she loved us too." I purposely didn't ask what I wanted to ask. Do you remember your parents? Did you see your mother die? Who killed your mother? Do you miss either of your parents?

Luke finally replied, "Did your parents fight much?" He went over to Baxter, sat down on the floor, and began to scratch behind Baxter's ears.

"Yes, I guess all people argue at some time. It's not the disagreement. It's how you choose to argue. You know, I was married, and while the beginning was wonderful, the arguments started, and I have to say, I was probably as bad as my husband was."

"Did you hit each other?"

"No. Not once."

"Then why did you get a divorce?"

"Nope, not going there. State secret."

Luke got up and said he was supposed to be home. I didn't ask why or what he was doing. I figured he must not know about the meeting. I received a text from Colin asking if an hour would be okay. I responded. "Of course, the coast is clear."

With everyone gone, I was finally alone. It was too early to Zoom with the kids, but I was starting to get some fan mail, so I thought it would be good to get that out of the way. I turned on my computer and remembered the webcam video recordings. I opened the program and noticed the previous night's activity had two indications of significant motion. I hit the playback, and in the first instance, it was a large elk with a beautiful rack. I copied the picture and sent it to both Bill and Miles. Who responded quickly with a thumbs-up.

I had difficulty rewinding to the second signal. Finally, I was able to go back to ten minutes before the incident. When fast-forwarding the recording, it wasn't working. I was going to have to read the damn manual. As it neared the time of the incident, I readied my phone camera to record another shot of the buck. I watched as two men appeared on the video. They were dressed in camouflage military-like uniforms carrying rifles and were looking toward the house. I checked the time. It was almost two in the morning. *Holy shit.*

I continued to watch and observed the men standing and staring from side to side and then gazing up toward the house. It was dark, but amazingly it was easy to discern their faces. They were unfamiliar and appeared to be in their thirties or forties. Both men were tall, overweight, and wore balaclavas. Were they hunting? Whatever it was, they were on my land, hunting season hadn't begun, and it was the middle of the night.

I didn't send that to my family. They would have insisted I leave the house immediately. I continued to watch as both men stood and then turned and walked back into the woods. My wonderful carefree life here ended right then. I went upstairs where I could get a better view. I used binoculars that Bill had given me as a welcome home present. I saw nothing that looked out of place. Digger was grazing peacefully in the paddock. I unlocked my gun from the safe and loaded it. I set it near my bed. As I was returning downstairs, I heard Colin calling out. I peered around the corner, and both Colin and Charlie were at the door. They didn't bring Luke, thankfully.

What could have been a difficult conversation turned into a relief for me. "Hey, come in," I yelled as I hit the main floor. "Anyone want any coffee, hot chocolate, or tea? Looks like fall is finally starting. Is this normal?" I casually asked.

"We can have the occasional snow, but then it can still be hot for several more weeks." Colin came around and helped me with the drinks. He put his hand on my shoulder as he sidestepped behind me.

"So, tell me a bit more about hunting season? Are there various seasons? What are the restrictions? How do you get a license?"

"Well, nothing is open yet. It all starts next month." Colin opened the cupboard looking for the cookies. He reached around from behind and found my stash of Tim Tams.

"Drat. My stash of Australiana food. How about you take the lovely bottle of wine instead?" Sitting next to the Tim Tams was the Penfolds wine.

"No way. Collie, toss those cookies over here. I've heard they're delicious." Charlie sat down at the bar and folded his hands.

"Alright boys, is nothing sacred? Can you hunt any time of the day or night?"

Colin stared at me. "Why are you asking?"

"I need to be ready. I want to make sure Digger and Baxter are protected. And I might want to participate myself."

Both Colin and Charlie glanced at one another and then gave me a long stern gaze. "So, we had a think about your reluctance to travel to Australia with Luke."

"We talked to him, and he doesn't want to go without you." Colin took the cups over to the bar and sat down next to Charlie.

"Does he know why you want him to go to Australia? Does he talk about his father?"

"We're starting to have that discussion. It didn't get far. Luke imploded. That's why we came alone."

"So, what does he say?" I still had to decide whether to tell them about my webcam video.

"He didn't say anything about his father. He said he wasn't going unless you were coming too."

"Well, maybe I should talk to him. He was over this morning, and I could see he was troubled. Does he know what's happening? Is it in the general news yet?"

"Maggie, I think he knows more than he's letting on, but he won't discuss it. I've tried, but he barricades himself in his room."

"If I send him back over, can you talk to him?"

"When will the parole board make their decision?"

"They've made it. The board won't announce it until next Friday. That's why I need to get Luke to a safe place as soon as possible."

"I have a problem. This may be your problem too." Both men looked up. "My brother and bro-in-law set up a webcam to spy on creatures of the night. We were hoping to see a bear or maybe even a cougar, but I wasn't expecting this. I came around the bar, stood in between them, and opened my phone. I flipped to the pictures and replayed what I had taken from the camcorder playback. Colin asked me to stop while he put on his glasses. Both men peered at the screen and then asked to have it played again.

"Do you recognize anyone? Could they be poachers?"

Both men replayed the video several times. Charlie responded. "I don't know these men. The video is clear despite it being night. What system do you have?"

"I don't know. What do you think these guys are up to? Could they be poachers?" I was hoping for a safer explanation.

"They don't look like any of the people I saw at Sarah's murder trial. Could it be the son of the former owners of this property?" Colin watched the video once again while Charlie went to the window and stared down toward the creek and small valley where Digger grazed.

"Maggie, let's go down and look around. Have you got your gun ready?" Charlie turned to me, and I could see he was upset. I went up to my room and retrieved the rifle. The three of us went down to the creek. There were no tracks where the men stood when videoed. They stood on granite rocks. Baxter quickly picked up a scent, and his hackles rose. We followed him into the woods, and we came to a trail that went back to the state land.

Colin pointed to a path that I had ridden and knew it went over the ridge and toward the road where there was a parking area. It was too long to follow, but we let Baxter travel further to ensure they hadn't doubled back. We returned to the creek on my property. "We need to contact the sheriff's office. Maybe Tom Sutton knows who they are."

"Hey, what's that?" Charlie pointed to a cigarette butt next to the path. He pulled out a piece of paper and used it to pick it up. He carefully wrapped it up and placed it in his pocket. Up at the house, Charlie called Tom. He didn't talk at all about Luke or any pending attempts at kidnapping. He mentioned I had shown him a video of two men with rifles on my property last night. Tom asked me to send him the video directly to his phone. We waited for a few minutes, and Tom called back. He wasn't sure, but one of the men looked like a heavier version of Calhoun's son. Tom suggested the Calhoun son might have returned to look for hidden money.

"In any case, they were in violation of several laws. I think I might have to come and spend some time with you tonight."

"No, that's okay. I'll be fine." I turned and watched both Colin and Charlie shake their heads.

"Flip you for it." Charlie reached into his pocket and pulled out a coin. "Heads or tails, old man."

"Heads, Charles, and don't get smart with me."

"I don't need babysitting. I'm a big girl, and I'm packing." I stood facing them with my arms folded.

They both stared for a moment and then laughed. Charlie flipped the coin and smiled. "Oh, happy day."

He showed the eagle to Colin. "Some men get all the luck."

Chapter 35

Charlie drove up to the house at dusk. He parked his car so that it would be evident to anyone looking from the woods.

"I don't need a babysitter. Remember, I have Annie." I crossed my arms and shook my head.

"Annie?"

"Annie, get your gun. Geez, you Americans and your guns. I've only been here a few months, and I'm already getting ready for a gunfight."

"How about a glass of the Penfolds?" Charlie stared out the window, but the interior light reflected on the window obscuring his vision.

"You're trying to get me drunk, so you can have your way with my Tim Tams."

"Among other things. Seriously, Maggie. I'm worried. We can't get the feds involved with the Luke problem pending. It's bad enough that we even told the local sheriff's department. By the way, Collie says the sheriff doesn't know who they are, and they know the Calhoun's son is back in Florida, so it isn't him."

"That's a relief to me. Why would these guys target my place if they're looking for Luke?"

"Collie thinks they may be hunting illegally. Is there any chance you would reconsider traveling to Australia? What if Doug took Luke, and you were on the same plane but in a separate area, and you met up outside the airport?" Doug poured the wine. I had some celery and cheese.

"Hmm, I didn't think of that. How long do you think it might go on for? How long would we have to hide out?"

"I don't know, but if it goes well, it will only be a few weeks." Charlie took a sip of his wine, and the pleasure on his face was unmistakable.

"And if it doesn't?" I took a sip of the famous Australian wine. "On second thought, maybe I should go over there. This wine is delish."

We turned off the lights and walked out onto the deck. We sat down, and Charlie poured a second glass of wine. One glass of wine was always my limit. I fingered the locket he had given me. "I like the locket, by the way."

He smiled and touched my shoulder, but nothing more. He continued to stare into the woods. "Do you mind if I ask about your divorce?"

"Yes. I mean, no. I was traded in for a younger model. No-fuss, no-muss. I was in love and didn't have time for him, anyway."

"So, you had another lover?"

"My job. That and the kids were enough."

"How did your children cope?"

"You know—the usual. Good and bad. Eventually, we all got over it. As if. The boys love me, no matter what, and my daughter tolerates me. Do you have any siblings, Charlie?"

"My sister died several years ago. She was fifty-two. She never married. My parents were different. I chose to ignore them, and my sister spent her life trying to help them. In the end, they died of self-inflicted issues."

"That being?"

"Drugs and alcohol. My dad died of liver cancer, but he drank to the end, and my mom medicated herself with prescription drugs. She was a pioneer. She was self-medicating well before it became popular."

"I'm sorry." I wondered who was going to inherit his empire, but I didn't ask.

"I left for college and only returned when it was absolutely necessary. I escaped in my marriage and work. Don't feel sorry for me. Other than losing Linda, my life has been wonderful. I'm a survivor. I love my work, and I love helping others. My work allows me to help a lot of people."

"Yeah, I see that. I know my new friend, Sandy, is thrilled. Her school will thrive, and hence many students will fulfill their dreams to get an education. Have you thought about helping kids who want to get into the trades?"

"Oh, here we go. I wondered how long it would take for the next assault on my pocketbook." He laughed. "Got a suggestion?"

"No, not really. My sister mentioned there was some program on television that encouraged kids to get into the trades. Finding a plumber or an electrician was almost impossible back home. We all can't be brain surgeons."

Just then, Charlie stood up. He stared intently toward the woods. This made Baxter stand, and he walked toward the deck railing and growled. I waited to see what Charlie saw. Just then, there was a flash of light, and eventually, a distant roll of thunder rumbled in the distance.

I stood up, walked over to Charlie, and peered into the woods. He put his arm around me, and we stood together without a word. I could tell he was nervous. I liked him, but I was reluctant to let it go further. I didn't reciprocate. I gave him no indication that I was receptive. He got the message and then simply removed his hand and turned to the house and said it was getting late and we should go to bed. "I'll sleep in the downstairs bed, Maggie."

Phew, no fuss, no muss. I knew I was not one hundred percent against the thought of Charlie becoming more than just a friend, but not yet. As ridiculous as it was, he didn't make my heart jump. I'll admit the serial killer did move the odometer, but only for a second. What is it about the human connection and that unknown electric force that can cause such a disruption to a person's neuronal balance? It had been several years since I felt any true desires. I blamed my ever-shrinking ovaries and life.

The following day, I arose early as usual. I made coffee and then went back upstairs to write. It was over an hour before I returned and found a note from Charlie saying he was heading home. He quickly reviewed the camera recording and saw no unusual human interference and then asked if I knew there was a bobcat in the area? Then he asked me to call him when I was finished with my work. He was heading back to Los Angeles with Colin. Doug would be over tonight to take over the guard duties.

I wasn't excited about these men's interference. I was about to call him when I heard a knock at the door. It was Colin's wrangler, Gabe Turner.

"Hi, ma'am. Mr. Chandler sent me over. He wanted to let you know that I will be patrolling the area. I'll be on the far side of your creek. We want to make sure you and Digger are protected. Mr. Chandler is keeping Luke away from the public, and so if he comes over, will you bring him back? They don't want anything happening to him. He said to say sorry, and in a day or two, this will all be over."

My suspicion was that Luke would be heading to Australia or somewhere soon. I guessed that only a handful of people knew Colin's plan. "Gabe, thanks. I appreciate your concern, so please thank Colin for me. He needn't worry. I'll be careful and do my best to make sure Digger and I stay safe."

"You do that, Ma'am. I would hate to think about how the boss might take it if either of you were injured."

That made me happy. "Gee, would he put Digger and me in the same category? I'm totally flattered."

"Mr. Chandler thinks you hung the moon, ma'am."

"How about I join you on a reconnaissance ride around the back of the property and into the forest?"

"Well, I don't suppose the boss would mind. Could I interest you in catching me some fish at the lake? I'd love to take some home for Betty Lou. It's our fifth anniversary tomorrow."

"You think bringing her trout is a plan to make her happy? Gabe, you are a charmer." I shook my head and laughed. He looked embarrassed and admitted he might have to come up with something else. "I'll meet you down at the barn in half an hour, and we can begin our patrol if that's okay with you?"

Gabe went back to his horse and walked him down to the corral where Digger was grazing. I showered and dressed for riding. I checked my phone and saw a message from Charlie asking if everything was okay. I replied that it was more than all right. I had a riding and fishing date with a good-looking cowboy.

He immediately replied, "Say hi to Gabe and tell him I have arranged the dinner and flowers for tomorrow." These guys were a circle unto themselves.

I approached the corral, and as I rounded the corner, there was Gabe astride his sorrel mare, and Digger was saddled and ready to go. I tied my traveling fly rod case to the saddle and used an old stump to stand on and mount. Digger hadn't been ridden for a few days and was fresh, but of course, he didn't put a hoof out of place.

We crossed the creek and took off toward Saddleback Lake. As we walked along the trail, I saw Gabe searching the sides of the track for any signs of recent human activity. He occasionally stared at the tips of the mountains that surrounded us. Neither of us saw anything. Suddenly, both of our horses bolted backward as a bear stepped into the trail. Gabe lost his stirrup and almost came off. Digger was behind him, and the protection of Gabe's mare was what saved me from disaster. We stared at the sow bear, who had two cubs in tow. Without saying a word, we turned and rode back a few yards and out of sight while we could hear the bear amble off into the brush.

"You okay, Maggie?"

"If I said barely, would you laugh?"

"I would. If I can bare my soul and say I might have to change my jocks after this."

This started us laughing. It was a nervous laugh, but the tenseness of the moment passed. We reached the lake and dismounted. I set up my rod. I already had a killer fly on the line. Three casts and wham, first fish. Gabe stood back away from the lake. His position allowed him to watch a large area. The two horses were tethered to a line he created from his lariat. Gabe watched most of the lakeshore and the mountains behind the lake. He could also watch the horses for any indication that they heard or smelled something.

I held up fish number one. It was average in size, and he nodded. I threw it into the small cooler I brought. I caught two more, and he circled his hand, indicating he wanted more. I moved out on a log and was able to reach a deeper spot. With two more in the bag, I was now almost bored. He looked at his watch and smiled. He gave me the okay sign with his thumb and forefinger. I felt proud that I had contributed to his anniversary dinner when it struck me that this must be a ploy, so I would fish with a guard.

"I forgot. Charlie asked me to tell you he had the flowers and dinner plans all set for you." I spied him suspiciously. He nodded. "Should I clean the fish now or leave it to your wife?"

"Suit yourself, she's expecting. Not sure if fish guts are on the menu right now."

"Are fish on the menu?"

"Not really. It's easier to guard you if I know where you are."

"Bastard. So, you're my guard?"

"Yes, ma'am. Until Doug relieves me."

"I could say something like male chauvinist pigs, but I guess that's a bit old-fashioned. Who put you up to this, Colin or Charlie?"

"Not sure, I suspect both. Orders came from Mrs. Gillard. I would never want to upset her."

"No good would ever come from upsetting the cook. That's for sure." Gabe only smiled. "Shall we head back? I have a hair appointment."

As we tightened the cinches, we heard an unusual sound. Two men with rifles came around the bend and were as surprised as we were to see each other. They stopped abruptly. I tried to smile. "Hi, are you guys lost?" I struggled not to stare at their rifles.

The men stared at me. "I think we just found what we're looking for."

Chapter 36

Gabe did not hesitate. "Yes, it's a great lake, you'll enjoy it. We just caught five trout."

Gabe's gun was still in its scabbard and on the side away from the men. He quietly mounted, and then he nodded to me to do the same. "Maggie, I need to get back. We're late as it is. Gentlemen," he said as he smiled and tipped his hat. "Good thing you guys brought guns. We saw a bear on the way in. She didn't look so happy to see us." He reached down, and I thought he would bring up his gun but instead pulled up a can of bear spray.

The men appeared to be ready to shoot, as well. They both raised their guns slightly. When they saw the can of bear spray, they laughed and relaxed. "Yeah, we're ready for any unauthorized encounters. You can't be too careful."

My heart was racing as I walked Digger over to a rock and mounted. I didn't talk. I let Gabe direct our response. Gabe kept his horse positioned so they couldn't see his rifle. We turned and walked toward home. He was in front, and I rode behind, protecting the gun from their sight. We rode a short distance from them, and Gabe reached down and brought the rifle up and checked that it was loaded.

"So, what time is your hair appointment?" Gabe's voice was stern and measured.

"One o'clock. I can't be late." I think my voice was wavering. I tried to sound casual. "I hope those guys brought fishing gear." I was concerned they would follow us, and I didn't want to let them think we were worried.

"One o'clock? We need to make tracks. Can you lope?"

"Lead the way, junior." I laughed. It was a nervous laugh, and anyone who knew me would know I was scared shitless. We were back at my corral before another word was spoken. We knew it would only be a few minutes before they would catch up to us if they decided to follow.

We unsaddled Digger, and Gabe quietly asked, "Are they the guys in your video?"

"I think so. If not, they're surely cousins."

"Maggie, I'm not leaving you. I suggest we go up to the house, and you pack a few items while I keep an eye on things. You can't stay here. I don't know what they're up to, but I can't see it is anything remotely legal."

"Uh, roger that. Who is over watching Luke?" I couldn't explain why I had concerns, but I think Gabe knew the story.

"Two other wranglers and Mrs. Gillard are in the house, and there are other men stationed around the perimeter of the homestead. I think we're okay in that respect, but I believe it's best if we call Tom Sutton. The sheriff's department needs to know in case these guys are illegal hunters. What do you think?"

"For sure, let's call the sheriff, and I have no idea what they're up to. It must be illegal, whatever it is. I want to protect Luke." I had to be careful. I wasn't sure what anyone knew. I doubted these guys were here to get Luke, but who knew for sure.

"Maggie, we all know about Luke. We're all aware that he may be in danger. We were hired for two reasons. We're all horsemen, but we all are also ex-military."

"You're kidding?"

"Nope. Living the dream. I loved my time in the Seals, but I love horses too. The pay ain't bad, either."

"Am I the only one who didn't know this?"

"No, you're one of the few that does know it, now. I would never say anything except I think your life's in danger now too, and you need to trust me. I'm not just a cowboy. And, by the way, Betty Lou's ex-military too. Now pack a bag, and we'll get the heck out of Dodge. You can come and stay with us over at Mr. Chandler's house."

"We need to get Digger over there too."

"I'll arrange it. Pack your bag."

"I'm not missing my hair appointment for anything."

"Yeah, Betty Lou would say the same thing."

I packed and loaded my car with Baxter and a few clothes. By the time I was done, a horse trailer had come over the ridge to collect Digger. I was glad I had opened the lock yesterday, but I would lock it once again. All the possibilities ran through my mind about what those guys in the forest were doing. Illegal hunting was still a strong possibility. Another possibility might be that they knew about mythical money buried on the property. They could be here for Luke. I'd heard there were illegal pot growers in the past, but aerial and drone footage and a heavy law enforcement presence had wiped out most of them. What hadn't been wiped out with the legalization of marijuana, the short growing season in this area, made the farming of marijuana less than profitable. Thank the snow for that gift.

We waited for Digger to be loaded and followed him out of the property. Gabe set the security camera footage, including the one near Digger's barn, to go to his phone as well as mine. I planned to go to Carol's real estate office, where she would do my hair. Then I would head to the Chandler estate to stay with Luke for the night or until Tom Sutton, or one of his deputies was able to identify the men and move them along. Doug would now join Luke and me and stay there for the night. Gabe felt it was easier to have us all at the Chandlers until he was confident we were all safe.

Gabe took his horse and headed back through the woods to Chandler's estate. I followed the trailer out to the road and stopped to lock my gate. I then drove to Carol's office. The office was closed, and I called Carol.

"Check your messages, Maggie. I left one saying we would meet at my house."

"Oh, okay. I'll be right over."

Carol lived out of town in the direction of The Sanctuary. She and Hal had a small property with an iconic barn that was often photographed. The barn was painted red and was over one hundred years old. It had even been used in a few movies. I had not been to her house, but I sure knew where it was, and I knew there is nothing worse than being late for a hair appointment, even if it is a friend doing one for a friend…

"You bring the books?" Carol opened the door and was standing tapping her foot, making sure I knew I was late.

"Oh, damn. I forgot. I can go back and get them. I had a small problem, and it completely slipped my mind."

"Yeah, that happens when you get older. Knowing how old you are, I should have called and reminded you."

"Eat dog excrement and die, Carol. You're as old as me." I laughed as she pointed to a seat in the kitchen.

"The usual?"

"Can you make me look a little more like Farrah Fawcett?"

"The current or the 60s Farrah? I could do the current, but it would require a wig for the younger model."

"Yeah, I heard she died. It's a tragedy. I was so looking forward to comparing her aging process to mine. I may have been the winner."

"Maggie, look in the mirror. You need a reality check."

"No, I need a facelift, a tummy tuck, and a boob job, and then I will be ready for the seventies."

"Or you can face them as the rest of us do with alcohol."

"Yeah, that sounds like more fun. Back to Farrah."

"In your dreams, sister. Say, what's going on with you and Charlie these days? Do I see a spring in his step?"

I smiled inwardly, but then I was reminded that he didn't tick all the boxes. "I have given him a new purpose. I am helping him divest his fortune on needy causes. I think that's what rocks his boat."

"Don't laugh. I think that is why he loved my sister so much. Charlie works to help others. Don't get me wrong, he is ruthless in the boardroom. You would not want to cheat him. He didn't get where he is by being a sucker."

"Yeah, I get that. It's early days. I'm not really looking, you know. I enjoy Charlie's and Collie's company, but it's nice to go home and be able to fart and only worry if it offends the dog."

"Well, who knows if you are the one to bring him back to life, but by all indications, he's coming out of his fog. Hal says he even hums now."

"Hey, did you hear a car?"

Carol had just finished applying the dye and foils when she walked to the counter to start some water for coffee. She cocked her head, and then we both heard a knocking at the door.

"Stay here. It might be Charlie, and we can't let him know you aren't naturally blonde."

"Uh, he spent the night. I kind of think he knows." Carol looked shocked. "It's not what you think."

"I believe you. Thousands wouldn't. Stay put."

I waited for several minutes. I heard quiet talking, but I didn't hear anything after that. The bell rang, indicating my time was up with the color and foils, and still, Carol was not responding to my calls. I walked out of the kitchen into a foyer, and she was nowhere to be seen. I opened the front door, and she had walked over to the barn. There was a truck parked in front of the barn. I suspected someone wanted to scc the interior.

I was well overdue to get my hair dye rinsed, so I did it myself in her bathroom. I removed the foils, found some shampoo, and washed my hair in the sink several times. I yelled out, but Carol still didn't answer. I found a conditioner and applied it, and then one final rinse and threw a towel around my head. I knew the Chandler men were expecting me, so I decided to forgo the haircut and walked out to tell Carol I would come back tomorrow.

I felt guilty not telling her about the two men we saw while riding, but there was no time. I yelled to her once more, and then I got into my car. I started the engine and, with a sudden pang of guilt, turned it off and went to the barn. I opened the door of the barn and saw the two men whom I had seen in the woods. Carol was showing them some of the antique farming equipment where it was stored in the barn. She turned and looked at me, and there was no mistaking the strain on her face. I was sick. I knew that, for whatever reason, these men were targeting me. They're the same men I saw at the lake.

"Hey, Carol. I finished our project, and I'm about to leave. The guys are waiting for me, so I better skedaddle. Did they call you? I had my phone off, and I see I missed several calls. They are expecting me, and if I don't get going, they will have the whole county over here."

"That's okay, Maggie. Get going, and I'll finish you up tomorrow. I'm just showing these gentlemen all of Hal's toys. I explained Hal would be back in a few minutes, and he was better at explaining what these contraptions did." I don't think any of us missed the wavering nervous voice. I was sick seeing the fear in her face.

I looked at my watch. "Yep, you could set the national time by that man's arrival. You have fifteen minutes." I watched the men stare at one another. The heavier-set man smiled and said, "Oh, great. We'll just wait then. Why don't we all go into the house, and then we can have a chat."

"Yeah, I'd love to, but I'm late as it is. Say, did you guys enjoy the lake?" I was fooling no one. They peered at one another, and then one of the men reached into his jacket and brought out a large revolver.

"Game over, ladies."

Chapter 37

Carol shot a distressed look at me, and I returned her stare and shook my head. I still didn't have any idea what this was about.

"What do you want with us? I think you have the wrong people."

"Just shut up and get in the truck." They opened the barn door, and the man holding the gun pointed it toward the vehicle.

Carol put a hand on my shoulder and calmly said, "I guess the haircut is going to have to wait."

"Yeah, I guess," was all I could say in return.

Carol stared at the gun. "Do you guys want to tell us anything? Your names? Life stories? Why you want us?"

"Carol, it must be for our good looks." I was stalling and simultaneously trying to calm my friend.

"Well, that would be true for me, but you?"

"Shut up, you two. You, wet head, get in the front, and you," he said, pointing the gun toward Carol, "Get in the back."

I saw no option, and I complied. My heart was racing, and I knew that if we were going to survive this, we needed to do as the men said. As we drove out of the property, I saw Eric's car slowing down to turn into Linda's driveway. He stared at us, and for a moment, I now had hopes that we might be able to get away from these men.

"Who's that?" Both men had gray hair and beards, but the larger rotund man was clearly in charge.

Carol started to speak. "Eric, our…"

I quickly cut her off. "He's a deputy sheriff. Was he coming to get his hair cut too?"

"Yep. Eric's not going to be impressed that I won't be here to do the honors. I hope you guys are prepared to suffer the consequences."

The thinner man looked at his partner. "What do we do?"

"Shut up and let me think."

Eric pulled into the driveway and blocked the exit. I was convinced this was an innocent but fortuitous move on his part.

The two men stared at each other, and then the larger man pointed his gun at us and yelled, "Get out."

We did, and then he pointed the gun at Eric and then back at me and told Eric to move his truck. Eric saw the situation and quickly backed out of the driveway and onto the road. The men jumped into their vehicle and then pointed the gun at me, and told me to get back in. My heart sank. I gazed around at Carol, who said, "I won't let her go alone. You'll have to take me too."

I shook my head. "Nope, one is enough. You stay and let me deal with these two gentlemen."

I climbed into the front seat, and the heavy-set man entered the back seat again. He yelled at Eric and Carol. "If you try to follow us, I'll shoot her."

Carol was beside the truck and turned to me. "You still owe me for the color and foils."

"I won't forget. Can you get Baxter? He's still in the car."

The heavy man shouted at the driver, "Let's go. The boss will be pissed if we don't get her back to the camp soon."

I was scared and weak with dread. I was trying to think about why these men wanted me. Was I going to be used to get to Luke? I had no idea what was going on. I started to talk, but the man sitting behind hit my head with the gun and told me to shut up.

The strike caused a minor laceration, and I began to bleed. I held my hand up and could feel the wound, which was small and superficial. The blood was minimal. I was sick with dread. After a few minutes, they pulled over, and the men pulled me out of the truck. They zip-tied my hands, placed a hood over my head, and then made me lie down in the back seat of the car. The heavier man then moved up to the front. I heard them take off, and I lay in the back, trying to sense the direction we were heading. Blood slowly dripped down across my face and into my eye. I couldn't wipe it away. I was paralyzed with fear, and as hard as I tried, I could not break the zip ties.

I felt the truck pull off the main road after what seemed like an hour and begin an incline on a gravel road. My cell phone was still in my pocket, and thankfully, it had not rung. I was sure I was out of any cell range. If by any chance I could get away, it would still have GPS capability due to an app I had installed when I started to ride into the woods.

The truck finally stopped, and I was pulled out of the vehicle. The hood was removed. It was difficult to see as the sun was so bright at first, but I quickly adjusted and peered around at a densely forested area on the side of a hill. I was shoved from behind, and I stumbled, but the smaller man caught me and held my arm as I was forced down a short trail that led to a large cavern. My hands were freed, and I was forced to climb down a rope ladder into the cave with several tunnels leading in different directions. It was dark, but there were small led lights that guided us through a long tunnel.

The hood and zip ties were placed on me again, and I was guided farther into a tunnel, where it sounded as if several men were gathered. It was surprisingly warm, but there was a dampness that told me there must be running water somewhere. It seemed like forever, and then one man finally spoke.

"You the vet?" His voice was not familiar. It was deep with a slight Spanish accent.

"I was a vet. What are you doing?"

"Don't worry about that. Did anyone search her?" I felt him reach down, and I was sick. I knew they would discover my cell phone. No one would find me in this cave, anyway. He pulled out my keys and a wallet but didn't mention my phone. Did my phone fall out of my pocket when I was lying prostrate in the car? Oh, please, Lord, let it be true. I knew it would be found soon. I'm sure there would be a search party out for me. He took me over to what felt like a table and pushed me into a chair. He cut the zip tie. "How is your dictation?"

"I don't know what you mean." He removed my hood, and I sat facing a table and a notepad.

"If you turn around and look at anyone, I'll put a bullet through your head."

I felt a hard object pushed against my head. "Okay, I'll do what you want. Please put the gun down."

"Pick up the pen. Write only what I say."

I did, but my hand was shaking so much. I was hopeful that because these people were hiding their identity, they planned to keep me alive and let me go. I had reason to hope. "What do you want me to say?"

"To Charles McLeod. I am being held as a hostage. My captors want a ransom. The money is to be transferred into an account overseas. They say they will kill me if you don't comply. I will be set free once the money is in the account. The sum is to be fifty million US."

"Is that all?" So, I was being held for ransom. It didn't appear to have anything to do with Luke.

"No, I need you to say something that will ensure he knows it's you and that you are alive."

I considered this and then wrote, "Yes, I am an expensive friend. I hope you can be as generous to me as you were to Sandy. Sorry to continue to dip into your pocketbook once again, Maggie."

"Is that it?" I was shaking, and my bravado did not fool the men.

"I don't want to hear another word from you. Put the hood back on." I did, and then he put the zip tie back on my hands, and this time he put my hands in front. He led me to a cot, and he took my shoulders and pushed me gently onto the cot. He handed me a cup and told me to drink the contents. I was relieved. If I was going to die, at least I would be asleep. In a short time, I felt the effects of whatever it was overcome my strong desire to stay awake. I prepared to die, and I thanked them for their kindness. The one person who spoke laughed, and then that was it. I died.

Chapter 38

Well, I kind of didn't die. Funny, but here I was in what might be purgatory. I couldn't see, I couldn't move, and I felt awful. My head and back ached, my joints were stiff and sore, and I had to pee. My bladder was at eleven on the ten-scale.

"Hello? Anyone here? I need to go. I promise I can do it without looking at you. Please let me up for just a minute. I'll go, and you can tie me up again. Hello?"

I received no response. I could hear an echo when I shouted even louder. Still, there was no reply. My hands were zip-tied to a stake, which I could feel had one edge that might help saw through the zip tie of the tie going around the stake. I rubbed my head against the wooden slats that I lay upon. My feet were also double tied to a stake at the end of this makeshift bed. I continued to rub my head, and the hood was slowly rolling up and was almost off. I was still having difficulty seeing, and when I finally got the hood off, I could not see any better than I could with it on. It was completely dark in the cavern. I could smell and feel moisture.

My hearing was still impaired from the drug. I thought I heard rushing water that was growing in intensity. I attempted to move my hands back and forth, creating a sawing motion. The noise in my head was becoming thunderous. I swear an avalanche of water was headed my way. It sounded far away, but it sounded like water was coming down the cave. I tried to remember what the tunnel looked like, but I wasn't sure I was even in the same area of the cavern. When I wrote the note, I didn't dare look up. I knew if I had made eye contact, they would kill me for sure. Right now, they needed me alive to ensure that I was worth sending the money.

The air temperature was dropping. The noise was becoming deafening. I was convinced I was going to drown or be swept away in a torrent of water. I attempted to saw the zip tie with my hands, but my range of movement was so small that I wasn't making any progress.

I felt water starting to touch my body where I lay. It wasn't as fast as it sounded. Then there was an enormous sound of a possible cave-in, and the water rose abruptly. The water was cold and muddy. It was almost high enough to cover my body. I held my head above the rising water and continued to saw. The pallet I lay on lurched, and the stake that secured my hands gave way. I slid my hands up and down and over an end of the metal stake and slid them off. I then reached down and was able to rock the stake holding my feet and slid my feet off that stake as well. I was bound but free. I attempted to stand but fell over into the rushing water in the process. I gasped as water covered my face. I was propelled in the torrent and put my hands in front to stop from hitting my head as I was swept down in the current. I could not orient myself to go feet first and protect my head.

It seemed like I was in slow motion, and it was going to be forever. I wanted this to be a dream, but it was not. It was real. I was freezing and drowning. I was hitting walls, and debris was hitting me. I finally could grasp a large rock and use it to climb up far enough that I was above the waterline. My eye stung, but since it was so dark, there was no point in attempting to open them.

I clung to the rock for a few moments. My hands were starting to lose their grip, and I was so cold I felt like I might lose consciousness. I was ready to give up. I knew there was no one to come and rescue me. I remembered I wasn't more than a few hundred yards from the entrance when I met the other men. I had to be closer to the outside and light. I quickly opened my eyes and saw a faint glow. This gave me hope and made me try once again. I thought I could feel the water receding.

One thing was better, my bladder was empty. The muddy water had probably washed away the urine. I could stand, and I felt a jagged protruding rock, and once again, I attempted to saw one of the zip ties. This time I was successful, and I was able to free my hands. I still had to undo my feet and legs. My eyes stung when I opened them, so I only did for a moment. I thought the water was still receding, and if I could just hang on for a few more minutes, then I would be sure this was true and not only wishful thinking.

I stayed where I was, and after what may have been an hour, I opened them again, and the water level had dropped several feet. I was overjoyed. I was going to live and get out of this cavern. I was possibly only yards from the entrance. I knew I could not climb up without freeing my feet.

I waited until the water had dropped another few feet, and then using my hands, hopped with both legs down the ledge. A boulder gave way, and I fell. I hit the water once more, which partially cushioned my fall. I did hit my thigh, and the pain shot through me. I prayed my leg wasn't broken. I knew it was not fractured when I reached a wall, grasped another sizeable protruding rock, and used it to stand.

There was an accumulation of debris, and I felt around and cut myself on a sharp object. A sharp object—! I reached down more carefully and pulled out a piece of glass from a jar. I sat down in the now-foot-high water and raised my feet. By carefully feeling, I was able to cut the zip tie that bound my legs together. I was free, and I was not wasting any time. If the kidnappers were still present, I was determined to get away and not let them think anything but that I was dead in the water deluge.

I inched slowly toward the light and finally found the great cavern that led to the outside. The light was enough that I could clearly see the ladder. My eyes burned from the mud, but as the water settled, I was able to wash the grit out from under my eyelids, and the pain was bearable.

I was exhausted, and the climb out of the cavern was at least two stories. I could not afford to slip or fall. I sat for several minutes, gathering my strength. I gazed upward and listened for any sounds that might come from my captors. Finally, I summoned my inner resolve and began the climb to freedom. It took several minutes, and I did slip once but was able to hold on while my legs dangled for a moment before I found my footing and resumed the climb out of the cave.

As I neared the top, I stopped and once again listened to the forest's sound surrounding the entrance to the cave. It was drizzling, which may have obscured any noise that was made by a human. Then again, maybe someone was able to track my phone and was looking for me. That was probably unrealistic. A girl can dream. I smiled to myself, thinking of how many times I said that to my daughter when she wanted something well out of her reach.

I finally climbed the last few steps and peered over the edge and into the forest. I slowly stood up. My thigh was throbbing, and I hurt all over, but I could stand, and I was alive. I was now chilled. The sun was obscured by clouds, but it appeared to be early morning, which gave me time to get a long way away from here before dusk. I carefully walked on pine needles to hide my tracks. I was no survivalist, but I was determined to get out of here alive and back to town.

I thought about who would be looking for me and how I would be found. From observing the surroundings, I decided there must have been a monumental rain that flooded the cavern from someplace up the mountainside. I could see no tire tracks, and much of the road had washed away. I walked along with the remnants of the road but off to the side and out of vision. Would a drone be used? The kidnappers didn't seem very sophisticated, but they did have an overseas bank account.

My only goal was to get out of this area and get to someone who could get me back to town and the sheriff's office. I was not warming up and was shivering badly for the first two hours. My legs, and especially my thigh, throbbed. I had to stop several times due to overwhelming cramps in my calves. I even tried walking backward for part of the time. I came to a second road, after two hours of walking.

I wasn't sure which direction to go. I was frustrated to the point of tears. I went left, but after thirty minutes, I realized this road was getting smaller, and I retraced my steps. I regretted the precious time, but it could have been worse. When I was back at the junction, I sat down away from the road and rested. It might be ten or eleven in the morning, and I still had plenty of daylight.

I stood up and realized resting was a colossal mistake. My muscles were seized and cramping. The pain was excruciating. Either I keep going, or I take a break for several hours. At least I had a road to follow.

Two hours later, I thought I heard a motor engine. It was coming in my direction. I was torn. If it was someone looking for me, I would probably cry, but if it was the kidnappers returning, then I had to hide. But how would I know? I didn't know how many men were involved. I could recognize the two men who abducted me from a distance, but I never saw any of the men in the cave. I heard more than one voice, but I had no visual cues to go by.

It was a truck, and there were two men with shepherds in the back. I didn't recognize the men, and I decided it was best to hide from them. With much reluctance, I let them pass. I waited for thirty minutes and expected them to return soon. If they were the kidnappers, they would probably search the waterlogged cave entrance and come back right away. If they were from a search and rescue unit, they may turn the dogs loose and be up in the area for a while. Then again, they may be illegal hunters. I simply could not take a chance.

I walked further down along the road but off the main path. This slowed me down enormously. After an hour, I heard dogs approaching. *Oh, please, Lord, let them be tracker dogs.* The game was up. Either they were the good guys, or they were the bad guys, but either way, I was going to be found.

In less than a minute, one of the dogs came upon me and barked furiously. The shepherd didn't seem intent on harming me. I even patted his head and told him to go away. That was not going to happen. Through gritted teeth, I tried to get the dog to leave, but he stayed at my feet, sitting, wagging his tail, and barking. I walked on, and he put his head under my arm and playfully grabbed my hand in his teeth. I wasn't about to test his limits. "Git, you lousy mongrel. Outta here now. Vamoose."

I then heard a voice yell, "Maggie? Maggie Kincaid? We're the canine patrol. Are you out here? Jock, where are you?"

I gave what must be Jock a withering look. "Traitor. I thought we were better friends than this. Here I am," I shouted. I gave up and turned myself in.

"Stay put, and he won't hurt you."

That made me laugh. Jock was sitting by my side and had his head under my arm. He was wagging his tail and obviously proud of himself.

"So disappointed, you lousy dog, so disappointed." I was sure they were the good guys, and I was officially rescued. The relief was overwhelming, and I broke all my rules on public displays of emotionalism.

Two uniformed men rounded the bend on the road, and I stepped out as they approached. "Hi, I'm Maggie Kincaid. I think I may be the object of your search." I started to cry, and one of the men put his arm around me and said it was okay. "Jock has brought many people to tears. We're used to it. We often have tears and, occasionally, a marriage proposal, but you need to know we're both married. I'm Terry, and this is my partner, Ken."

"How about Jock? Is he taken?" That made them laugh, and then even more tears followed.

Both men were in their late forties to early fifties and had salt and pepper hair. They wore hats that had insignias on them. Both men seemed to take this in their stride.

"How'd you know where to look?"

"We tracked your phone, and we lost the signal a few miles back, but we both are spelunkers, and we know there are several caves up here. You're lucky you weren't in one of them. We had a hell of a storm last night, and one is subject to flooding."

"Yeah?"

"Many people have gone in and never returned. It's called Lost Cave."

I described the cave. "It has a rope ladder going down into the main cavern, and then it shoots off in several directions?" Both men stared at me.

"It must not have rained as much up here," said Ken as he gazed at my clothes.

"No, I'm guessing it rained fairly hard."

"Maybe we better save this for when we get you back to the sheriff's office."

"Will you buy Jock a steak for me?"

"Ken, this lady needs a ride home. I'll stay with her if you go get the truck."

"Terry, you say that all the time. When are you going to man up and walk back up the hill so I can have a rest?" They both laughed, and Ken took off at a jog.

I shook my head. "Ah, youth."

"He's fifty-four. I'm fifty-five, but I had a knee replacement last year."

"And I'm old enough to bc your mother."

The truck arrived. What is it about dual cabs? *Doesn't anyone have regular trucks in America?* They started to help me into the front passenger seat. I felt vulnerable. "Do you know if they've caught the men who did this?"

"No, we've been out of range for the last two days except for check-in to make sure you hadn't been caught. If they have, we haven't been told. We're from the next county. Your county is too poor to pay for Jock's upkeep."

"Do you mind if I sit in the back and lie low in case we pass anyone returning to the cave?"

"Sounds reasonable."

"I was made to wear a hood, and I never saw their faces. Except for the two guys who took me from my friend's house, I wouldn't recognize them, but they would know my face."

"Maggie, you're headline news. Everyone in America would recognize you."

I peered into the rearview mirror and was shocked. "Not now. Man, I'm a mess."

Ken offered me some water and a granola bar. "Yeah, but you're alive."

"Thanks to you two."

"And Jock."

"I was drugged. How many days was I missing?"

"Three."

"Oh, boy. I need to let my kids know I'm alive."

"Yes, and you need to get to a hospital too."

"Can you let me use your phone to call someone when we are in range?"

As we descended the mountain, I heard another vehicle approach. I was down low and asked if either Ken or Terry recognized the car.

"No, but it looks like a news van. I don't recognize the logo, though." I felt the truck stop.

Terry rolled down his window. "You guys lost?"

A man responded. "No, we had a hunch the missing old lady was up here."

"Yeah, so did we. You guys from around here?" Ken laughed as Terry responded.

"No, we're from Atlanta. Good luck finding her. The easy money is that she's dead and buried up in the mountains. The ransom was paid, and the men who did it haven't been caught. We've got money riding on it. We sure would like to lose that money, but—."

"Be careful up there. The wilderness isn't for amateurs." Terry rolled up the window and reached back, and patted my arm, which was under a blanket. "One hour, and we'll have you back at the command center."

"Command center?"

"Yes, they've taken over the fairgrounds. There must be two hundred people looking for you. You've got some high roller friends."

"Really?"

That was it. I woke to Ken shaking me awake. "I think you're in safe hands. Want to sit up as we drive into the fairgrounds?"

"Does anyone know I'm alive?"

"You must be exhausted. We've been on the phone for the last twenty minutes."

"I guess it's out of the question for you to drive me home so I can shower and change first?"

"Totally, Jock needs publicity, and we need to keep our jobs. Sheesh, Maggie, you would think you were a media star or something."

"Well, the good news is at least my hair got dyed just before this happened, but I didn't get the trim. I heard that 'old lady' remark, by the way. Was I described as a grandmother?"

"Uh, yeah. Pretty much. That's the media for you."

The truck slowed down, and with great effort, I sat up and gazed around. My eyes were still scratched, slightly painful, and probably red. I had a black eye, and my pants were torn. Ken had given me his jacket to wear. The sun was shining, and it was warmer than up on the mountain.

I couldn't guess how many people were at the fairgrounds as we pulled in, but they were smiling, waving, and clapping. The truck pulled up in front of a pavilion that said Cherokee County Fairgrounds. Several people rushed to the car. I saw Carol and Eric from a distance. Numerous deputy sheriffs attempted to shield me from the reporters and well-wishers. I waved, and both Ken and Terry supported me as I descended from the truck and entered the pavilion. I was immediately taken into an office where Colin Chandler and Charlie were waiting. The three of us hugged, and I had another cry.

The moment was finally broken when Charlie said, "You have to be the most expensive friend I have ever had the pleasure and displeasure of knowing."

"Yeah, well, are you familiar with a canine search and rescue team from our neighboring county?"

"Oh, great. Here we go again."

Chapter 39

Colin asked if we three could have a private moment. At first, the FBI agent who appeared to be in command said no, but Colin whispered something to him, and the room was vacated except for Colin, Charlie, and me.

"How's Luke? Is he okay?"

"He's under lock and key at home. He was worried sick, but we called him and your family and let them all know you escaped and have been rescued been. Jesus, you gave us a scare. Poor Carol's beside herself."

"What's going to happen with Luke? Are you still going to take him to Australia? I don't think what happened to me is related. Do either of you think otherwise?"

Colin examined my face and lacerations, which were minor. "The FBI thinks there may be a connection, but they can't link anything yet. Did you find anything out? Did they mention Luke?"

I recounted the events as much as I could. I didn't discuss my escape and how lucky I was to be alive. I explained that other than the two men who abducted me, I never saw anyone, and I only heard their voices. I told Colin and Charlie I was so sorry to cause such a problem. Finally, I asked the question that needed to be asked. "Charlie, did you pay the ransom? I'm so sorry if you did. I'm happy to pay you back out of my allowance."

Both Charlie and Colin laughed. "You are going to have to wait for that answer. This may require more than your allowance."

"Yeah, well, if you still want me to take Luke to Oz, I think I might be able to go now."

Charlie punched Colin. "I was thinking about full-time servitude, but that might do fine."

Eric entered the room and announced he was taking me to the local hospital to be examined. I was under strict orders, and I would have a deputy sheriff present. Of course, I refused and was quickly shut down.

I emerged from the small room, and there were Ken and Terry with Jock and the other dog. I limped over and hugged Jock and shook both men's hands. "Thanks again, guys. I'm hoping to get you some funding. I pointed to Charlie, and then when I had his attention, I hugged the men and Jock and gave the thumbs-up sign. Charlie reciprocated with a shake of his head and a smile.

Terry patted my arm and said, "Next to a marriage proposal, I can't think of a better way to thank us."

"Oh, the money will go to Jock. You guys will only be admin." I hugged them and walked toward the door.

"Maggie, you owe me." Carol was standing by Eric.

"Huh?" I had no idea what she might be thinking. "For what?"

"The color and the mess you left in my sink." She then started to cry, we hugged, and I cried too.

"Can you finish the trim later when I get done at the hospital? I want to look good for the media."

Eric stared at my face and shook his head. "In your dreams, sister. You'll be lucky to get out today at all."

"What if we could go fishing later?"

"Oh, trying to bribe the doctor, are you?"

"Is it working?" I smiled up at him. "I could cook us both dinner. I have some frozen trout."

"Let's ride, cowgirl. Your chariot awaits." We walked out a side door of the pavilion, and an ambulance was waiting with the back doors opened. There was Larry, the backhoe driver. I stared around, expecting to see his friend Ron who picks up the dead horses. "I think Ron would have been a better option." Larry guffawed while the comment went right over Eric's head.

I smiled and waved to a few people who were standing by. I mouthed thanks and then was ushered into the ambulance and gratefully accepted a chance to assume the horizontal position. I was stiff and sore as I lay on the gurney of the ambulance. I borrowed Eric's phone, called my sister, and asked her to call my kids and tell them I was alright. I couldn't say too much at this point, but I was headed to the hospital and would call everyone tomorrow. Christy insisted she fly over, but I asked her to stay home until I knew more. At this stage, all I wanted was to suck on the inhaler that makes you happy. I had seen the device on television.

"Not in your dreams, Kincaid. You're not worthy."

"It was worth a try." I smiled weakly.

"You'll be lucky to get aspirin."

"The big pharmaceutical companies must love you. Not."

"I'm not on their Christmas list. That's for sure."

"How do you expect us unmarried women with no love lives to get our kicks?"

"Fly fishing."

"Oh, yeah."

"Don't I even get a siren?" Larry revved the siren for one short beep.

"You're not siren-worthy. Who do you think you are, anyway?"

"The object of the biggest manhunt in this county in days."

"I won't fish with you if you get a big head."

I felt my face. It was swollen and painful. *Too late for that.* We pulled into the hospital emergency drive and were met by two nurses and an emergency room doctor. The nurses removed my clothes and gave me an old-fashioned gown. I was auscultated and radiographed, and blood was taken. They were required to obtain blood to monitor my various bodily functions and assess what drugs I had in my system.

Because I was unconscious or could not recall at least two days, they radiographed my ribs, leg where I had a large bruise, and my cranium. A female FBI agent was in attendance, and I would be under protection by at least one agent all the time. Nothing was broken, and my head showed no unusual damage or bleeding.

I was placed on an intravenous fluid drip and given some jello to eat. I asked for gin, but that request was sadly unfulfilled. I put on a brave face, which required all the humor I could manage, but then the agent and I were on our own, and I turned away and did my version of a breakdown. I cried silently and must have fallen asleep when I felt a nurse wake me and tell me she needed to reassess me. I was so annoyed that I was sure I upset her.

I turned to relieve the pain I had from sleeping in one position too long. As I rolled over, Charlie was sitting in the chair next to my bed. He was smiling and reached out and patted my hand. The agent sat across the room and would not leave the room, so Charlie held my hand and didn't speak. I wasn't awake long.

I was given the okay to go home in the morning. A new agent was assigned to me. He and Eric took me to the sheriff's office. I was still in the dark as to who abducted me and if the ransom was paid. I was now clear-headed, and I knew the FBI, Charlie, and I would have to all come clean.

I was asked to go first and escorted into a room with only three agents and me. I told the agents everything I knew. I explained finding the two men I was convinced abducted me on my nature webcam. The agents had the images. I described the encounter at Saddleback Lake when Gabe and I rode to the lake to fish that same morning of the abduction.

I explained how I was taken into the truck, hooded, and driven up into the mountains. The hood was removed to negotiate the ladder going down into a cave, but I could not look at anyone once I was deep into the cave. I thought there were at least four or more other men in the cave. I explained writing the ransom note and how I was asked to write something to show that I was alive.

I was not present for the interview with Charlie. Still, I was told that without hesitation, he offered them money, which he had to gather from several different sources. He began to transfer money into an account in Belize. He deposited sixty million dollars and then asked for verification that I was still alive and didn't hear anything again. The money was emptied from the bank account set up by the kidnappers. Interpol could trace the money back to the States, but they weren't disclosing anything more.

My phone was on and was traced to the highway leading north into the mountains. When the signal was no longer pinging off towers, the locals suggested that I may have been taken to any one of twenty sites. Only a few people knew about the caves. Fortunately, the canine search and rescue men were knowledgeable and followed that up.

"Basically, you were left for dead. The toxicology report isn't in, but it looks like you were given Rohypnol. It probably should have killed you. Maybe they wanted to keep you sedated until you were needed for further confirmation of life. Still, the weather set in, and from what we can tell, they couldn't negotiate the mountain road with whatever they were driving."

My heart was racing as I heard this. "Do you have any idea who these men are?" I wondered where the discrepancy in the amount came from. I clearly remember writing fifty, not sixty million.

"No, that's why we want you to think about what you heard and saw. We've identified the two men who abducted you. They're from a neo-Nazi group in Louisiana. We know they shaved their beards and heads and boarded planes at the airport. We are onto them, is all I am going to say. The problem is they are not the ones we want, and we doubt they even know who is behind this."

"So, am I still a target?"

"We don't think so, but until we know for sure, you are our guest. We think if you go home and we have an agent with you, you'll be safe."

"If I wanted to go to, say, Australia to see my children, would that be alright?"

"You're free to go, but we don't advise it. We have no jurisdiction there, and we can't ensure your safety. This may be a large international syndicate, and they may have operators in many countries."

"If I really want to go back. How would I do that?"

"I can't advise you, and again, we strongly feel your life might be in danger. These men didn't plan for you to survive. Most likely, they know you did."

"I barely remember anything. I heard voices, but I didn't hear names or see anything."

"Could you identify a voice if we played some from a recorder?"

"I doubt it, but we could try."

"So, what is your relationship with Mr. McLeod?"

"Friends. Just friends at this stage. Nothing more. I only met him a few months ago."

"So, why do you think they chose you to entice his money away from him?"

"Well, we might be becoming better friends, but it hasn't happened yet." My head was beginning to throb. "I don't really know."

"Are you aware that Mr. Chandler's grandson is under threat if his father is released from prison?"

I suppose I was expecting that. It's in all the papers. It was now common knowledge that I had befriended Luke and had helped him regain some confidence and emotional stability. "Yes." I knew enough to not say more than I was asked.

"Are you aware of Mr. Chandler's efforts to keep Luke away from his father if he is released?"

That was tricky. "Well, would you want your son or daughter to be with him given the circumstances?"

"I'll take that as a yes."

I smiled and nodded. "My head is killing me, and I think I need to go home. Do you mind if we end this? I'm happy to continue later, but I need to get something for my head and maybe to eat. The hospital food was delicious, as you can imagine, but I think I need something that can be chewed."

"Yes, that's fine for right now." The agent turned to his two colleagues and asked them if they had any other questions. Everyone seemed to be happy that I had given them all I could remember. I saw Charlie as I came out of the interview room and smiled. He stood up and immediately walked over and kissed my cheek.

"I'm so sorry about all of this. I should have been more aware of any potential plot to use you as a hostage. I want to have you come and stay at The Sanctuary where I can protect you."

"Thanks, but I have friends who are getting paid to do this for me." I pointed to the FBI agents.

Charlie frowned. "The people who kidnapped you are dangerous. Why not have your friends come, and you all stay at my place?"

"I want to go home for a while. I need to call my children and a few others. How about I go home, and then if the FBI says it's okay, I'll come and spend the night."

"Oh, I forgot." Charlie reached into his pocket and handed me a brand-new phone. "I already checked, and you have a new unlisted number. I'm sorry I didn't have your contacts to transfer, but considering the circumstances, the next few calls are on my tab.**** I'm so sorry about all of this, and we need to talk. Almost losing another close person makes me realize how special you've become to me."

A surge of pleasure shot through me like a bullet. That was it. I was smitten. "Thank you. Not just for the phone either." He kissed me once again on my cheek as he and one of his accountant-type employees went into the interview room.

Two FBI agents and I left for my property. I was met by Baxter, Luke, and Gabe. They were over waiting for me. Baxter was beside himself and turned in circles and howled as I ascended the stairs to the deck and door. I didn't have my keys. I looked at Luke, who smiled a produced a key that would allow me to enter. I hugged him and shook Gabe's hand. "Is your grandfather home?"

"I don't know where Grandpa went today." Luke looked at the two men who were with me.

"Don't worry, Luke, they're the good guys. I introduced everyone and headed straight for the bathroom and my stash of paracetamol. I knew relief was on its way. I returned to the kitchen. I craved sleep, but the stairs were daunting. I was so stiff and sore. My thigh was screaming. I offered everyone coffee and Tim Tams. The agents had never tasted these and immediately took photographs and asked if they were sold in America.

The pain meds were kicking in, as was my desire to sleep. I showed the agents where anything was that they might need in the next hour or so. I thanked Luke and Gabe for caring for my horse and dog while I was gone and slowly climbed the stairs, showered, gowned, and went to bed. *Oh, my beautiful warm bed—how I have missed you.*

It was late afternoon before I emerged. Two other agents were sitting downstairs with the ones from the morning. This time they had a recorder and wanted to play some voices. I made us all crackers and cheese. They had gone through all my security tapes and found nothing that looked out of place. They did see a bear on the outside webcam this time.

I asked to have a moment to call my children in Australia. "It's going to be a few minutes. They all live in separate states. I need to call my brother and sister too."

As usual, I was admonished for leaving Australia and coming to this crazy gun-toting country by my daughter and then given the third degree by my sons. My sister and brother and I did a Zoom call, and I tried to keep my black eye hidden, but of course, that was impossible.

"Maggot, you need to get out of there. This is crazy. Come and join Miles and me in San Francisco. The sun is shining, and it's a glorious time to be here."

"Yeah, for all of two weeks. No thanks. Besides, I have four hunkalicious FBI agents here to keep me company." I glanced over at the four agents. I turned my laptop toward them, and they all smiled and said hi.

"Oh, Maggot. I'll be over tomorrow."

"Christy, they're half our age. By the looks of their hands, they're all married, anyway." We talked for a few more minutes, and then I returned to the men and sat down at the kitchen table to listen to the recordings.

They played several voice recordings, and I could see this was a test. On about the third voice, I recognized the lead FBI agent's voice. "Oh yes, that's him for sure."

"Are you sure?" The men were all looking at one another and shaking their heads.

"I am sure it is the man I talked to this morning in the interview room. Agent Mark Jones? That was a test—right?" I smirked and suggested we get back to authentic voices.

I didn't recognize any other voices, and the session was ended when Charlie called and asked if I would come and spend the night at his place. "I'd feel better if you came here. It's more secure, and there are plenty of security cameras for the agents to watch from the office. Besides, I miss you."

This brought another surge of pleasure that was so foreign to me. "I'll ask and call you back."

The agents called their boss, who was happy for us all to stay at The Sanctuary. They'd been there during the kidnapping, and Charlie was summoned from Los Angeles. It was a better setup logistically. So, thirty minutes later, we arrived, including Baxter.

Chapter 40

We were greeted by Charlie and Roberta. I introduced Roberta to the two new agents who accompanied me. Roberta took my overnight bag and offered to take me to my room. The female agent, Gloria, asked to stay with me. We were escorted to a large bedroom with an ensuite that had a spa. The water was already full and warm.

I turned to Gloria and grinned. "The last one in is a rotten egg."

"Uh, not on company time. Your spa awaits you, madam. I'll be out here doing the hard yards while you enjoy yourself."

Roberta showed me how to turn on the jets and control the temperature. "Mr. McLeod thought this might be good for your injuries. Is there anything else I can get you?"

"No, thanks. This is wonderful. I can't thank you enough."

"Oh, Mr. McLeod will be so pleased."

"Roberta, if you don't mind me asking, how is your brother?"

"Hanging in there, Dr. Kincaid. Thanks for asking."

"Remember, it's Maggie. Besides, I may be working for you to pay back what Charlie spent to get me free."

She looked at me quizzically. "Ma'am?"

Maybe she didn't know. I decided to drop the topic. "Just a joke, Roberta."

"Dinner is at half-past six."

"I won't be late."

After Gloria examined the room, I shut the door, stripped down, and entered the deliciously hot water. I turned on the jets to a low level and let the bubbles massage my body. I turned in all the comfortable positions to maximize the massaging of my thigh, back, and arms.

"You okay in there?" Ever on duty, my silence probably worried Gloria.

"Do you want me to sing so you know I'm still alive?"

"Uh, no, thank you."

"Ten more minutes."

I finished washing my hair, which still needed a trim and put on some slacks and a sweater. I wasn't too bad for an old broad.

Gloria and I went into the living room. It was a more modern carpeted room with crème-colored lounges and a large fireplace. It wasn't warm enough to have a fire, but I was chilled. I might be getting a fever. Charlie and the other FBI agent were discussing matters, and they abruptly stopped when we entered. "Did we miss something?" I turned to Gloria, who shrugged when no one answered.

"Maggie, would you care for a glass of wine?"

"Maybe just a small glass, but don't open a bottle unless you're having some." He peered at me, smiled, and shook his head.

"I'll add it to the tab. Yeah, I've been thinking about that. You weren't the object of the abduction. You were the pawn, and it's me who owes you. You could have been killed. I'd never forgiven myself if that had happened."

"Don't you think it must be someone you know and knows we are friends. That must be someone local. But they also had to be sophisticated enough to have access to an overseas bank account."

Gloria stared at me and then seemed to consider what I said. Dinner was called. We all headed into the dining room. The other agent, Mitch, asked to be excused for a moment. His phone had buzzed. "It's the boss. Be right back."

Roberta brought in trays of meat and vegetables as well as salad and bread rolls. "That is almost worth getting kidnapped. This looks delicious. Thank you."

Gloria helped herself to the meat and vegetables. "Mr. McLeod, I'm going to have to guard Maggie for at least a week. I don't usually like the evening shifts, but I may make an exception."

Mitch returned and sat watching Charlie and me without further comment. After dinner, Mitch suggested that Gloria and I sleep in the same room. This seemed to upset Charlie. I hoped he didn't think I was going to sleep with him tonight.

"Do you mind if Maggie and I have a brief private moment?" Charlie took my hand and waited for their response. My heart was racing, thinking where this was going to lead.

We walked out to the sunroom and sat down together on a wicker love seat. He put his arm around me, and his tears began to flow. "I am so sorry. I've never had anything like this happen before. I'm so sorry to have put this on you." He wiped his eyes and stared out of the glass walls. There was enough daylight that we could see the garden beds alongside the building. "I would do anything to make this go away."

"If you knock say ten or twenty million off what I owe you, I might forgive you." It took him a second, but he smiled and then laughed. "Charlie, I guess this is the burden of running with the A crowd. I'm reconsidering my options here, FYI. Rural Australia's only real threats are snakes and sharks. That's a bit tamer than what I'm experiencing here."

"So, I guess a marriage proposal is out of the question?"

"You're kidding, aren't you?" I was shocked.

"I was wondering if we could open negotiations for a merger in the future."

"Never say never. How much in the future?"

"We could start negotiations now." Charlie was so nervous.

"I'm open to negotiations, but I play hardball. You know it's not the money, but I'll need a prenup. I need to protect my assets."

"Yes, I know that."

"I need a certain amount of freedom. I need to ride and fish. I need to be able to do that with my male friends."

"Yes." The affirmation was tentative.

"You didn't sound very convincing."

"Yeah, I'll work on that."

"I need to see my grandchildren regularly."

"We could move them out here."

"Want to bet? They think they were born in God's land. We need to sleep in the same bed unless one of us has insomnia or is ill."

"Agreed."

"We stay four nights at my place and three at yours."

"Nope. If you want us to stay at yours seven nights, I don't care." That made me happy. I knew he would be away for much of the time.

"Before we get ahead of ourselves, let's test the chemistry." I turned to him, and he to me. The first kiss was tender and sweet.

"Mm, better do another just to make sure." We did. It was longer, and we held each other afterward.

"B plus. And I'm not going for an A with two FBI agents in the next room." I smiled and stroked his face. I could feel faint stubble. He was smiling but still nervous. I was too drugged with pain medication and lack of sleep to feel anxious. I had doubts, but they were receding quickly.

"We'll resume negotiations another time. You need to get to bed." He took my hand and pulled me up off the loveseat.

"I'm sure they'll leave us alone in a few days." I turned to the agents who were politely gazing out of a window at the last of the sunlight.

"One could only hope."

Chapter 41

Charlie was in his office the following morning with his accountants and two other men. They were all flying to Texas this afternoon, where they proposed an acquisition of a new company. I planned to learn more about Charlie's business later. It would be way too presumptuous of me to start looking around.

I slept well, considering our 'merger' discussion. I must be getting old. I never slept when I first fell in love with my ex. It was early days. I was on the fence about giving up my independence. It's okay for a future partner to agree to allow the other partner to go fishing with a much younger man, but would this agreement last? Time will tell.

I ate breakfast with my two FBI sidekicks. They would take me back to my house after breakfast, and then they would be replaced by another lot of agents. I was going to see Charlie again in two days when he returned. The FBI allowed him to resume his endeavors. As I finished breakfast, I walked past his office and stopped at the door to say goodbye and thank him. He stood up and smiled.

"Thanks so much for last night." It was awkward.

He walked over, took me in his arms, and kissed me in front of the other men. "See you in a few days." Two men sitting at the desk whistled. I was so pleased and yet embarrassed. *For God's sake, I'm almost seventy, but I feel like a teenager.*

I returned to my room and then remembered I needed to tell Roberta thank you for all she'd done. I walked down the hallway and heard the men discussing their strategy for the meeting they would have tomorrow morning. I came to the room where Roberta was changing the sheets that Mitch slept in. I overheard one of the men say something about waiting for a few more days until things settled down.

It hit me like a brick. Here was the voice of my captor. He was the one who dictated my letter. His voice and cadence were exactly how I remembered. My mind was clearing, and I remember hearing him talk, even after I was drugged. This was an inside job, and I needed to warn Charlie. I was sick. He would be so furious and upset. His life was probably in danger, as well.

I agonized about confronting him immediately or waiting until we left and telling Gloria and Mitch. Then I heard Charlie. "No, I've got the fifty million and ten extra in case things get tough, and I need to get rid of it before anyone starts snooping." I felt like I had been gut-punched. I quietly hurried and went around the corner. There was one of the men coming out of the bathroom.

He looked at me and asked if I was lost. "No, I'm looking for Roberta." My voice was wavering and maybe even high-pitched. I peered and pointed down the hallway. "Oh, there she is." I waved as she was coming out of another room. "Hey, Roberta. I need that recipe for the beans, and thanks for everything last night."

"You're welcome. I hear you may be becoming a regular?" Roberta put her hand on her hip and wagged her finger.

"I sure hope so." *Not.* I smiled and waved. "So much to do when I get home. Take care and good luck with your brother." I was sick with fright and disappointment. I tried to consider a logical explanation. I must have missed something that would explain this conversation in a way that didn't implicate the man I was now falling in love with.

I returned to my room, and Gloria and Mitch had left. They were waiting for me in the car. I went into the bathroom and made sure I had everything. When I turned around, Charlie was standing in the doorway. "Is everything okay?" He had a look that did not exude warmth and love. He was in a no-nonsense 'command mode,' and I could see he was not asking in a concerned way.

"Oh, darling, I was just checking that I didn't forget anything. I found Roberta, thanked her for the meals, and asked for her recipe for the beans. I hate leaving you. I know it's only a few days, but I need to get you past the B plus."

That made him laugh. "Phew, I thought you were having second thoughts. I'm sure with some practice, I can get past at least an A-minus." He took me in his arms and kissed me once again. This time it was more urgent and exploring. He held me after.

"Nope, that was definitely a straight-A. The troops will be getting restless. I need to go. I hate this, but I need to leave."

He put his arm around me and walked me to the front door. "Maggie, I know you understand that this will all be yours soon too. I am a businessman first, and you may hear confusing things. There are explanations for everything. So, if you have any concerns, please ask me first, won't you?"

"Hey, lover boy. Not sure what that was about, but if I have any, you'll be the first to know. Safe travels, darling." I turned and walked to the car. My injured thigh and general soreness hopefully hid my shaking legs. I turned to enter the vehicle and waved one more time. We drove out of the gates of The Sanctuary. I sat up and calmly said, "Can you take me to your leader."

Chapter 42

Gloria turned to me. I kept watching and turning to see if we were being followed. We were. No doubt.

"On second thought, can you take me home as we planned, and then we can meet your replacements."

"Do you want to tell us what's going on?"

"I overheard something." My mind was racing. Who was involved, and who could I trust? Was Colin Chandler involved? Did Carol know about this? Why would Charlie have me killed and then all but propose marriage?

Mitch was driving. He turned to Gloria. "We're still being followed."

Gloria turned to talk to me, but she was watching the vehicle behind us. "Do you want to elaborate?"

"Not now. I recognized a voice."

"From one of your abductors?"

"Yes."

No one had to ask anything more. It was an inside job. What I didn't want to disclose is that it appeared that Charlie was the mastermind. I couldn't come up with any other logical explanation. I desperately wanted one. Finally, I met someone who was all but into my inner sanctum, and I discovered he was a fraud.

We turned into my long driveway and pulled up to the gate. The car following us turned in as well. Mitch pulled out his revolver while Gloria got out to open the gate. I was not allowed to get out. One of the men came up to my window. My heart was racing. He knocked, and I turned to see him as he made a rolling motion with his hand, indicating he wanted me to roll down my window. I looked at Mitch, who was holding his hand and gun alongside the driver's door.

I opened the window, and the man handed me my phone. The feeling of relief was palpable. "Oh, thanks. For a second, we thought you might be the kidnapper."

"Uh, no. I haven't kidnapped anyone yet." He smiled and shook his head.

Gloria stood at the gate, waiting for us to enter so she could close it. "Excellent. Now hurry up, you two, I have to go."

I shrugged and thanked him again. The phone was on, and Mitch asked to examine it. After thumbing through it, he announced it had a tracker on it. We were in the house, and after Gloria returned, they asked me about what I knew. I was reluctant to say anything that might not be true, and I thought it was best to go to the command center and talk to the head FBI Investigator.

Mitch and Gloria looked at me, and then Gloria said, "Why are you asking to go to the top?"

"I just am. I'm not going to say anymore." We heard a car pull up and observed the next set of agents arrive to take over. The four of them conferred out at their car while I agonized about what I had overheard in Charlie's office.

The agents returned to the house. Mitch spoke for them all. "Let's step out onto the deck. Okay, we think it's best if two of us stay here and two go with you to the command post. We'll have you enter from inside your garage, so in case someone is watching from the woods, they won't see you. You'll be down low and not visible from anyone's view. We're calling the headquarters once we're away from the property."

I was a similar height to Gloria. We went into the garage together and exchanged clothes. Then Gloria went back into the house, and finally, all four agents were in the garage, and the two new agents left with me hiding in the back seat. I was taken to the command post, but instead of getting out, I was kept low in the car. The agent in charge of the incident entered the vehicle, and we drove to a remote location. I was asked what was going on by Agent Willoughby. He announced that he was recording the conversation.

"You know how you asked me to listen to voice recordings, and I was able to spot the one you threw in as a test?"

"Yes? Do you think you recognized a voice from yesterday?"

I hesitated. I was going to throw this whole investigation a bombshell or at least a curveball. "I think you know I stayed out at Charlie McLeod's place, The Sanctuary, last night." They nodded. "He and I are getting to be more than just friends."

"Yes, that's why we think you were targeted for the kidnapping. Is there something else?"

"Maybe, and maybe not. I'm praying it's perhaps not, but I can't ignore it. This morning when I went past Charlie's office, he had several men whom I had never seen before sitting around his desk. As I was waiting for his maid to emerge from a room, I heard one speak. They are heading to Texas to do some sort of takeover of a business. I heard one of the men talk, and I swear on a stack of bibles that it was the man who asked me to dictate the ransom note. I'm sick. I don't want to be right, but deep down, I think I am."

"What did he say?"

"He wanted to wait until things calmed down."

The agent was sitting up and beginning to take notes while I sat in the back seat. "Anything else?"

"This is the point. Charlie mentioned having the money to buy the business. He said he had the fifty million and then ten more if it didn't go well."

"So, they have the exact sum they paid in the ransom."

"Sir, not exactly. When I was asked to write out the ransom note, it was fifty million, not sixty. I don't know how the amount changed. Why would anyone pay more than was asked? I mean, ten million more? I don't get it."

Agent Willoughby let out a slow whistle. "Money laundering. That's why."

"Damn, I lose." The second agent sitting in the car punched his open hand.

"So, what did you lose?"

"Willoughby, you're a savant," exclaimed the second agent.

"Anyone who wants to let me in on the bet?"

Both men hesitated. "Where are they going this afternoon?"

"They're flying out to Texas to buy a tech firm of some sort." I felt my eyes watering. My perpetual headache was re-emerging, and my new life was in tatters. I didn't know who was who anymore. I wondered if Hal was in on it and if so, were Carol and Colin as well? Who were the good guys? Were there any good guys anymore?

Patty Tilmouth, the local vet, and her brother, Eric, were honest. I would have bet my life on Colin and Charlie. Now I knew I was probably wrong. I only survived by chance. Did they want me dead? I was so confident last night that Charlie was going to be my last and forever love.

"Charlie McLeod has been on our radar for years. He's hidden his secret life well. CLM has a plant near the Mexican border where they make illicit drugs and sell them on the black market. He's amassed a fortune. McLeod's only problem is getting the money into the mainstream. This time, it appears he did it right in front of our eyes. He sent the money from nefarious accounts to the offshore bank and was able to bring it right back, and now it looks legit."

"I think I'm going to be sick."

"Really, shit. This is a brand-new issued work vehicle. I've got to use it until we leave the state. Get out if you're going to puke."

"Not that kind of sick. Who else is involved? Is it any of the locals?"

"We don't think so. McLeod uses one pilot for all the transport, but the local one appears to be innocent."

I didn't want to ask about Colin Chandler. I wondered how he kept up his lifestyle without working for so many years.

"We looked at the old movie star guy, and so far, we can't make a connection. There may be a few of The Sanctuary barn crew, but it looks like he has these suits that come and go as he needs them for his illegal endeavors."

"The suits are the guys I saw last night and this morning. He isn't all bad. He funded my friend's school for kids in Atlanta and Alabama."

"This is the thing. Other than a bit of jetting here and there, it seems McLeod uses the money for philanthropic activities. I'm guessing there's going to be a hue and cry when the funds dry up."

"So, why is he doing this?"

"The guy gets off on wealth redistribution, but he is selective, and he genuinely wants to help people. I heard it was to atone his dead wife, and someone said you were the same, and that's why he is attracted to you."

The guilt I was beginning to feel was overwhelming. "So, Charlie's Robin Hood, and I'm Maid Marian. I didn't mean to make him rob a bank."

"Yeah, we get that. Charles McLeod's not all bad, but how he funds his philanthropy is a problem. That, and you almost died."

"Yeah, but who would have thought the cave would have flooded. Isn't that a once in a hundred-year kind of thing?"

"True, and we got the tox report on your blood. It was Rohypnol. I don't think he really meant to kill you. He sure didn't want it to be linked to him. That's why he had those men stalk you for a few days before abducting you."

"He spent the night at my house protecting me. Well, that's what I thought, anyway. So, he's on his way to buy a company with his drug money that is now legit. What happens to the company?"

"We're aware he's doing that. He told us his plans, and we agreed to let him go. We didn't roll up here on a turnip truck, you know. He is paying far more than it's worth. The company was folding, and Mr. McLeod is not only buying it for more than its worth, but he is also saving the jobs for several hundred people. He can turn it around in a heartbeat. As we said, he's not all bad."

"He gave millions to my friend Sandy's nonprofit school. What happens when Charlie is caught?"

"It depends. Some of the institutions McLeod helps are stand-alone and come from legit funds, and some aren't. Was it a lump sum?" Agent Willoughby was writing down names as we talked.

"I don't know." I needed to call Sandy.

"Okay, we've probably told you enough. You're now aware. If you continue to consort with McLeod, you'll be under indictment for anything that might be construed as consorting with a known criminal. How do you feel about wearing a wire? If we get him on tape admitting to it all, then it is much easier for us to prosecute him."

"You want me to snitch on Robin Hood? How much danger will I be in?"

"I won't lie. If you confront the man, there's no telling what he might do. It might help if you can get the names of any accomplices. We can be close. I know we can arrange it."

"Can I think about it? I hate that all of this has happened. I realize it's ill-gotten gains, but let's face it. He has done more to help people than you or I or probably anyone aside from Bill Gates in America. He is unknown to the public, and he's done it for years if what he told me is true. It doesn't seem like he wants any fame or glory. He is just a philanthropist."

"His drugs have killed lots of people on the way."

There was a pause while I stared out of the car. "Can I have twenty-four hours?"

"We're probably going to have to arrest him tomorrow or when he returns from Texas."

"I'm guessing you know about Luke, Colin Chandler's grandson. Does any of this have to do with him?"

"We don't think so. We've tried to make the connection. CLM's drug dealings are far more sophisticated than what Luke's parents were in. They were almost end-users. They did sell some to fund their addictions, but the group that wants to get to Luke appears unrelated to Charles McLeod."

"I don't suppose there is any way you can do something to protect this boy if I wear a wire?"

There was a long silence before Agent Willoughby answered. "I can find out. I don't know. We'll give you some time to decide, and we can see where we can help the boy. Is that acceptable?"

"Nothing is acceptable." I paused, thinking that if I woke up and this was simply a nightmare, I would run to Charlie and throw myself onto him. "But it is what it is. Isn't it?"

They drove me back to the house. By the time I arrived, there were agents all over the property and back into the woods. My phone had rung several times. The calls were answered by the agent assigned to protect me. The agent took names and numbers and said I had a migraine and had gone to bed, and she would inform me when I woke up. The calls were from Charlie, Carol, Colin, and my family.

"The good news is we found no bugs in your house, and no one is apparently watching from the woods. We removed the tracking device on your phone, and they will know that, so I would only mention that you saw it and removed it if he asks. He probably won't, but just so you are aware of what may come up."

"Thanks," I paused. "Who are you?"

"Nancy Pollard. Sorry, I should have introduced myself." Nancy pointed to an older man sitting at the kitchen table, talking on his phone. "That's Hugh. We're your babysitters for the next twenty-four hours." She extended her hand, and I shook it. My hand was shaky, and I was reaching my limit.

"That migraine isn't that far from the truth. Do you all mind if I go upstairs and rest for a while?"

"Do you want your phone?" It was probably tapped, and that is why the FBI wanted me to have it again. My guess was that the FBI was not sure I wasn't involved, and they were going to make sure I wasn't letting Charlie know they were onto him.

"No, thanks. You guys can be my answering service." I had hot chocolate and a grilled cheese sandwich and went to bed. I didn't wake up until there was a knock at my door. It was around five in the afternoon. Was I still recovering from the trauma or becoming depressed from all that had happened in the last few days? The knock became louder.

"Come in." I was dressed and had a quilt over me. I sat up; Nancy entered my bedroom. "Is it something important?"

"There's a young boy on the phone who said it was urgent." Nancy handed me the phone.

"Hello?" I was trying to not sound drugged.

"Maggie, it's Luke. Digger is sick. Can you come over?"

Chapter 43

Luke was speaking so fast I was having difficulty understanding him. He said Digger was black and wouldn't get up. That was all he could tell me. I asked if Dr. Tilmouth had been called. He didn't know. He was asked by Gabe to come and get me, but Mrs. Gillard would only let him call me.

I told him to open the security gate so I could drive up to the barn. I threw on some jeans and a long-sleeved rugby top and came downstairs. I explained that my horse was next door and was sick, and I needed to drive over and see him. I asked the FBI agents to transport me next door. They were more than willing as they thought they would meet the famous Colin Chandler. *Even FBI agents can be star-struck.*

I asked them to hurry. We entered the property through the open gate and drove around the house and up to the barn. The sun was setting when we arrived. I'd slept the whole day away. I knew I needed to get off this sleeping kick.

The barn lights were on, and I saw a vet truck parked at the end of the shed. Luke was standing outside of a stall door. I ran down the aisle and found three ranch hands in the stall. Digger was sitting up, which was a relief. His hind limbs, flanks, and abdomen were covered in feces from rolling in his stall. He lifted his tail and passed watery diarrhea without even standing. It smelled horrible. The vet wasn't Patty, and she appeared relieved to see me.

"Hi Dr. Kincaid, thanks for coming. I was told this is your horse. He looks bad. I wasn't sure if you wanted me to keep going or just do the kindest thing."

"I'm Maggie, do you mind if we dispense with the formalities?"

"Yes, ma'am. I'm Denise. I'm sitting in for Dr. Tilmouth while she attends a vet meeting." Denise was slightly overweight with black curly hair and a smile that would make you forget your problems. I almost did. Her accent indicated she was from the South.

"Denise, what have you found so far?"

"Ma'am, the men here said he was okay a few hours ago. He ate his breakfast." She looked up, and the men nodded. "They came to feed tonight and found him like this. His heart rate is eighty-eight, his gums are brick red, his temperature is way below normal, and you can see he's in pain."

"It doesn't look good. Have you got any intravenous fluids in your truck?"

"Yes, ma'am. So, you want to keep going then?"

"Let's give it a go. Let's get some blood for the lab and check if you have tetracycline in your truck too. Has he had any Banamine?"

"Won't you fry his kidneys with all that?"

"Sure will. Good call. We'll give those after we get Digger rehydrated. Look for the largest catheter you can find. I know I saw a twelve gauge in her truck and intravenous sets behind the bandages on the driver's side. Oops, I'm having an Australian moment. On the passenger side."

I entered the stall, and my two FBI buddies both started in with me, smelled diarrhea, and said they would be down the hallway if needed. I lifted Digger's upper lip and was appalled by what I saw. His gums were brick red, as Denise suggested, but they also had a purple tinge, which to me was one step closer to the grave. I'd seen horses look this bad and survive, but not often.

Luke came up behind me and tearfully asked if he was going to be all right.

"I don't know, but we're going to do the best we can. Digger's awfully sick and dehydrated. He has toxins floating around in his blood, and they do horrible things to the horse's organs, like the kidneys. Luke, the problem is, we don't know what's causing it. It may be something he ate or a virus he picked up. We're going to shotgun this as it's the only thing we can do. We also have to worry about laminitis." I knew ninety percent of this would go over Luke's head, but the staff could learn as well. "Often, if horses get something called endotoxemia, it comes from the bacteria in the intestines. The toxins then travel through the blood to the feet, where they shunt blood away, which results in damage to the lamina, which then causes a separation of the hoof from the inner foot and the bone. It's kind of like someone pulling your toenails off the end of your toes. The bad news is Digger has to walk on his toenails."

"Maggie, what can I do?"

"Pray, Luke, just pray."

Denise was brilliant at getting the intravenous fluids going. "Damn, sister, you're good." I was rewarded with that smile again. We were going to run out of fluids reasonably soon. I called Eric, who had a key to the vet clinic and knew where the extra fluids were kept. He would be much faster than if we went back to get them. We gave Digger some Banamine, which is like Tylenol for horses. It's more potent and can damage the kidneys, so we waited until we had a few liters of intravenous fluid into him and then gave the anti-inflammatory medication and continued with the intravenous fluids.

"Denise, have you ever seen a horse with Potomac Horse Fever?"

"No, ma'am." I laughed to myself. *You can take the girl out of the South, but you can't take the South out of the girl.* I ignored the 'ma'am.'

"This sure looks like the ones I saw before I moved to Australia, and even in Australia, we had cases like this. They responded to tetracycline, and I don't know what it was, except the lab found a spirochete. So, shall we get out the oxytetracycline?"

"Yes, ma'am." Man, I like this woman. She knew the dose and put it into the intravenous line, and Digger lay quietly in his stall. We put ice boots on his feet to keep the toxins away from the area that controls blood flow. Digger was trained to stay down, and we kept telling him to stay where he was. This was a tremendous asset to our treatment.

Eric showed up and joined us. He brought enough fluids to see us through the next two days. After two hours of intravenous fluids and the tetracycline, Digger wanted to get up. I was sitting down on a bale of hay inside his stall. I could reach down and stroke his head. With a lunge, he was up and staggered for a moment and then lifted his tail and dropped his penis and urinated enough urine to drown an army. This was good and bad. It was not concentrated. It was either that his kidneys could not concentrate the urine, or the protein in his blood was so low that the fluids could not stay in his system, and hypovolemic shock would kill him

We took the opportunity to pass a nasogastric tube and give him some anti-diarrhea powders and some more electrolytes. Poor Denise was exhausted. I had her leave me all the drugs I thought I might use for the evening and told her to go home. Digger even looked around for something to eat. His mucous membranes were still purple rimmed, but the overall color was returning to normal.

I'd given my phone to the FBI friends who were now sitting in an office down the way. Mrs. Gillard brought everyone food. Nancy walked down and said that I had received several calls and messages. She handed me the phone. One was from Colin, saying he was flying back and would see me tomorrow. "Things were looking up." I wondered what that meant. There was one from my sister who left a brief message, "Maggot, call me or die trying." That was two hours ago, and it was too late to call now.

The final one was from Charlie saying he would stay in Texas longer than expected and would be home the day after tomorrow now. He said he loved and missed me. This was the first time he said that. I was sick hearing it. Why couldn't it all be a big mistake? At least it gave me another day to decide if I would be used to get the evidence needed to secure a conviction.

I ate some chicken and salad and went back into the stall with Digger. He was looking brighter and apparently feeling much better. He nudged me looking for food. "Sorry, beautiful boy. Not yet."

Despite his improvement, he was kept on fluids all night. We slowed down the rate, and he wanted to stand. I felt the feet and digital pulses behind his fetlocks to monitor the onset of laminitis and found nothing that indicated he would go down that path. I was convinced that Digger was going to live. I thanked everyone for their astute observations and their help this afternoon and evening. It was one in the morning, and everyone was exhausted. I said I would stay with him, and I would adjust the fluids as needed. No one was experienced in this, and Digger was my responsibility.

Luke had fallen asleep two hours ago and was woken long enough to get him back up to the house. I was alone with Digger.

Nancy was sleeping in the office on a cot while Hugh sat at a desk and watched a monitor covering entrances to the barn. As Digger continued to improve, his diarrhea abated, and I had time to rest in between picking up the motions, doing observations on him, and changing the intravenous fluid bags. Digger's temperature rose to low normal, and his heart rate dropped to fifty-two. It was almost normal. I sat down on my hay bale and closed my eyes. Digger had been nuzzling me earlier, but now he stood away and was sleeping, standing on his feet.

I was startled awake when I felt an arm reach around and pull me to a warm body. Colin had come in and surprised me. I was dead to the world. It made me realize how vulnerable I was. Hugh stood at the door and smiled. Apparently, he saw Colin come through the office, had recognized him, and allowed him to come to see his old horse. Colin leaned over and kissed the top of my head.

I smiled and took his other hand and held it. Then the tears came again. This time I made a mess of myself with snot and the whole nine yards. "Sorry."

Colin pulled out a handkerchief and wiped my face. "Nothing to be sorry for. You've been through a lot these past few days. I'm the one who should be sorry. You entrusted your horse to me, and I almost killed him."

"And you? How's the case going? I'll take Luke to Australia if you think it might protect him. I need some time to think about things."

Colin hugged me and smiled. "Maggie, thanks. It seems things are changing for us both. Luke's going to be safe for a long while. In looking at the evidence, no one ever entered his father's DNA into the databank. He was a match for another murder and two sexual assaults. In the words of our attorney, 'He ain't going nowhere.'"

"Oh, poor Luke. Does he know?"

"No. I'll tell him, eventually. When he wakes up, I'll tell him he's going to live with either his grandmother or me until he's ready to leave home."

"Helen must be pleased. Any chance she's moving back?"

Colin slumped a little, and his grip on me tightened. "No. It seems that her husband has decided he will live on her ranch, and they are reconciling."

"Oh, Collie, I'm sorry."

"Yeah, me too. Helen's the love of my life. I'm an old geezer, and I probably don't have many years left. I guess with you and Charlie getting together, I'll be back on my own."

Sadly, I now knew that wasn't going to happen. I couldn't tell Colin that he was losing both his wife and a best friend soon. I couldn't see how Charlie would escape prison, but who knew. I knew I wouldn't marry him, anyway. This was going to have to wait. I felt terrible for the knowledge and for the pain that so many people would endure in the next few months.

It was time to change the intravenous fluid bags. It was getting cold, and I was feeling the chill. Colin saw that and gave me his jacket. I showed him how I assessed Digger's condition. His heart rate had now dropped to forty-eight. He had no bounding pulses in his legs, and his hooves were warm. His temperature was now back up to normal, and he had experienced no more diarrhea in the last two hours.

It was almost daylight. I was cold and aching all over. Two ranch hands and Gabe showed up at the barn. I remembered Gabe had his wedding anniversary. "Hi cowboy, how was that anniversary dinner the other night?"

"We had it last night. A good friend had gone missing, so we postponed the dinner. Yes, it was great. Thanks for asking." I realized I was the friend.

"Can I show you how to care for Digger for a few hours?" Gabe nodded. I then showed him how to stop the intravenous fluids and cap the catheter. He knew how to do the rest. Colin, my agents, and I went to the house. Colin directed us to the kitchen, where he began to prepare bacon and eggs. While he cooked that, I poured coffee for everyone and made toast.

"What the hell are you all doing in my kitchen?" Mrs. Gillard emerged in her bathrobe. "Out, now, the lot of you. Colin Chandler, you're going to give me a bad reputation. Breakfast will be served in the dining room. Now get out." We all moved into the dining room, and Luke wandered in and sat down next to me.

"Maggie, is he?" Luke didn't finish his question.

"Yes, he's fine, Luke. Thanks for your help yesterday."

Luke seemed pleased. "Maggie, what does it take to be a vet?"

"Music to my ears, beautiful boy," and I glanced at Colin, who seemed pleased. "Luke, you can be anything you want. You're smart, you learn quickly, and you have grit. You might want to consider going to a regular school this year." I hoped that was okay to say, but it was true. I didn't look at Colin this time.

Hugh and Nancy nodded. Hugh said, "Luke, the FBI is always looking for good men and women."

Luke didn't realize they were FBI. "Oh, really? Maybe I should look at that too, Grandpa. Then I can help keep the bad guys in jail."

"Luke, you have many years to decide what you do in life. Maybe you could be an actor like your grandpa. We know you can act." Colin and I laughed, knowing how long Luke pretended to be deaf. Luke laughed at that, as well.

I was shaking with a lack of sleep. "I need to get to sleep. I'm going to head home. Luke, can you do me a favor and come and get Baxter and take care of him for me today?"

"Can I ride over in the FBI car? Do you have a gun? Can I see it?" Hugh was Luke's new interest. I was passé. Hugh and Nancy took Luke to the car. That gave me a second to speak privately with Colin. I still wasn't sure if anyone else was involved and knew what Charlie was doing. It was a delicate subject.

"Collie, I'm concerned about the money that Charlie lost in paying my ransom. The FBI guys aren't saying anything, but I think the tracers lost it. I'm sick thinking he lost so much money. I mean, fifty million is a lot of money. I don't care who you are."

"Maggie, I wonder the same thing, but Charlie has assets we don't even know about. He's my best friend, but even I don't know about most of his business dealings. All I can tell you is Charlie would have paid twice that amount to save you. He loves you, and he would go to jail for you. So, if he robbed a bank, don't be surprised."

"Thanks. I'll keep it in mind." The guilt I was feeling was enormous. Charlie wasn't all bad. Thankfully, he seemed to keep Colin out of it. Who knew about the others?

I hugged him, and as I slipped into the car to head home, Colin grabbed my arm and hugged me one more time. "Don't think if I was ten years younger, Charlie McLeod would even get a look at you."

Chapter 44

I was exhausted. Baxter had waited for my return and was doing doggie circles when we arrived home. I quickly fed him, and Luke took him back home for me so I could sleep. I noticed I was sleeping a lot, and I wondered if this was how my mind dealt with the mental trauma of the past few days. Was it the heavy sedation that is causing me to be foggy?

There was another change of the guard, and Gloria and Mitch were back on duty. They came with a few other agents who decided that rather than wearing a recording device, my house would be bugged. They placed microphones in the living room, my bedroom, and out on the deck. I couldn't imagine Charlie getting into my bedroom, but I had to admit that is where we would have headed if I hadn't overheard that voice in his office.

He would be back tomorrow, and I would invite him over for dinner. If he returned too late, then I would see him the following day. I slept downstairs in the guest bedroom while they set up the devices. I slept for several hours and then had lunch and decided to walk over to see Digger.

Gloria and I went down to the creek. I suspected it was the creek that harbored the snails that, then through flies, eventually infected Digger with what I was sure was Potomac Horse Fever. His symptoms and his response to treatment screamed PHF or its cousin. Denise had taken samples and sent them to the lab. We would know for sure in a day or two.

Denise was at the barn when I arrived. She was smiling and taking more blood to monitor his blood count. My guess was he was critically low on white cells. He was vulnerable to other infections until he rebounded and was able to fight any further assault on his immune system. Denise appeared tired, but she still had that Pepsodent smile. "Somebody is feeling better."

"Thanks to you." I wanted her to feel like she was the one to save him. "Now you know, all things are possible."

"No, thanks to you. You know where I was headed. Digger would be six feet under if you had left it to me."

"Well, I had to learn that lesson too, and I'm happy to pass on any knowledge I have. By the way, I gave him about a one percent chance of surviving when I came last night. I think you and I know. We both got lucky."

"Digger got lucky. Thanks for the lesson."

"I think I would leave that catheter in, just in case we need to use it again."

Denise listened for abdominal sounds. "I tubed him with some more diarrhea meds, and he still hasn't had a motion. I'm keeping up the anti-inflammatories and the tetracycline. I don't see a hint of laminitis, and he is quite sure that he needs to eat, and he is being held hostage from his food." Denise gazed at me and then covered her mouth. I knew she realized the reference to the hostage might be too close to reality.

"Yeah, well, even hostages need to eat. Why don't we start to introduce some food and see how he does?"

I went down to the house, and Colin was in his office with Luke. They were going over a plan to get Luke into a school. Colin jumped up, came over, and asked me to join in. "We're thinking of introducing him to the school after Christmas. He would be going to the seventh grade. He would need to catch up on several subjects." Colin was going to hire a proper tutor so Luke would be ready and not fail due to lack of preparation.

I declined to stay, saying I wanted to call my kids and assure them I was all right. I picked up Baxter and Gloria, and I walked back to my property and house. "You ready for tomorrow?"

"No. To be honest, Gloria, I'm scared shitless. Charlie's basically a good man. I hate doing this."

"Do you still love him?"

"Probably in some ways. Charlie's always been kind to me. Why he had me kidnapped and used me to legitimize his money was bizarre. I wonder how much those other men influence him."

"If it helps, we think he had no intention of killing you. We think he planned to hide you and then do the transfers and then have someone find you. They needed to keep you in the dark, so to speak, and the easiest way was to drug you once you wrote the note."

"Why did he change the amount from fifty to sixty million?"

"We suspect one of his men did that without his knowledge. We don't know. Was that your first clue that something wasn't right?"

I didn't answer. "I guess I feel like I'm in this too. You know I had no idea, don't you?"

"Yes. No doubt whatsoever."

As we emerged from the woods that separated Colin's and my property, Sylvia and Trent were standing in the driveway with Carol. I waved and began to walk toward them. I was wary. It's hard to believe they all were as unaware as I was about Charlie's business dealings. Carol and Hal must have known or suspected something. Maybe they heard about Digger. Anyway, they have always been kind and helpful. As I walked toward them, I saw Carol and Sylvia hugging. I was quite a distance away, and even across the meadow, I sensed that at least the women were crying.

With my bruised thigh and injuries, I couldn't run, but I turned to Gloria, who could see this as well. She shrugged. Carol ran to me and hugged me and cried. "Maggie, we're all so sorry and worried. It doesn't look good."

"What's going on?" I had no idea why they were upset.

"You haven't heard? Oh, my God, Trent. She doesn't even know. Oh, you poor thing. Let's go up and sit you down."

"No! Tell me now. What's going on?"

"Charlie's plane went down. It went off the radar, and they think it crashed into a mountain in the Rockies."

"Oh, Carol, wasn't Hal flying it? Oh no. This can't be. It's got to be a mistake. I'll bet he made a side trip and didn't tell anyone. I turned to Gloria, who rushed up onto the deck and ran inside. There were three FBI agents in the house, all on phones and talking to others. They were nodding a shaking their heads. Mitch came down to where the cars were parked.

"Dr. Kincaid, Maggie, can you come upstairs?"

I was weak and starting to shake. "Mitch, these are my friends. Carol's husband is a pilot for Charlie's company. Carol, was he on the plane? Have you heard from him? It isn't making sense. He isn't due back now. He shouldn't even be in the air now."

Carol was trying to help me. "No, Maggie. He wasn't coming back. He was flying the smaller plane. His copilot flew the men in the new Cessna. Hal's still in Texas."

Mitch supported me as we went up to the deck and main floor. I sat down on the sofa, and Carol sat on one side and Sylvia on the other. I was speechless. I couldn't talk. Who was going to tell Colin? Did he know yet? "Has anyone told Collie?"

Trent stood up and asked for his number. I handed him my phone, and Trent went back out on the deck. I couldn't hear the conversation. Trent was on the phone for several minutes. Trent returned inside the house and handed me my phone. "He's on his way over."

I didn't want to see anyone. I was filled with guilt. My friends all thought I was the poor grieving lover, but in truth, I agreed to get the information that would help convict him. I did still love him, but he did almost get me killed. I wasn't sure who really knew what. At the same time, I had crazy thoughts that it was all a mistake, and every good thing he did was so overwhelming that they would ignore all the bad. Maybe Charlie was innocent, and the men who worked for him did all the drug-related portions of his wealth accumulation, and Charlie knew nothing about it. Deep down, I knew it wasn't true.

I remember Carol saying he had his dark side. Did she know about this? It was hard to believe that her husband worked for Charlie and was oblivious to what was going on. I sat in a daze watching the agents talking on their phones, turning to observe me, and then talking to one another. Gloria finally came over and asked to speak to me privately. We went into the downstairs bedroom.

I enviously eyed the bed. *I wanted everyone to leave and let me sleep. I knew that with sleep, I could escape this nightmare.* I turned to Gloria. She looked out of the window and then turned back to me. "I'm so sorry. I know you're going through hell. I can see you're torn. You loved him, didn't you?"

"I did, but I'm not sure now. I still feel Charlie and his men put me in grave danger, even if they didn't mean to kill me. It's hard to let that go."

"We need one more favor from you." Gloria paused while Mitch entered the room. He came over and put his arm around me and sat me down on the bed. *One step closer to sleep.* "You can't discuss this with anyone. Any one of your friends could know about this or be involved. Are you okay with that?"

"If I could protect Charlie and his philanthropic endeavors and it could go on forever, I could live with that as his legacy." I stared at both and could see that it probably wasn't going to happen.

"We're here to collect information. We think your life is no longer in danger. We were concerned that if confronted, Charlie or one of his men would want to silence you. We now need to make sure that your friends were not involved in any way. It may be weeks before any of this becomes public knowledge. Can we get you to agree not to discuss it?"

"Does it ever have to become public knowledge?"

"We don't make those kinds of decisions. We're assigned to gather the facts. Charlie McLeod isn't a well-known public figure. Despite his wealth and charities, he was hardly known in the public arena."

"What will happen to all of his charities? Do you know?"

"No, do you know if he has a will?" Gloria glanced away, knowing this would be highly inappropriate at this time under different circumstances.

"No idea. The Sanctuary house staff would probably know. You could ask Roberta. I'm guessing he has lawyers who deal with these things. We never discussed it."

"Can you tell me what you did discuss the other night at dinner?"

I smiled, thinking of that moment when I was so innocent. "We discussed a merger."

Both Gloria and Mitch furred their brows. "A merger?"

I nodded. "We had what we called a preliminary discussion about moving in together. Charlie wanted us to live together, and he was throwing out some ideas about how that would work. He was not a very sophisticated man. There was no ring or any engagement. I have a feeling he wasn't going to ask me to marry him. Maybe because he was still in love with his deceased wife, Linda. Perhaps he wanted to keep my involvement with or knowledge of his illegal activities a secret? I don't know. I think he knew me well enough to know I would not be a part of anything illegal or even unethical." I gazed longingly at the bed.

"So, had you agreed to move in with him?"

"Does it matter?"

"Maybe." Mitch was to the point. He didn't skirt around issues.

"I agreed to continue negotiations. That was the purpose of our next meeting. I think we were both on the same platform, and tomorrow was going to be the decider. Well, not now, hey? Can I have a few minutes to be alone?"

"Sure. I'll tell everyone to leave if you want."

"No, actually, I better go out and see Colin. He's going to be devastated. They were best friends. His loss is far more significant than mine. I think my loss began when I overheard that voice. I've had several hours to adjust to the end of my fairytale."

"We have no legal authority to record anything anymore. We were only allowed to record you and Mr. McLeod's conversation. We won't remove the devices while you have company. However, we caution you that this is an ongoing investigation, and anything is still on the table."

"Yes, I understand. I only wish it was over. Do you know if they've reached the crash site? I take it there are no survivors?"

"We don't know. It doesn't sound good."

Chapter 45

The following week was a blur. I saw Colin briefly that afternoon and then went to bed. I emerged from the fog a week later for a private memorial at The Sanctuary at Linda's memorial plot. I dutifully pretended to be the grieving unconditional lover. Luke and Colin were by my side, and I know Colin was grieving far more than me. By then, I knew that while Carol and Hal had no actual knowledge of Charlie's activities, I guessed they had their suspicions. Colin and the others had none. I saw at least two people who might be FBI agents.

While the wreckage had been spotted from the air, a severe snowfall hampered any attempt to gather human remains, and the task was to be abandoned until spring or maybe never. The area was not easily accessible. I knew Charlie would want any remains to be scattered with his wife's ashes, but that could come later. The ceremony was brief. After Colin gave Charlie's beautiful eulogy, we all were asked to go up to the house where Roberta had prepared some food. I didn't know everyone, but most of the guests came and told me how sad and sorry they were. Everyone had something nice to say about Charlie. Roberta was distraught. We hugged, and I tried to help her with the food.

"Dr. Kincaid, are you still trying to get me in trouble with the boss. You know you're going to get me fired." We laughed for a minute, and then we both cried. "Can you come with me?" I followed Roberta into his bedroom. I'd never been in there.

It was a beautiful room with two large beds and windows that looked out over the paddocks. There were several pictures of Linda at various ages and one wedding picture.

What surprised me was there were also several pictures of me. My books were on Charlie's bedside table. He'd apparently read them all. "How long has he had my pictures up?"

"Months. Haven't you been back here?"

"Never." I was stunned. This man had practically made a shrine to me.

"Maggie, that isn't why I brought you here." She opened the side drawer next to his bed and pulled out a small box. She handed it to me. "I know he would want you to have this."

It was an engagement ring. The diamond was large, and the setting had small fish carved into the inner gold band. I held it and began to cry once again. Roberta and I sat on the bed and hugged each other. "Put it on, Maggie. I know he'd have wanted you to wear it. I'm so sorry it's me and not Mr. McLeod who gave it to you."

After several minutes we returned to the living room. It was cold, and the guests were beginning to leave. Light snow was falling. This was my first snow, and outdoor activities were going to be limited from now on.

Colin saw the ring immediately. He shook his head. "I thought it was with him on the plane. I'm so glad it wasn't. I hope you like it?" He held my hand and peered closely at the ring. "My friend in Los Angeles made it for me, I mean for Charlie. Do you like the fish? Charlie was worried you would think it was too crazy."

"No. I love it, Collie. I'm going to pretend it's from you both. I'm so blessed to have had you both in my life." I gazed over at

Luke, who was standing next to his grandmother. "I mean, all three of you." Colin continued to hold my hand.

"I'm afraid I have more bad news." He stared over at Helen. "Luke's going to move to Helen's ranch and go to a school near her. The school caters to gifted children. Luke's not gifted, but the school is far above what our local school can do for him. He can make a fresh start."

"Oh, Collie, I'm so sorry."

"No, this is for the best. You let your kids go, and he is the last one for me. I can see him any time I want, and he'll come back for the summer. We'll see how long that lasts."

Luke saw us observing him, and he smiled and waved. I waved back with my free hand. Colin wasn't letting my hand go. I think he wanted to hide the ring from everyone's vision. I didn't care, as I knew the intent of both men. Helen saw the ring and nodded, and she motioned me to join her in the sunroom.

"Maggie, I'm so sorry for you and for Collie. He feels as if he lost a brother. When we lost our daughter, I thought we were going to go mad. I know we're all different, but I hope you and Collie can find some comfort in each other. Collie thinks the world of you. You know you're the first person he's shown any interest in for many years. His current wife was a reaction to my leaving him. He married her on the rebound, and he's told me many times how much he regretted it. He knows that despite the ups and downs, I love my husband. I hope you two can support each other."

"Helen, thanks. I think you give me too much credit. It's you Collie will love to his dying day. He's never said anything, but I can see it."

Helen shook her head. "You're wrong. We've both moved on. He was too much of a gentleman to come between you and

Charlie, but perhaps, in time, you two might find each other. I see you have the ring. Charlie and Collie asked me about it. Collie and I thought it was with Charlie on the plane, and we decided it would be too painful to tell you about it. Collie asked me if I thought it was crazy to have another one made."

"Really? Now I feel awful. I've hardly talked to Colin in the last few weeks. Oh, Helen, this is too much to bear right now. I'm still in shock."

"I'm sure you are. I'd love to have you come over and spend some time with me. I hope you'll consider it?"

"Maybe, in time, I'll come over and see you all. Thank you for everything. Take good care of my adopted grandson, will you?" We locked arms and returned to the gathering. Colin was talking to Carol and Hal. Hal would continue to fly and work for CLM for the probable short-term future. Carol mentioned how Hal hated himself for allowing the change of pilots that fateful day. Sylvia and Trent came and hugged both Colin and me. They'd driven me over here, and we were going to leave in a few minutes. I said goodbye to everyone I knew, and I returned to my house and resumed my life.

I slept most of the days. With the shortened days of autumn, it was easy—too easy. I returned phone calls and messages from my children in Australia and my sister, and rarely my brother. I told my publishers and agent I was unable to do any more books for the foreseeable time. I had fulfilled all my contractual obligations. I rarely heard from the FBI. Agent Willoughby had been replaced by another agent who was overseeing the investigation. I was not in Charlie's will, and I received nothing, as I had expected.

Colin came over when he was home at his ranch. We had occasional meals together, and one evening we even played catch in the barn's aisleway. Digger occasionally stuck his head out of his nearby stall to observe us make a pathetic attempt at recreating our summer with Luke and Charlie. It didn't last. Colin's shoulder was playing up, and our hearts weren't in it. At one point, Colin turned away, and I knew he was wiping a tear. I suspected it was for the loss of Luke too.

Colin's current wife sent papers asking for a divorce and a substantial payout. Colin was happy that he would be free from the woman but was fighting the alimony. He was spending more time over at Helen's ranch, much to the consternation of Helen's husband.

I declined all invitations to dinner from anyone else and even refused a ride to the hot springs with Sylvia. Digger was going to stay over at Colin's for the winter. He was healthy again, but we all decided that Digger would be safer if he could stay in a heated barn when winter really set in. The prediction was for a harsh winter.

Occasionally Colin would ask me about the case. I hadn't heard anything for weeks, so I didn't have to lie to him. We met in late November, and he cooked a turkey dinner. "Are you trying to impress me with your culinary skills?"

"Always, sweetheart. Pass the gravy. Oh, have you heard anything about your kidnapping case?"

"No, it's all gone quiet. I think the feds are trying to round up all the kidnappers before they go to court." I hated lying to Colin, but if I could keep Charlie's involvement a secret, I would. I had no choice. The FBI was working with other agencies now, and I was asked to sit tight.

Colin visited his other children and grandchildren in early December. He reported he was banned for a few weeks from Helen's, as her husband was on the warpath about Colin's continual presence. Luke was doing well in school, and with the tutors that Colin and Helen engaged, Luke was almost caught up to his age group. He was still considering veterinary medicine, but law enforcement was also on the list.

Colin called me in mid-December. "Maggie, I've had enough winter, sweetheart. Pack your bags and get your passport. We're going fishing."

"Thanks, Collie, maybe next year."

"Not taking no for an answer, goddammit. Either you get ready, or I'm coming over and dragging your sorry ass out of bed and throwing you on a plane. Your choice."

I didn't want to do this. I was comfortable in my sorrow and grief, but Colin had been so lovely and caring over the last months, and I knew he was not a man to cross. "Where're we going? I've always wanted to go to Patagonia."

"You'll have to wait and see. I'll send Doug over tomorrow morning, and you'd better have your butt in gear, or there will be hell to pay. Am I clear?"

"Yes, sir." I did laugh. I could see myself getting onto a plane to who knew where, having a drink, and sleeping for another ten hours. How bad would that be? I didn't need drugs or alcohol to sleep—ah, sweet depression, my reliable, ever-present companion.

Chapter 46

The following day, I was packed and ready to go. I had my passport and fishing gear. Doug Cameron showed up, gave me a hug, and asked if I was prepared for an adventure.

"Can't wait." I lied.

"Yeah, I hear that in your voice. Well, Colin's worried about you. You know how he feels about you, and he's determined to get you out of this funk. Colin told me that enough is enough. He's grieving as well, you know. I'm taking Baxter over to stay with Luke while you're gone."

I fingered my ring. I thought more about it coming from Colin than I did Charlie these days. I had two lovers, and none of us was exclusive. I'd loved them both. Colin loved Helen, and Charlie loved Linda until his death. It would have been unthinkable last year, but here I was.

Doug dropped me at the airport, where I was directed to a flight to Los Angeles. I was met in LAX by a concierge who escorted me to my next flight, on Air New Zealand. She handed me a first-class ticket and wished me well. It was strange. I thought Colin would be going too. I was seated and offered a drink. Here I was in first-class, and all I wanted to do was sleep. The seating was luxurious. They knew my name and even one of the attendants knew I was an author and had read one of my books. She had horses in New Zealand. We talked for a few minutes while the rest of the passengers were boarding.

Just as it seemed the plane was ready to depart, Colin walked in and sat next to me. I leaned over and kissed him on the cheek. I was close to tears once again, and he took my hand and held it as the plane backed away from the terminal, and then we took off for Auckland. Of course, the air attendants were all over him. He was a famous movie star. I never saw this adulation back home. He was oblivious to their adoration. It made me chuckle.

"What?" Colin had no idea what I found funny.

"You. You and your fans."

"I'm an old man, but I still have my good points. You should bear that in mind."

"Collie, I can't imagine being your age, but I hope I'm half as robust and mentally with it as you when I get to be eighty."

"I'd advise you not to say that to me when we're alone on the river. The water is mighty cold, Maggie. You might regret it." He squeezed my hand and continued to hold it. We both had a laugh, but it did make me think how much happiness he'd brought to my currently miserable life. When had I begun thinking of my life as bleak? That's not how I ever thought of my life. Even when I went through my divorce, I thought that as bad as it was, I looked forward to my next adventure. I resolved to get myself back on track—line in the sand.

A flight attendant walked over before dinner was served. "Mr. Chandler, can I bring you and your daughter some more bubbly?"

I couldn't stop laughing. I leaned towards Colin and whispered, "Now that's hysterical."

"At least she didn't say, granddaughter." Even Colin saw the humor in her assumption.

When she returned, Colin thanked the air hostess. "Can you send this annoying woman back to the cattle cars?"

We talked for a while, and then he fell asleep. I joined him soon after. It seemed as if we had only departed, and the crew was waking us up for the landing. "Did we time travel, Collie?"

"Yeah, it does feel like it." He rubbed his chin and felt the stubble. That was the only indication that time had passed. He went to the bathroom and returned shaved and refreshed.

We landed and then caught a private plane for a trip to the South Island. We arrived near Nelson and were picked up by a helicopter and taken to a remote property along a river. There was a landing pad in front of the main building. Colin and the pilot began retrieving our bags and rods. "You head on in, and I'll get the gear."

"I can help." I turned to take my suitcase.

"Maggie, you need to learn to accept help. You're too independent for my liking." I knew enough not to cross him. This man was used to getting his way. Colin handed me a small bag then pointed to the stairs leading to the door. I saluted him and climbed the steps to this large mansion-like lodge. I opened the door to what appeared to be the central building expecting to be greeted by the hosts. Standing in the foyer was Charlie McLeod.

Chapter 47

There were no words to describe my shock. I stared and didn't move. Finally, I woke up from a terrible nightmare. Was it over? It had been the longest and worst nightmare of my life.

"I know what you're thinking, and it's not a dream, darling. It's real. Don't worry, it's okay. I'm in witness protection. The FBI knows where I am. I chose the venue, and they've approved it. It doesn't cost them anything."

I turned to Colin, who had joined us in the lodge. He smiled. "Don't blame me. I only found out a few days ago. Are you okay?"

"No, I'm not okay. Are you Collie?" Colin explained he had received a phone call from an undisclosed overseas number. He thought it was a prank and hung up immediately. When the phone rang again, he realized it was Charlie, and he described his reaction from complete joy and relief to fury. Colin understood my response to this shocking turn of events. He put his arm around my waist and supported me as we entered the foyer. My reaction ranged from disbelief to pure anger. Why did this man do this to us?

"Does somebody want to tell me what's going on?" In a million years, I couldn't imagine an explanation that would justify this inconceivable outcome. "Who else knows you're alive?"

"No one that you know. You were never supposed to be part of this. I have so much to explain, and I will. If you can forgive me once you know everything, I can die a happy man."

"New Zealand? Is this a fishing lodge?" Colin gazed around at the complex, consisting of the main building with several smaller cabins. "Does it have a name?"

"It does, but I'm calling it The Next Sanctuary."

"Not very Māori sounding. Who owns it?" Colin had been to New Zealand more than I. We were both aware of the strong influence of the Māori culture, especially in the rural areas.

"Maggie owns it." Charlie smiled at me.

I was dumbfounded. "You're joking, of course."

"Not hardly, darling."

"Are you trying to buy me off? You know I can't be bought."

"I think you said you could be bought when you needed to be."

"Uh, yeah, but only for other people. I can't be bought, you know. This is crazy, and I have no interest in owning a fishing lodge. On second thought, Collie, do you want to split it with me?" I never told anyone, but I did consider going to New Zealand and opening a small B&B for fishing tragics when I retired.

"Yeah, I could be happy here. At least for half the year."

"The question is, do we allow guests? There may be one too many guests here right now." I wanted to hit Charlie for what he had put me through. Both Colin and I stared at Charlie. I saw that Colin's sentiment was similar.

"What's the point of having guests that don't fish?" Colin smiled, and we high-fived each other.

"Hey, wait. This isn't how I expected things to go." Charlie frowned, and I could see his apprehension.

"Oh, did you think we would greet you with open arms? First, you let me be kidnapped, and then you almost get me killed. Let me think." I gazed up at the ceiling, pretending to search my memory. "Oh, yeah. Then you faked your death and left us grief-stricken for months."

Colin added, "Maggie, you're right. A fishing lodge is small compensation for the hell you and I have been through." We were joking, but we weren't joking. I was furious, and I didn't think Colin was far behind me. Charlie could not see what the last few months had done to Colin and me. This was a flaw that somehow, I had not seen until now. His grasp of human emotion was lacking. I wonder if his dead wife had ever let him have it. I doubted it.

"Can I explain?" Charlie saw our reaction to his attempt to win Colin and me back. I think this finally made Charlie realize how grief-stricken and saddened we had been in the last few months.

"Can you?" Colin's face reddened, and for the first time, I saw the hurt that this had caused him. Colin was fit and robust for his age, but then who was I to judge. My birthday had come and gone while I wallowed in my pity and slept. I was now sixty-nine. Eighty wasn't looking that old now.

I gazed around while Charlie stood silently and hopefully considered his actions. The main building where we stood must be the guest dining room. It was modest compared to the fishing lodge I'd stayed in when I came for fishing trips over the years. However, it was still beautiful with a large double-sided stone fireplace, several dining tables, and an expansive covered veranda around the entire main facility. Leather chairs were scattered around the fireplace and on the porch. The view of the river down the hill was a prominent feature. I could see facilities for livestock and a few paddocks that needed grazing or mowing. I couldn't see any cattle or horses.

"How about we get something to eat, and I'll explain it? There is a significant amount of detail I need to keep to myself, but the most important thing is, I am not a crook."

"To paraphrase a former president." Colin was as out of the loop as I was. "Where's the kitchen? Old men need to eat."

Charlie showed us to the cabins. We each had our own. *Phew, I was worried there were going to be unrealized expectations.* The cottages were luxurious and well maintained. Each had a porch with wicker chairs that allowed for a view of the valley and river below. Inside were king-sized beds with crisp, clean linen and bathrooms with heated towel racks. There was no television, but there was an assortment of books. Each room had a recliner, table, chairs, and two dressers.

My cabin was decorated with art that appeared to be original and depicted fishing scenes and western horse packing scenes. I studied one, and the signature of the painter was Todd Mulholland. There was a single painting of a woman on a horse that reminded me of Digger.

I peeked inside Colin's cabin and found it identical to mine, except the paintings were of various trout species. The detail was meticulous, and they each had a different fly next to the mouth. Collin was lying on his bed.

"You need any help, Collie?"

"You may have to pry me off the bed. If I wasn't so hungry, you'd never get me out of here."

I reached down, took his arm, and pulled him up. "These paintings are amazing. Who's Todd Mulholland? He must be a local artist, but one of the pictures in my room looks like the American West."

"I'm impressed, and you know I paint too. I'm gobsmacked, Maggie. What are you thinking?"

"Shock, anger, elation, and hunger. Come on, old man, old ladies need to eat too."

Chapter 48

We returned to the main building where Charlie was preparing our sandwiches. "Sorry, there's no staff. We need to cook and clean for ourselves. Food and any mail are delivered once a week. We're on solar with a battery backup. Haven't run out yet, but it's summer. There's a backup diesel generator." Charlie pointed up toward the mountain on the other side of the lodge. There's a spot up the hill that you can walk to and get phone reception. Do either of you have a New Zealand sim card?"

"Nope." This was going to be difficult on many levels. I didn't mind going off the grid, but I needed to warn my family. I wasn't sure how Colin felt. Did he already notify his family and friends?

Colin peered inside the refrigerator and found the beer. "I'm good. Helen and my family know I was going bush. Is that what you say, Maggie?"

"I guess. I'm going to have to think about this. What about Luke, Collie?" I turned to Charlie as he carried the plates out on the veranda.

Colin appeared to consider this. "Uh-huh. What about Luke? I may be a short-timer here." Colin brought the remaining plates out, and I carried the drinks.

I might be as well. I was torn between my need to be with either man or any man. I couldn't conceive of a story that would justify any of this.

"How'd you get fresh lettuce?" *What the hell am I worrying about lettuce? This man has some explaining to do.*

"There's a large garden behind the cabins. I'll take you there later. You must see it all. There are over seven thousand acres. There's another river over the hill." Charlie pointed to the opposite spot where he got reception.

"Is there a tractor? The paddocks need mowing. Is there any livestock?" Again, I was avoiding the obvious questions and concentrating on the trivia.

"I can't communicate with the outside world. I'll explain. You can buy some cattle. There are deer, and you can hunt, Collie. You two are going to have to pretend you are up here alone. There's an old John Deere in the barn that's down past the pasture you see over there." Charlie pointed to the grassy paddocks. "I would be wanted by a cartel if they knew I was alive. These men have far-reaching interests, and, despite no evidence I survived my plane crash, they may still be looking for someone who tipped off the FBI."

I waited to hear more, and I wondered how Colin felt about this turn of events. We sat on the porch. Compared to home, the warmth of the Southern hemisphere was wonderful. We ate, and Charlie and Colin each sipped a beer. Any alcohol at this stage and I would be under the table. I sat next to Colin and across from Charlie. I wasn't choosing sides at that moment. I needed more information. When we were both done eating, we stared at Charlie, who was looking at his folded hands resting on the varnished wooden table.

"Colin, Maggie? It's complicated."

"Yeah, I get that, sport. Is that dickhead ex-son-in-law of mine involved? Is Luke in any danger? You better be telling us the truth." Colin put his arm over my shoulder. "I don't want you hurting my girl anymore. If you think any cartel is dangerous, they would be nothing compared to how I would react if I thought you were messing with Maggie."

I squeezed Colin's hand dangling over my shoulder. "Thanks, but I can take care of myself. Remember, I used to geld horses for a living."

Colin shot me a look and laughed. "Oh geez, who am I to be talking. Do I need to lock my door tonight?"

Charlie continued. "Seriously, yes, the dickhead is involved, but only at a lower level. I've asked my contacts about you all, and they think everyone is safe. They won't promise that Luke will always be safe, but I would have turned myself over to them if I thought any of you were in danger."

I glanced at Colin. "How sure? One hundred percent sure or reasonably sure?"

"Maggie, I won't let anyone get hurt. Let me tell you both the whole story. Charlie went to the kitchen and returned with two beers. "I got involved several years ago before Linda died. When you have a loved one who is sick, and the doctors offer no hope, well, you'll grasp at anything to keep them from dying. There was a doctor in Mexico that had a clinic. I think you know what I'm talking about. He preyed on people like Linda and me, who were at our most vulnerable. He had a cure for Linda's kind of cancer, but we had to travel down and come to the clinic. Sadly, that's where it started.

"We had to pay upfront, and then when the first round of treatment wasn't working, we had to pay more. At some stage, the doctor realized that money wasn't the object. Despite Linda's declining health, he asked me to come to his villa, where I met him and several men who wanted me to invest in their company.

I asked for more information. They said they had a drug that his research team was developing that would be even better than what they were currently using. They wanted me to stake them, and they would use the newer drug on Linda.

"I was beside myself. I wasn't thinking clearly. I said I would be happy to help and asked the doctor how much money he thought it would take to get the drug ready to try on Linda. I offered more money if they could develop the drug sooner. I think you know where all this was heading.

"They said it would take no more than a month, and why not take Linda home, and they would personally bring the drug up to us when they were sure it was ready. They gave me some drugs to give her while we waited. The local magistrate came to the next meeting and vouched for the doctor and his associates. He told me his own wife had responded to the doctor's treatment and was alive and well. I wasn't sure if I could trust them, but I had no other option. Linda and I flew home.

"When we arrived at the airport back here, there was a drug-sniffing dog. I think you know where this was going. I was a fool, and now I was being arrested for possession of heroin. The FBI and then the CIA both became involved, and that's where my life of crime began and ended. The rest of the details can't be discussed, but let's say I would do anything to get these men and the doctor in jail."

Charlie put his head in his hands and grimaced. "I've been on a mission ever since. It turns out that the cartel has associates in the jurisdictions of both countries. People high in our own government and judicial system are involved in protecting these men. The money they've made is in the hundreds of millions. Many people have benefitted, and hence, looked away from actively prosecuting this cartel. The culmination was the purchase of this small company in Texas. I had to pretend to wash some money to make it look as if I was as involved as them in illegal activities."

I was having difficulty understanding it all. "So, my kidnapping was supposed to be staged?"

"Yes, FBI men, including the two men who you saw on your property and at the lake, were supposed to kidnap you and hide you out for a few days. I was to pay the ransom and get it back from an account in Belize. That was to show I was doing things as bad as them. The first problem was that two men from the cartel showed up to make sure the kidnapping went to plan. Then they decided to drug you and leave you."

"So, I was going to be left in a cave all night by myself without being drugged?" *I'm supposed to love this man who took such risks with my life?*

"Maggie, this all happened without my knowledge. Of the six men in the cave, only two weren't FBI men. None of this should have happened like it did. Two men were going to stay with you, but they knew it would appear more like a set-up, so they all left. Two of the FBI agents were going to return in a few hours, but the rain set in, and it all went to hell. I'm so sorry. I'll do anything to make this right. There was so much at stake. The FBI and CIA weren't going to stop the sting down in Texas at that point. They were sure you were dead. They all were sure no one could have survived the flood inside the cave."

"Yeah. I was thinking I wasn't going to survive it, either. No point in crying over spilled milk; better soldier on and get the bad guys." Colin took my hand and shook his head. I leaned into him and stared down at the river.

"Charlie, let me guess." Colin shifted as he sat forward. "The men you met in Texas were all in the cartel, and you set them up.

The FBI or the CIA gave you a get-out-of-jail card. Conveniently, you left the meeting early, and son of a gun, you and a pilot were killed on your way back to The Sanctuary, and that was the end of it all. They've all been arrested, and if they thought you might have set them up, you're forgotten and off the hook because you're dead."

"I can't say any more about it. If I'm dead, my associates and I are no longer in anyone's crosshairs. I must lie low for a few years, and when and if they all go to prison, I might be able to resurface. I may be asked to testify, but that hasn't been determined. CLM is defunct, and The Sanctuary is to be sold. There will be no more Charlie McLeod. I'm Todd Mulholland, when and if I resurface. I chose New Zealand because of you two. I can be happy anywhere as long as I have you two by my side."

Colin shook his head. "You do realize this bizarre, ridiculous story would be a good movie. I don't think anyone would touch it, though, and it reeks of BS."

I gazed down at the river. "It could be a book, though. So, you've taken up painting?"

"It's been my salvation. I painted pictures for your rooms, and then I've done more. I'll show you tomorrow. I hope you like them." Charlie had lost weight, and his paunch was gone. He was tan, and his hands showed evidence of physical work.

I had a lot to consider. I was torn between walking out of this property and staying to see how this ends. I needed solitude. "Gentlemen, I'm going fishing. I do my best thinking when I have a rod in my hand." Both men stared at me and laughed.

"What?"

Colin began to laugh even harder. "We'll let you think about what you just said, Maggot. Isn't that what your sister calls you?"

I got up and turned away to retrieve my fishing rod. I stopped when I realized what I had just said. "Oh, Jesus." I kept walking and raised my hand. "I got it. I'll be back later."

"Aren't you tired?"

"Nope, I've done enough sleeping for the entire year. I need fish and water. I need to be alone, and I'm considering my options."

New Zealand fishing proved to be everything I knew it would be—difficult. I went down to the river and sat on a rock overlooking the flow, pools, and possible areas where fish might hide. Ninety percent of fishing down here was sight fishing. I knew I had to see a fish and hunt it down, or I wasted my time. I had to train my eyes to see my prey. This would take days and maybe weeks. Was I up to the task? I considered my options.

New Zealand trout fishing was all catch and release—kind of like my retirement and new life. It was rare that a fish was kept. We caught them, played them on a line, captured the fish in a photograph and returned them to the rivers.

Technically, I could work here. My Australian vet license was transferable. Do I learn a new skill, or do I go home and sleep? Which door do I open when I return to the lodge?

As the light faded, I found myself fishless after two hours of effort. I stared up at the lodge and cabins. There were lights on in all three cabins. I turned back to the river and, in the dimming light, made one last cast and had a strike. I was slow setting the hook. The trout got away. The story of my life… Well, that story was ending. I walked back up to the lodge to search for a snack and maybe some medicinal alcohol. I saw the remnants of two cigars and cake crumbs. Now, I turned to the cabins to make possibly the most important decision of the remaining years of my life. I have the choice of three doors, but which one would I choose?

Acknowledgments

My readers and editors are gratefully acknowledged. The readers include Julie Laughton, Jodee O'Leary, Jeannie Olson, Jane Gropp, Sharon Spier, and Sandra Fletcher. Thank you for your advice and encouragement. The editors include the primary editor, Marilyn Anderson, and Denise Piggott, who did proofs and general advice about the storyline. My family and the staff of Adelaide Plains Equine Clinic also gave me space and time to write this story before I departed. The usual comment was that I was writing about myself. At this stage, I was still living in Australia. My reply was short and sweet. "I wish." Spoiler alert: It came true.

Elizabeth Woolsey DVM

Elizabeth grew up in postwar California, convinced that she was the daughter of Roy Rogers, and she was switched at birth. She spent her youth emulating him. Sadly, DNA evidence has proved her wrong. Thus, she followed her other father's footsteps into equine veterinary medicine. She subsequently migrated to Australia, where she practiced equine veterinary medicine near Adelaide, South Australia, until her retirement in December 2020. She began writing about her experiences as a horse vet and published her first book, Horse Doctor an American Vet's Life Down Under in 2005. A few years before her father's death, she discovered a treasure trove of personal and historically significant letters. She knew this would make a great book, not only for her family, but also for WWII enthusiasts. She published Jack's War, Letters to Home from an American WII Navigator 2015. While veterinary medicine has been her passion, fly fishing, horseback riding, and writing occupy her leisure time. Her new books include stories about women and men in equine practice. She now writes from her log cabin in North Georgia.

https://www.facebook.com/elizabeth.woolseydvm

ewoolseydvm@gmail.com

http://www.horsedoctorpress.com/

Horse Doctor Adventure Books:

Small Town Secrets

The Travels of Dr. Rebecca Harper Series

Book 2 Troubled Waters

Book 3 Lauren's Story

Book 4 Past the Present

The Catch and Release series

Catch and Release

Catch and Keep

Also by Elizabeth Woolsey (Herbert)

Horse Doctor: An American Vet's Life Down Under

Jack's War: Letters Home from an American WII Navigator

Made in the USA
Columbia, SC
03 March 2022

56756123R00180